T0413216

The Art Thieves

Also by
ANDREA L. ROGERS

Man Made Monsters
Chooch Helped

the
Art
Thieves

Andrea L. Rogers

LEVINE QUERIDO

Montclair | Amsterdam | Hoboken

This is an Arthur A. Levine book
Published by Levine Querido

LEVINE QUERIDO

www.levinequerido.com · info@levinequerido.com
Levine Querido is distributed by Chronicle Books, LLC
Text copyright © 2024 by Andrea L. Rogers
Illustrations by Rebecca Lee Kunz
All rights reserved.
Library of Congress Control Number: 2023939965
ISBN 978-1-64614-378-8
Printed and bound in China

Published in October 2024
First Printing

For Nex and all the kids who deserve better.
And for Angel Smith and the other people trying
to make this world better for our kids.
Wado.

A

Side A:
Who Do You Love?

Side B: Summer's End

Side A

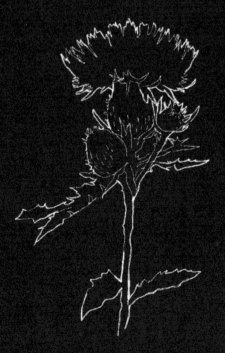

Who Do You Love?

Turning
Tide

E-mail from Stevie #1

TO: Angel Wilson (LawAngel@ICWA.law)
FROM: Stevie (stevie@hmail.com)

Thanks for coming to see me, Auntie; but by the time you read this, it will be too late. No one will have started to panic, yet; but in less than two months nothing will be the same. What came first, manufactured GMO printable Chicken or Egg Flu? I wish it mattered. But let's just say, maybe go back to wearing a mask, bathing in sanitizer, and avoid 3-D printed meat and eggs for a bit . . .

I want to apologize for my silence. Obviously, it frustrated you. I'm sure you feel like I'm wasting your time. You have no way of knowing that most everything you do in your life right now is a waste of time. Consider this e-mail my gift to you. My last chance to help someone a little before it all ends. At least for ninety days. Not just for you, but for most of the people you love. I hope after you read this, you will understand that the last thing you should do is bother with my case, though, I know you. You will try to save me, like you have saved all the Indian kids you could.

You shouldn't bother. Not because I killed Levi, the way the detectives implied. Even thinking about that, typing those words, makes me feel sick. You shouldn't bother because you have a limited amount of time to be with the people you love. The last thing you should do is spend time on any more cases—unless you can get someone sent back to home and family early. Otherwise, the only things you should focus on are spending time with Jane and anyone else you can think of.

Go do Ceremony. Stock up on food and water. Decide what kind of life you are willing to live when it all falls apart. What you're ready to do, for you and your child.

We didn't kill Levi. You know I could never. Would never. I did quite the opposite, really. I wouldn't call what my friend Adam did kidnapping, either. I mean, maybe . . . technically. My dad surely thinks so.

But Levi Lives.

You and I may be dead before the New Year begins.

The unfortunate thing so many of us never understood is that human beings are meant to care for the earth. The world is out of balance. Our ceremonies and sacred plants and stories are important. We are connected to the world, not meant to only exploit it—not be a cancer on our own planet. Living here with other living beings should have always been a life of reciprocity and cooperation. There are plants like river cane, a bamboo native to this part of the world, that do better with human interaction. In turn, it used to provide the basic materials for our way of life. Now it is nearly extinct. So much damage has been done, but so much could be made better. It was always a choice. It may be again.

So, you see why I can't possibly speak, why I can't possibly even tell this story. If I spoke, I would choke. Even while I type this, tears fall. If I started talking, the detectives would assume I'm lying or insane. At least until September 8th. The plague starts then, and then the civil wars. Border skirmishes by Christmas. Ho! Ho! Ho! Bring out your dead.

Sorry about the gallows humor.

Donadagohvi.

I hope we see each other again. Maybe even in this world. Possibly even this timeline.

Wado.

For everything.

Stevie

A
City
of Fire

There were no tense voices that morning. It was the first time in the last fifteen days that I wasn't jolted awake by disharmony. I wondered for a moment if it was the calm after the storm, which is kind of an appropriate thing to say since the planet is in a cycle of drought and superstorms, ice and fire, polar vortexes and heat domes. On this side of the world, it's hot and moist, but the ground is cracked in places previously lush. Kind of like my parents' marriage.

This is where the captions at the bottom of the TV screen would read "scoffs."

What's funny is they never talk about going off-planet. This is our world, as much as it needs healing. Colonizing space never appealed to my family.

While I was enjoying the quiet, my phone buzzed with a text from my mom reminding me to get my little brother fed and ready for school. I had forgotten that my dad (I quit calling him Walter long ago) had left town for work. He's a crime consultant and a hunting and wilderness guide. This trip was the crime thing. Before he left, he told me he was worried about my mom. Dad was all for getting back to the land, too, but my parents had never been what you'd call preppers before. They just came from people who'd had to be self-sufficient.

Dad had said, "When we're alone, she cries a lot." He didn't look at me when he said this. I rarely saw Mom cry. Mostly only when she was really angry. Working on an Indian Child Welfare case, fighting injustice. That's why she went into law.

"She holds me like she's grieving some nights," Dad went on. "If things get too weird . . . call me immediately." Then he told me he was following up leads on a missing persons case somewhere near Big Bend. The drought has caused water levels to drop all over the world. Old mysteries were being solved, but not in the way families might have hoped.

My parents. Their marriage had undergone stress tests before. The summer I was eleven, I went to my estranged father's house on a mountain in Nowhere, Colorado. For once I was temporarily glad to visit him, because it had been abnormally strained in Texas. Walter and my mom had started fertility treatments. I guess making a baby is stressful when you're on a schedule. But two weeks into my court-mandated visit with my bio dad, Walter had to come get me. Bio dad had gone on a bender and left me alone that second week. I had finally hiked down the mountain one morning to a place with cell service, and called my mom. She was perplexed when she awoke to me asking her how to make pasta at that higher elevation on a woodstove. She called the local sheriff. They picked me up, took me to the cabin to get my things, and confirmed my father was still absent. Then they took me to the police station to wait.

At some point they brought my father in and locked him up.

Walter had arrived that evening and taken me to get food. We stayed in a hotel that night, but while I was in the bathroom, I overheard him talking to the local police on the phone. We're not white, so we're pretty wary about calling the police. Walter spent a brief period training to be a cop, thinking he could change the system from within. As a Black cadet, he was quickly disabused of that notion. Instead, he put all his experience hunting and tracking—along with his psychology classes and savings—into independent consulting. Basically, he's a private detective.

Anyway, Walter was able to get some things done over the phone. After I went to bed, I heard him leave. He was back when I woke up though. After having had a talk with my father.

On the drive home, he said, "Stevie, I want to ask you to think about something."

I looked at him.

"This thing with your dad, doesn't seem to be working out."

I burst into tears.

Walter pulled the car over into a rest area. He got out and opened my door and held my hand like I was a little kid as we walked to the vending machine. He gave me money to buy what I wanted and I settled on a sugary soda and peanut butter cups. He bought a packet of trail mix and a water. We sat on a bench that overlooked the rest stop's playground.

I offered Walt one of my four peanut butter cups and he ate it and listened. He was good at wait time. When he wanted to, he could sit in silence and never seem uncomfortable at all. He could give you his full attention. That was the A part of ADHD, I guess.

Finally, I spoke, trying not to cry. "He just left me there. Said he had to go pick up groceries. We hadn't even had lunch."

"Stevie, I'm sorry. We didn't know how he'd gotten the last year."

"He was always this way. Mom made things work. I think he only takes me so he doesn't have to pay child support."

Walt didn't say anything.

"I don't want to go back. If he's around, I'll have to take care of him."

Walt laughed. Two crows sat in the tree overhead calling loudly.

"Are they talking about us or to us?" Walt asked.

"I think they just want your trail mix."

Walt tossed some nuts and dried apples towards the base of the tree. We sat in silence, willing the birds to accept the gift. Finally, one did, then they both turned and flew away. We watched them disappear.

I was still watching after the birds.

"How do you say 'crow'?" Walt asked. I knew what he meant.

"Ko-ga," I said. But I always did it like it was a crow talking.

Walt laughed.

"What did you want to ask me to think about?"

"I talked to your mom about legally adopting you. She said I needed to talk to you."

"What would that mean? How would that change things?"

"I'd legally be your dad. As if I were your natural father."

"I wouldn't have to stay with him anymore?"

"Not if you didn't want to. And even if you don't want me to adopt you, we can work on that."

"So, you'd be my dad? Not just my stepdad?"

"Ouch. I don't think there's any such thing as *just* a stepparent."

"I know. But, it would make things different"—I tapped my skull—"in here"—then I tapped my chest—"but not in here."

Walt swallowed.

"Is it expensive?"

Walt laughed again. "All that matters is how you feel about it. You don't have to decide now."

I knew. I knew what I would say when he and my mom sat down with me the next day.

It was one of the best things that ever happened to me. When we got home, there was a positive pregnancy test in the bathroom. Romance blossomed between my parents once more. By the time my little brother was born, Dad was officially my dad too. Even through the postpartum difficulties of my much-wanted brother, Levi—even through his diagnosis with life-threatening allergies—my parents were partners. We were all pretty happy.

But that was before Mom became obsessed.

A few weeks earlier, I had graduated from high school along with my two best friends, Loren and Jess. Our celebration was overshadowed by a nearby reservoir catching fire, the air of our outdoor graduation smoke-filled. The masks some of us still wore didn't do much for our red and irritated eyes. You really are living in the Pyrocene when water burns.

It wasn't really a surprise. Where previously the city had planted trees, dead saplings now stood twisted and broken. Wire ran from gnarled wood to stakes to save the plants from too much wind and, though the city watered and mulched for a while, the trees seemed to cook as if they were in an air fryer. The dead saplings jutted from the earth like bone-dry fingers. We threw our graduation caps into ash-filled air.

At the end of the summer, Jess, Loren, and I were supposed to go to the University of Texas at Austin. Mom wasn't thrilled about that. She said it was too far if things went bad. No: "It's too far *when* things go bad." That's what she said. "And you won't even drive." She said that like I was unaware. Like it was a surprise to me.

My phone buzzed again with a second text from her, making sure I had seen the first. At the same time, the door to my bedroom opened. My baby brother, Levi, ran in and jumped in bed with me, leaving the door wide open behind him. I stopped myself from asking, "Were you born in a barn?" You have to be proactive about not turning mindlessly into a younger version of your parents. Instead, I said, "Let's sleep five more minutes, kiddo." Cuddling that kid made me stupid happy.

From Mom's locked office I heard ringing and then the shrill scream of a fax machine.

Then, silence.

I breathed in through my nose and out through my mouth, the way our parents had taught me and Levi. I had enough to be anxious about without Mom's whatever-this-was.

My phone dinged with another message. Now she was texting me from inside her office.

"The killer is in the house," I muttered, then hollered down the hall more loudly: "I'm up!" I didn't want her venturing out and into my room.

"What killer?" Levi whispered. He stared at me, his beautiful curly hair framing his head like a corona, his brown eyes opening wide.

"I kid, kid." I tousled his hair. "What are you doing up so early?"

"Why did you say there is a killer in the house?" he whispered back.

"Well, you know as well as I do, there is some killer cereal in this house."

"Mom says sugar is the silent killer." Levi was not yet worried about whether he sounded like a parent.

"Oh, yeah, well who wants some Fruity Sugar Crunchy Circles?"

"Me! Me! Me!" Levi shrieked, and just like that the silent killer was forgotten.

Stay in My Corner

We had to be extremely conscious of food ingredients in our house, super careful with what we gave Levi. A lot of his food was homemade so we could be sure it wasn't contaminated with tree nuts. Each time he had an allergic reaction and we went with him to the hospital, we were grateful to leave with a somewhat healthy kid. We tried to keep an EpiPen on hand wherever he was. We only bought processed stuff that stated it was processed on lines separate from tree nuts.

That morning, I set him up with his favorite cereal and then started making our lunches. I washed an apple, sliced it, then put some lemon juice on the cut edges before packing it. Then I made Levi a turkey and cheese sandwich on white bread. Mom wandered in, half paying attention to her phone. "How are you getting to work today?" On cue, the doorbell rang.

"Loren's taking me," I said as I went to let her in.

"What's your mom doing here?" Loren whispered as she entered. All summer Mom had been gone at dawn.

"Other than playing with the fax machine?" I joked. Quietly. Loren rolled her eyes. Loren was a computer programmer and wrote apps. For fun. She was all about the latest tech. "Dad went out of town on a case."

"Can you say which one?"

I shook my head.

Loren shuddered.

When we stepped into the kitchen Mom smiled, "So, you're taking Levi to school, yeah?"

"All summer, Ms. Jones." This was something Dad and I had worked out. He gave Loren gas money, and she got Levi and me to school and work. The school part was easy because Loren worked there. My job was a short walk away, though she usually just dropped me off first, unless I needed to check in with Levi's school for one reason or another. Sometimes I rode with her and then walked to work anyway, just so we could talk longer. Then I could stroll through the arts district. The gift shop at the Modern Art Museum didn't open until the museum opened for the day, so I was generally super early. That was the cost of not driving in a city where it was nearly impossible to function without a car. When the guards let me, I loved wandering around and seeing the art while the museum was empty. I was looking forward to sitting and drawing another sketch of *The Ladder*.

Mom turned her attention fully to Loren. "How are swim lessons going?" The dirty look I gave my mom then was authentic. In middle school, Loren had been at a swim party that ended in tragedy. I assumed water was nothing short of terrifying for her. But Dad and Mom were obsessed with whether Loren could swim (among many other things).

They thought paying her to take Levi to lessons would help her learn.

"Levi has no fear," Loren replied, smiling.

"What about you, though? Picking anything useful up? You gotta use that brain for more than programming if there's an emergency."

"Well, actually, if Levi gets into trouble in the water, he's more likely to drown me if I get in with him. You're supposed to use a pole to reach them or throw them a flotation device."

"I'm more worried about you, dear."

"I don't know. It sure seems like nothing but drought from here on out. Have you seen the Trinity? Besides, I'm going to make enough on my app to buy a boat."

Mom frowned, but she had that coming. The tense discussions I kept overhearing her and Dad in, my friends and I had come to call *the denouement of the world.* From the side-eye she gave me then, she knew I had told Loren a few things, the puzzle of the vintage fax machine that screeched at random times that my dad didn't seem to notice. Our parents really tried to keep me and Levi from hearing them—from scaring us—but I caught bits and pieces of their arguments/ conversations about go bags and buying preserved food and moving off grid and rising temperatures.

Mom wasn't like this before they married, or even after—not until the last year. But shortly after Grandma died, she became obsessed with disaster news and climate-related tragedies. They sold our house with the pool while housing prices were at an insane high, six months before a nationwide drought made it super expensive to fill the pool or water the cracking yard. They'd put their windfall in savings and good camping and hunting gear. We were living in Grandma's house while they considered/debated their next move. Mom seemed to believe civilization was doomed and wanted to move back to land in Oklahoma. Dad had his doubts, but didn't mind the idea of getting out of the city. He could do his jobs from anywhere. He was a kind of green book for hunting and fishing when he wasn't doing the private consulting thing.

"How about if I make dinner tonight?" I announced, apropos of nothing.

Mom frowned. She was a lawyer. She knew a deflection when she heard one.

"I meant to ask you to do that. I'll have groceries delivered. Probably going to be late. Don't let Levi stay up past his bedtime this time."

"Funny way to say 'thanks,'" I answered as she turned to walk out.

"Not today," she shot back from her bedroom. Then, she stopped and came back to where I stood. "You're going to need to get behind the wheel again, Sissy. Especially now."

Mom was all about the parting shot. My stomach clenched up in knots. Since the wreck I'd had just after I got my license, I didn't drive. I didn't want to drive. I got anxiety riding in a car for a long time. I had to see a therapist and get medication to deal with it. I had learned to mostly ignore the big trucks towering around the car while in the passenger seat, though without distraction my head was on a swivel, watching out for wreck potential. Sometimes I read. Sometimes I talked and talked and talked to whoever was in the car. Sometimes I just listened to music and closed my eyes.

It was so different when I was behind the wheel—when I had to watch the brake lights ahead of me and the objects hurtling towards me and the tons of metal boxes on wheels on either side of me. Just thinking about it gave me tension in my neck and upper back. I didn't see any reason to ever drive again. I would plan my life around public transportation and walking. I'd live in an apartment with a dozen roommates in a walkable city for the rest of my life if I had to. Okay, that was an exaggeration. But I'd be happy to live with Jess and Loren.

Once in the car I asked Loren why she never used her key on mornings she got to the house early.

Loren laughed, then looked in the back to make sure Levi wasn't listening. "Are you kidding?" she muttered. "Your dad used to be a cop, and both of your parents hunt and own guns. This young and gifted Black girl is trying to make it to adulthood."

"Okay, he trained for six months. Does that really count? And they're both really careful."

"I don't know, your mom seems a little more skittish these days."

"Right? I think maybe she's read Octavia Butler too many times."

"No one has read Octavia Butler too many times. She might be on to something."

I wanted to tell Loren about the most recent fight—the stuff I hadn't told her via text, the stuff Dad had said before he left—but Levi didn't need to know the details. How could I let a six-year-old know his parents were fighting about the end of the world?

"How's the app that's going to save us all going?" I asked instead.

Loren glanced at Levi again. Her app was supersecret—like, no joke. I barely knew what it would do or how it worked. Jess was the only one Loren had told everything to. All I knew is even while we were at work, the app was at her house, parsing through tons of data on religion, spirituality, and laws in order to compile a list of best practices for humans based on where they lived, what the planet was doing, what they felt was right or wrong, what was good for the majority—rules for living. It was like one of those quizzes that told you what kind of learner you were or whether you were an introvert or extrovert or whatever, except it gave you a set of beliefs to live by, responding to world conditions.

Loren didn't think of the app as a form of religion so much as a philosophy, because it was adaptable. "Training wheels for souls," she said. "Use it until you don't need it anymore. Once you understand cooperation is less expensive than mutually assured destruction, maybe you can be trusted to free range." Then she'd laugh.

More and more it seemed like "adaptable" was the best way to define the opposite of a lot of religions and governments. Governments had outlawed our own Native religions until the 1970s—even dancing was technically illegal.

While white children imitated Indians at summer camps and scout troops, Native kids died in boarding schools learning to be servants and tradespeople. The schools were often run by churches, for way too long. They were still finding graves. We were still trying to recover the language that had been beaten out of so many in schools.

Once Loren launched *Soulcraft*, it would take all the data people put into it to build a network that took seriously the three laws of robotics and encouraged people to follow them. It would filter out any ideas or beliefs that harmed other humans, and take into account the importance of the earth. People loved data. People loved direction. I hoped it would work. Humans weren't doing so great.

Before she could answer me about her app's progress, we heard a fire truck behind us. Loren pulled over to let it and several more emergency vehicles pass. They turned onto the highway ahead of us and we saw they were driving into smoke. By the time we got back on the road, it was obvious we would have to avoid the highway and detour through the city streets. The dry grass that edged the highway was on fire. I turned and saw Levi staring out the window.

"Stevie?" he said, his voice all tears and questions.

"I think I'm going to need to work a little faster if there's going to be a world worth saving," Loren whispered.

"Yeah, I like this planet," I replied. I thought of all the people settling on the various space stations and enlisting to travel to planets, to build New New Englands and New

New Spains. People who had taken their families to work in mines, in exchange for health care and debt forgiveness. I thought of how the Cherokee Nation and other tribes and Indigenous people were buying up properties from these exiting settlers, expanding back into the original boundaries of what was supposed to have been Indian land as long as the grass grew. "I know a whole lot of people who aren't going anywhere."

Come
and Get
Your Love

When I got to the gift shop office there was a note from my boss, directing me to make labels for a display of carvings by an "indigenous" artist from Costa Rica. The curator for the main collection had popped into our gift shop meeting the week before and told us about the upcoming summer exhibits and the artist, who the curator only called Adawi. He was a new "artist intern." He was going to be working, mostly, in the museum's Preparator's Workshop, a space in the basement. He would be shadowing some of the curators occasionally and learning the ropes of museuming.

I rolled my eyes. What did Christy even mean by "indigenous," small *i*? Sometimes in the U.S. "Indigenous" was accurate, but sometimes it was a lazy, offhand phrase, used either to lump a bunch of brown people together who may or may not be Native, or for whom no one bothered to ascertain a tribe.

I was familiar with a tribe in contemporary Costa Rica and Panama, the Bribri. The curator who had just gotten back from the region was doing a whole exhibit on contemporary art there and had arranged for an award-winning author from the Bribri to come give a reading later that month. I knew the names of some of the other tribes but could stand to learn a lot more about them. I quickly researched. There were eight tribes indigenous to Costa Rica and, also, tribes who had moved into Costa Rica from other territories where their right to exist was even more tenuous. Pushed off homelands; ethnic cleansing in the name of "progress." I typed the names of all the tribes into my document and saved the URL so I could come back to it when I wrote up the artist's biography.

Usually these interns didn't get paid much, painted a lot of walls, and moved really expensive pieces of art during installations. Sometimes they lived with a curator's family, or were given a studio space where they could work and live. If they had art pieces to sell, the gift shop gave them a small space to do so, and the artist kept all the proceeds from the sale.

I decided to not start work early. Instead, I headed for the side of the museum that housed its most important piece. *Ladder for Booker T. Washington* by Martin Puryear is a thirty-six-foot long ash and maple ladder that has its own three-stories-tall room. At one time, it was loaned to the National Gallery of Art and installed in its Rotunda. The few times it had been off display in our museum, I felt like the building's heart was missing.

First, though, I went to the security guard desk nearby to see who was on duty. I was lucky, one of the guards was Tex. The other seat was empty, so whoever his partner was must have been on rounds in the galleries.

I first met Tex when he taught art at American Indian Summer Camp. He left when the little kids got to be too much for him, but he'd reached out to Mom to tell me when the museum shop job came open. He was Native, like me, but he's Kiowa, not Cherokee. Tex heard me come in, but he kept his eyes on the screens. Of course; he had seen me coming from the gift shop on several of the many screens.

"Somebody else likes your piece," he greeted me, gesturing toward the feed from the room with the ladder.

A tall guy, with long black hair pulled back in a braid, and both sides of his head shaved, was walking around the ladder. He had his own sketchbook in one hand.

"Who's that?" I asked, sitting down in the empty chair.

"New artist intern."

"Oh, Adawi. The 'Indigenous' guy."

"What?" Tex said.

"Christy told me to make a sign for his art in the gift shop. Said he was Indigenous. But didn't know his tribe. Seemed like maybe somebody should have bothered to ask?"

"H'mph," was all Tex replied.

"Did you know there are eight tribes indigenous to Costa Rica?" I went on, reading from the notes I had made in my journal.

"Yup," he said. Then he named every single one of them. Then he told me about tribes that were also in Costa Rica from the surrounding area.

"Dang, Tex, you're the one who should be curating these shows."

"Yeah, well, that's just between you and me. I love art; they love to talk."

We watched the guy on the screen sit down. Tex stood up. "Watch this guy while I get us some coffee, yeah?"

"Sure," I said. On the screen Adawi was making broad strokes with his pencil, but it didn't look like he was looking at the sculpture. I leaned forward and zoomed the camera in, but I couldn't tell what he was drawing. He seemed to be looking at the walls of the room the ladder hung in.

"Huh," I muttered when he stood. He flipped his sketchbook open to another page and then he turned and looked right at the camera. He smiled a deep smile that made me grin back, though there was no way he could see me. I could see he was what some people called "ethnically ambiguous." His eyes and hair were dark, and his skin was brown, but any guesses at what his tribe or origin were would be merely that. He reminded me of a young Chaske Spencer, the way he looked in *The English*. He made some more marks on the new page of his sketchbook. It occurred to me that maybe he was sketching the camera on the wall. After a few strokes, he went back and sat down and finally seemed to start sketching the sculpture. I was still watching him when I felt someone standing uncomfortably close to me. I froze.

"Steee-v—ie."

"You're back!" I cried, whipping around. I felt sudden relief. And—I didn't mean to act so happy. But I didn't know how not to.

"Sorry I missed your birthday," Alan said. Alan was an artist and photographer who worked here with the Youth

Program. He had been gone on sabbatical from both the museum and the university he worked at and had been traveling that spring.

"You missed graduation!" I responded. "And the art show for the program." The art show had really been important to me.

"That too," he replied. "I got you something, though. It's at my apartment. I hope you'll forgive me?" I noticed Alan's hand was lingering a little too long on my shoulder. Suddenly, I felt a little uncomfortable and stepped back, still holding his eyes.

"It's okay. Graduation was kind of a letdown. Lots of smoke and ash. The reservoir caught fire. Did you get a chance to look at my portfolio?"

I wasn't attending UT as an art student, but I wasn't planning to give up photography either. I had gotten serious about photography when I was thirteen, even asked for a good camera for my birthday that year. The one I still used. Alan had always used my work as an example in classes and made sure to encourage me one-on-one. As a professional photographer, his opinion was sought and valued by more people than me. He wasn't hard to look at, either. Alan was a bit more tan now, with sharper edges and muscles from traveling. Office and studio life had left him looking a little soft.

"I just got back. Wi-Fi was spotty in most of the places. But I'll go look at it this evening and give you a call."

My heart sank. We had texted a few times while he was on the road, shooting climate disasters. He had never mentioned a lack of internet. Just that it was late wherever he was, and he was thinking about how he could help me promote my work.

"It's no big," I said, hoping the disappointment wasn't writ too large.

I remembered I had promised Tex I would keep an eye on Adawi. I turned away from Alan. The guy hadn't moved.

"Who's that?" Alan asked.

"New artist intern. Costa Rican wood-carver. Name is Adawi."

"Yeah?" Alan stepped closer, leaning around and against me, reaching over for the camera control. He zoomed the lens in closer. "Sketching the *Ladder*. That tracks."

"Huh?" I answered, getting up and stepping to the side so he was no longer leaning on me. The break room door opened; Tex returning with our coffee.

"Wood-carver," Alan said. "Hey, Tex."

Tex frowned. "No one mentioned you coming back. I'm going to need to make a call before you go any further into the building."

Confused, I looked between the two men, noticed Alan now looking a little displeased. "No reason for that. Just stopped by to see Stevie."

"Well, you know the gift shop hours, friend." Tex definitely didn't say "friend" amiably. "Stevie, take these coffees and I'll walk Mr. Hunt out." I took both cups.

"Let me get the door for you."

"I need to get going anyway," Alan answered. He turned and left the room followed by Tex, almost as if he had forgotten I was there.

When Tex came back, he sat down next to me without saying anything more. Normally, our silences were comfortable, both of us drinking our coffee and watching the various camera feeds, sometimes talking about the pieces they were focused on. Today was less so.

It wasn't until the camera feed got to the photography exhibit that Tex finally spoke: "When I was in college, I had a professor who liked to go take pictures in places where people were poor. This one time he was giving us a lecture and he had done these beautiful portraits of a young mother. Her baby was mixed. Our professor said a white tourist had fathered the kid's kid and left. He told us you could pay those Indians to pose a lot cheaper than here. He must have showed us a dozen pictures of her. When he got done, I said, 'What was her name?'"

"What was it?" I asked.

Tex shrugged. "He didn't know. He turned bright red. Said he had it written down somewhere."

"Eww," I said.

"He sold one of those photographs for a thousand times more than he gave that little girl. I got up and walked out of the class."

"Is that the one where the professor failed you?" I knew Tex had left college early. He shrugged.

The camera feed showed Adawi getting up from the bench.

"What do you know about this artist?"

Tex shrugged again. "That guy has terrific taste in art. But so do art thieves."

I laughed. "Well, is it cool if I go visit the piece? I still have about thirty minutes before I have to open."

"Go ahead."

"Aho, Tex."

Tex laughed, "That's not Cherokee, little sister."

"Shoot, you know I speak about as much Cherokee as I do Kiowa." It wasn't true, but it was what I always said.

"No reason for that to be a permanent condition."

"So you and my mom keep telling me." Then I slipped my headphones on and went to go sit with the *Ladder*.

Space Age Love Song

I sat down and began to sketch. While I tried to get the lines straight on my paper, I thought of Booker T. Washington and the artist, Martin Puryear. I had read an interview that the name came after the piece. That it just fit. Art was in conversation with the world. The more it said, the more it resonated for me. Like music. Sound waves like fluid connecting you to the musician, the singer. It was why I liked vinyl. Music broken into digital bits was just colder than the warmth of analog.

I considered the idea that education and jobs had been touted as the way for people of color to succeed—to climb out of poverty, even while the system was rigged with redlining; even with the burning of Black Wall Street in Tulsa, my mother's hometown. It was all a scheme organized to advantage those with the advantages, and test and winnow out those who started with significantly less money or brown bodies. I thought of legacy advantage in the Ivy Leagues and testing classes that weren't free. I thought of my father, who had joined and then left the police force when he realized he couldn't change it from the inside but would either be destroyed or corrupted from without. I could empathize, but I would never really viscerally feel the impact of a white world's regard on a Black man or woman, or even on my Black Cherokee brother. Get all the education you want, it wouldn't change the skin color people saw when they looked at you. It wouldn't change the names they called you when they had a tantrum.

The top of the hand-carved ladder was precarious, slim. If anyone could balance on the top, the fall from the great height would kill them.

I was startled from my reverie by the reentry of the intern. I took off my headphones.

"You mind?" He gestured to the other end of the bench. There was room for three or four people, but I scooted away from the center of the bench, leaving him three-fourths of the wooden seat.

"I'm Adawi," he said, extending his hand. "But, please, call me Adam." On his brown thumb there was a long white scar, and on his pinkie, a bandage, "flesh" colored, but not *our* flesh colored. Complexion-wise we could have been related—cousins, citizens of the same tribe. He noticed me noticing and started to pull his hand back, but I reached forward and grabbed it, shaking lightly.

"The hazards of working with wood," he said, as I burst out, "Sharp knives, yeah?"

We both laughed.

His hand was warm and strong, and I was conscious of holding the grip a few moments too long. I was glad I had grabbed his hand before he could pull away and also embarrassed. He held my hand until I let go.

"What kind of artist are you?" he asked. I was sure I looked surprised, but then he gestured towards my sketchbook.

"Oh, I just love this piece. This is where I come to think," I added halfheartedly, "about how to make the world a better place."

"Your drawing is good."

I laughed. "I draw this piece a lot. But my medium is photography. Mostly. Well, I mean, I like to take pictures. But at the museum, I just work at the gift shop and take classes."

Suddenly I was self-conscious. Here I was talking to someone who was my age and had traveled far from his home to study art—to make art. I felt so unserious. I thought of Loren, busy writing code that she said would indeed make the world a better place, the opposite of so much online content that subsisted on hate and divisiveness while just creating more. Jess and I spent our free time hiking or going to the movies, or we binged shows like Tananarive Due's series, *The Good House*. I did take pictures. I loved photography. But could it be the reason I moved? A love. Not a passion, I didn't think. I wasn't good enough. Was I?

I suddenly felt weirdly unmoored. I enjoyed photography and art, but maybe I just wasn't confident enough.

I decided to say the quiet part aloud. "I don't think I'm passionate. About anything. Except my two best friends, Loren and Jess. And my family. My whole going-to-college seems like—I don't know, doing something because everyone has been telling me that's what you do? Forever. Then what?" I didn't like it. And I didn't like to think about it too hard. It was just what you did. Education. That was supposed to save us, yeah? "I don't even *hate* anything, not even foods." I paused. "But too much citric acid gives me mouth ulcers. I definitely hate orange drinks." I froze. Where had this rabbit hole monologue come from?

"Okay," Adam laughed, "I will never ever offer you orange drinks."

"Wait, not all orange drinks. I like orange juice. Just not fake orange drinks. Makes my throat hurt."

We sat in silence. I watched him watch me out of the corner of my eye. Then he smiled. The kind of smile that was warm and contagious.

"It was really hard for you to come up with something you hate, wasn't it?"

I laughed. "But this sculpture. I love this sculpture. It's the most important piece here. I'm glad it has its own room."

We both looked at it after a moment.

"It deserves its own building," he said. "There is so much in it. The experience of the artist, the weight of history. It's in the wood and every stroke of the knife that made it. That there is one long golden ash sapling, cut in half, then carved and named to symbolize an impossible climb? Or a slow climb? Or a climb that is so hard."

"It can be interpreted so many ways. It just kind of depends on the viewer's life. Each time I come back here, I experience a different piece."

At the same time, we both finished, "It's perfect."

"It's the whole reason I'm here," Adam added quietly.

I looked at him. Suddenly I felt like we were in a church.

He looked askance at me. "Well, one of the main reasons."

"Yeah?" I asked, "What else?"

Adam turned and looked at me directly. "That"—he paused—"is hard to explain."

I wondered how this conversation had ended up here. I'm not a verbose person. I didn't tell people—especially people I had just met—what I loved or hated, or asked them those kinds of questions. I combed my brain for something else to say.

"Oh, what tribe are you?" He gave me a confused look. "I'm making signs for the gift shop to go with the pieces you're selling."

Adam frowned. "People in this country are very confused about Indigeneity. They don't know about the many tribes, do they? And your parent can be a tribal citizen, but that doesn't guarantee their child is." He paused. "Just list 'from Costa Rica.'"

I frowned. "I can do that." I took a breath. "But what tribe are you?"

It was his turn to breathe, a long, deep inhale. "My father was a white American and my mother was Cherokee. But I wasn't raised in the culture. I wasn't raised in any culture." He smiled. But it wasn't a real smile, at least not a happy one; it was the saddest smile I had ever seen. "I grew up in a commune, a utopia by current standards, a place where I was raised with one purpose. To make the future better."

"That doesn't sound so bad."

"Well," he replied, glancing at me from beneath the hair that had escaped the tie pulling it back into a braid, "it got me here. Sitting with you. So, it's not a bad thing."

Was I blushing? What the heck? What was this?

Was this guy slick or what?

"So, who is your family?" I suddenly remembered he said we belonged to the same tribe. That seemed to catch him off guard.

"Yeah, I don't know. My mom has all that info."

Ouch. Major red flag. Best-case scenario, we were cousins; worst-case, it was a family fairy tale. He did look Native. But Indigenous people weren't the only humans with black hair and high cheekbones. And maybe he just had a really great tan? Adam continued.

"I don't use cultural heritage to sell my art. I grew up in a commune, a very odd commune. Lots of what you call expats from America and Europe. Think Patricia Highsmith and James Baldwin and Gertrude Stein." He smiled. But that sad look was back in his eyes.

I wondered if it was a troubled place, the kind of place that people called "cults" and made documentaries about or raided to save kids from exploitation and human trafficking. I didn't want to push it, but I realized I did. I needed to know.

"But you don't want me to put 'Cherokee'?"

"No. The pieces I make aren't 'traditional.' They're not like the art of Indigenous people in the past here, or Cherokee artists, or in Costa Rica, even. I make what I make because it pleases me. Because I get the knife and the wood and my hands and I can't stop cutting until I'm done; because the wood wants to be carved and sanded into those shapes."

I nodded.

"Am I only a good artist if I am Indian?"

I let the question hang. Overhead, the opening strings of "A City of Silver & A City of Fire" by Louis W. Ballard began to play, alerting us that it was fifteen minutes before the museum's opening.

Adam stood. "Do you work in the gift shop all day?"

I nodded.

"Maybe I can come by? See the display."

I almost caught my breath.

"Sure, okay."

He reached out his hand, pulling me up from the bench. "It was nice to meet you, Stevie who hates orange drinks."

I laughed and we went opposite directions. I hadn't talked to a new person like that in a long time. Well, maybe Alan, but he was older—an adult, a teacher. Our text conversations this summer had been long and interesting. But in person?

Weirdly, I felt like Adam knew more about me than anyone else now, other than Loren, Jess, and my family. But Mom would still forget and hand me a Fanta Orange now and then. And she had known me longer than I had been alive. I hadn't had a conversation like that with a stranger—a young guy my age, no less—maybe ever. But something bothered me. The mystery. When someone tells you who they are, believe them. I wondered if Adam had any idea who he was. What do you do with a man who doesn't know who he is yet?

24
Frames

When I got back to the gift shop, I went into the office to make edits to Adam's sign.

"Costa Rican sculptor, Adam," I typed. Then I made a page for photographs of his pieces along with their prices. I got the box with his carved pieces and held each one, photographing them with my phone, touching the smooth wooden sculpted creatures that felt oddly warm and alive—comforting in my hand, like living stones polished by raging waters; tender expressions. A napping kit fox, a creature like a kitten, animals wrapped around each other and themselves. A flying bird, a fish streaking along a stream. Each one felt alive and substantial. When I was done, I put them back in the box and took them out to put them on display.

While I worked on the floor, Christy had come in and was counting money at the register, in case any early birds came in or an employee needed to buy a water or a chocolate bar. From the register where she was refilling the receipt printer for the few people who would want a hard copy, she hollered, "Those pieces look great. Have you seen the guy?"

I blushed. He was a little young for Christy to be saying it that way. Gross.

She came over to look at the signs I had made. She frowned. "It needs something."

"Yeah?" I was nervous she would ask me to add "Indigenous" back to the bio. Instead, she snapped her fingers.

"A portrait! That's what we need. You can shoot a portrait of him, right?"

I swallowed. "I'm not exactly a portrait photographer."

She looked at me. Agog. "What! Are you kidding? Those pieces of yours in the Senior Show? Of your friends and baby brother and parents? They were gorgeous!"

"Thanks?" I said. It was hard to always match Christy's excitement. She used all the exclamation points, all day.

"Tell you what. The shop will pay you to spend the afternoon shooting photos with the artist? I'll call Carole to come in and work your shift this afternoon? Plus, we'll pay for your materials and thirty dollars an hour to take pictures! I'm going to write an article for the friends of the museum, so I need more images anyway!" Christy didn't ask, she told. In exclamation points. "You have your camera?!"

I always had my camera. And like that, Christy had decided. She disappeared into the back to call the workshop and then Carole and arranged everything. When she came back, she said I could leave for the day at lunch, head to the security guard office, and Tex would take me to the workshop to meet Adam. It was like a car crash the way this thing had just happened to me. Except, I didn't think it was necessarily a bad thing; just not how I had assumed the day would go.

I texted Loren to ask if she wouldn't mind picking me up somewhere else if we went to shoot photos. She shot back a thumbs-up a little later. It was a group chat, and Jess added that they would be coming along too. Suddenly I felt nervous. This was starting to feel like more than a casual hang-out-and-take-pictures thing. I wondered if I should explain it was a paying gig, but thought preemptively that over-explaining would be a lady-doth-protest-too-much moment.

I didn't think about the photo shoot while I worked. The distraction kept my anxiety in check. At lunchtime, Carole came in, hugged me, and shooed me away. I liked visiting the Preparator's Workshop. It was where you could see all the magic happening. Also, it connected to a storage space for art that was off-exhibit, underground, climate-controlled, and never humid like the rest of the city. In that space there were rolling walls and shelves holding various objects. They slept in the dark, put away until they were needed for a show. It was like a bank vault for art: cameras always watching, doors locked up tight.

Once in a while, Christy sent me down there with Tex to assess the art others rarely saw, hoping to draw attention to the permanent collection and make connections with pieces in the shop. I looked with eyes that tried to memorize the work of artists too rare to display too often, or currently underappreciated. Even Vincent van Gogh was once a tough sell. Ask Theo. And, of course, there were the pieces which would forever stay in storage: irrelevant, mortal. I was grateful not to work in a museum with remains. That's bad medicine, as Mom would say.

The workshop, though well-ventilated too, was still a dusty place that smelled of acrylic. It was where plastic was molded into shapes to hold or protect or display priceless objects, and where wood frames were cut or built or repaired, hammered into cases. The dry air felt cool when Tex and I stepped out of the elevator into the bottom of the museum.

I had my camera out already, the bag hanging over my arm.

"No flash around the art," Tex reminded me.

"I know."

"Shooting pictures of the new intern, aye?" There was something in his voice that embarrassed me. Made me feel shy.

"Christy wants them for the shop."

He smiled. "I bet she does."

"Tex." I tried to sound disapproving, but really, I just laughed.

In the shop Bob was at the desk looking through a large binder, making notes on a large sheet of paper. It was a notebook on an upcoming exhibit. I saw a few other guys working, painting a false wall, loading up some tools into a rolling cabinet. But I didn't see Adam. Bob looked up when we came in.

Bob ignored me, speaking to Tex. "We're going to have to take out the biggest glass wall to get this piece in."

"Good thing it never rains anymore," Tex said drily.

Bob guffawed, then looked at me, remembering Christy had told him why she sent me there. "Adam's out back," he remarked. Then, "Hey, Tex, you going to Sundance this year?" Bob wasn't Native, but his wife was.

Dismissed, I headed for the big rolling garage door which was closed but had the exit door next to it.

"He's welding. Don't look at the flame," Bob called after me.

Jeez. It was already a hundred degrees out there. WTF?

"Good to know." I grabbed two bottles of water out of the large refrigerator in the corner before going out to the patio. The overhang jutted from the hillside slope where the bottom floor of the museum was buried.

I felt the push of the heat and sun immediately. Adam's back was to me. He was focused. Sparks flew, creating a halo, a starburst around him, a firework with Adam's form a silhouette. I lifted my camera. I took a picture and opened the lens up, a wide photo with flames and heat and white concrete flaring. I pivoted around him so that I got his body and welding helmet in profile. He was wearing a brown leather Carhartt jacket and a leather apron tied around his waist that caught and volleyed the sparks away from his body. He was completely focused. I stepped further out, my camera anchored to his figure. He noticed me in his peripheral vision. Seeing him see me, I froze. He turned off the torch and lifted his visor.

"Siyo," he called, his smile bright and white teeth shiny. His brown skin was diamonded with sweat. He really was beautiful. I wondered how often he had to shave the sides of his head to keep that scalp looking neat.

I had been about to say he was going to get heatstroke and he shouldn't let Bob make him weld in the Texas sun, but I was too surprised by his Cherokee greeting, though should I have been? Instead, I held out the bottle of water, which seemed like threatening a forest fire with an eye dropper. "You speak?" I asked, adding, "Cherokee?"

Adam took the bottle. "Tla," he said. "Tex told me you're Cherokee too. You didn't mention that earlier." He held up his hand and slipped off his welding gloves. A streak of black ink was smeared across the back of his hand. Cherokee syllabary, smeared, but legible. "I'm good with languages, though. There were a lot of them, where I grew up."

The way he said it was funny. Like he was making it up. Improvising. *Yes, and . . .* I thought.

"I wish I were good with languages," I said. I pointed my camera at him. He was drinking the bottle of water. The photo was totally an ad for H_2O in plastic. I guess if you ignored the ink smears and the harm to the environment when that plastic never decomposed. He finished the water quickly and wiped his forehead, leaving a trail of black ink. I took another picture. Then I showed it to him.

"Oh, man." He used the bottom of his shirt and tried to wipe the ink away. I looked away from his bare torso. We might even be able to mark those prices up a wee bit. Especially if they threw in a portrait.

"I'm almost done here. You should go back in. It's too hot." He picked up a temperature gun and aimed it at the concrete at my feet. "It's forty-six degrees."

"It's a lot hotter than that," I said.

He pushed a button. "One hundred fifteen Fahrenheit."

"That's hot," I said. I handed him the second water bottle I was still holding.

"You're not dressed for this by the way," he said, while opening it.

"Says the guy in denim and leather."

"You want to go eat in about thirty minutes?" he asked.

"Take me someplace you like?"

"You like barbecue? The best patio places around here are barbecue places."

"Sounds good. As long as I can wear denim and leather."

"Those are the only places I know," I replied.

Then I returned to the cool of the building. As soon as I walked in, Tex stood up. "Let's go look at some art." I didn't know if he wanted to see art or get away from Bob. But either was good with me. Bob was a women-and-kids-should-be-neither-seen-nor-heard kind of guy. I was not a fan.

At the storage side of the basement, we signed in to the clipboard hanging next to the digital lock. Old-school and new-school security working hand-in-hand. "What are we researching today?" Tex asked.

"Art focusing on animals," I said, thinking of the article Christy wanted to write tying the sculptures Adam made to our collection. Surely we could find some pieces in the permanent collection. We started with the moving shelves, rotating them up and down, looking at the photos hanging below the boxes in which the pieces were stored safely away. On my phone, I noted what artists and abstract animals I found. Then we went to the paintings.

Tex pressed a button and the first wall rolled out.

We walked along its length, noting the names and subject matter.

"So many white men," I said.

"Painting anything but," Tex remarked. He pressed the button and the wall retracted back into the bank of walls. He turned to me. "Just because we're not represented doesn't mean we haven't always been artists." Something in my chest kept me from saying anything back.

Tex pressed a button and the next wall rolled out.

I sighed. "What are you working on, Tex?" Suddenly the room seemed quieter. I waited. We were standing in front of a large abstract nude of a woman, her nipples large and dark, her brown skin a contrast to the white, sandy beach around her, a fuchsia flower in her black hair. She reclined as if she existed only for the painter, the viewer. Tex pressed the button and the painting retracted into the wall.

"When I was in college, I painted a lot of stuff like that. I was in a figure drawing class, so we all painted this same model—a local woman, nearly a girl—who made a lot of money posing for the art students; more than most jobs you could get with just a few years of college.

"She was beautiful. We all painted her from different perspectives, drew her from different angles. Some people brought in things for her to hold or wear. She smiled. She tolerated it. She bore it."

He stopped. He wasn't really answering my question.

"I never did that. And when the other students talked about her outside of class, I just walked away.

"But I never said anything. Never spoke up. I just kept painting her, drawing her. That professor liked my work, said my paintings were her as if seen by Kandinsky or Picasso or Manet or Monet . . .

"You could have called each painting by the model's first name and added the name of some important European artist. But at the end of that class, I asked her out to lunch."

Tex pressed a button and another wall rolled out. We walked down either side. He didn't speak. When he pressed the button and the next wall retracted, I couldn't stand it anymore.

"What did she say?"

Tex broke into a smile. "I married her."

I laughed. He meant his wife, Jewell. Then I remembered that she had passed less than a year earlier.

I felt the room's pressure drop.

"Oh, Tex." I felt myself tearing up. I didn't want to cry. You shouldn't make grieving people comfort you.

He just nodded. "Last month, I pulled out all those paintings I did of her." He took a deep breath, pushed for the next wall of paintings, abstract blocks of color purchased by oil magnates and donated after they hung over a corporate office a few years.

"And they don't look like her at all. Not my Jewell."

I listened. Maybe I was learning wait time from Dad.

"Listening is love. Our marriage wasn't always a party. But in her eyes, when she wasn't mad at me—and I promise you, I deserved her being mad more than once—but when I remember her looking at me? I knew that she saw me. I knew that she loved me. I never felt alone when she looked at me, Stevie."

I waited for him to go on. He pressed the button once more and the paintings retracted. He pressed it again and more rolled out.

"So, I got out the primer, and every weekend now, I pull out one of those paintings and I cover that canvas in white paint. I let it dry. And I add another layer. And when that one is dry, I sand it."

Tex checked his watch. "Those paintings, they weren't exactly lies. But they weren't her, either." He pressed the button. The paintings retracted back into the wall. I had forgotten to note if there were any animals in the last four.

"Lunchtime," he finished.

I followed him back to the shop.

"Wado, Tex," I said, as he turned towards the exit, returning to the guard station.

"Hawa," he replied. When he got to the top of the stairs, he looked at me, and then he looked up at the cameras high above us. They had pivoted towards us, recording our movements and words. *They're always watching you.*

I laughed. "I know," I said.

Motorbike

Adam came out of the back of the workshop where I was waiting for him. He was toweling off his long, wet hair that was no longer in a braid.

"You ready?" he asked.

"I can call us a ride. I don't have a car." I didn't say: *I don't drive; I can't drive; I have a license, but driving scares me.*

"I have a motorcycle."

That was unexpected. I hadn't practiced responding to "I have a motorcycle." Instead, I just said, "I've never ridden a motorcycle."

"I have an extra helmet for you. Is the barbecue place far?"

"No. Just left out of the parking lot onto Camp Bowie, right on Virginia, then left on White Settlement."

He smiled. "I promise I am a very good rider. I will be very careful."

I laughed, not lightheartedly, more like at a funeral. *I put the "fun" in "funeral."* I swallowed.

"Um, I don't know. My dad told me never to ride on the back of a bike . . ." I was following Adam to the underground garage where he was parked. He was carrying leather saddlebags and he put them on the motorcycle, gesturing I could put my things in for the ride. The bike was a replica of an Indian Chief from 1948 because, of course it was. I had seen one like it in the Smithsonian's National Museum of the American Indian a few years earlier. Bright yellow. But Adam's was black. Because, yeah, well, of course.

"It's just like riding a bike," he said, handing me the helmet.

"Except superfast and I have no control of the handlebars or the speed . . ."

Adam laughed. Then he stepped over the bike's saddle and sat down. I handed him back the helmet he had handed me and climbed over behind him.

He turned back towards me. "What if I told you I can see the future and I know nothing bad will happen?"

I looked into his eyes and reached forward, taking the helmet back. "Ever?"

"Not today," he said.

"I guess that would explain why you have the extra helmet," I replied, as I buckled it on. To myself I asked, "Wonder what you have in your wallet . . ."

"What?" he asked.

"Nothing," I replied. I gave him directions to my favorite place along the river with an outdoor patio. Patios were one of the best things about Texas.

I put my arms at my sides as he started up the motorbike. After the first turn, I gave up and put my arms around his waist. I kept my eyes closed the entire way. I felt dizzy, like I hadn't had enough water. I held on and we rode. I kept my hands clasped, trying not to move. By the time we reached the restaurant, I realized I was breathing when he breathed, the road and the vehicles around us forgotten.

At lunch I found myself talking about my two different lives. One in Texas, with my two best friends, Jess and Loren, even though I admitted that really they were each other's very best friends, had a connection from before I met them, communicated without talking.

"Jess, well, their parents are super religious, conservative. Jess would go by gender neutral pronouns with everyone, but their parents would lose their minds. Loren is pretty into them. If it weren't for Jess's parents I think they'd be a couple." I paused. This wasn't stuff we talked about to anyone. Well, Loren and I talked about it. Loren was patient. Focused on her work. She thought things would either change when we all moved away or they wouldn't, and Loren would finally move on. Jess was fragile about this stuff. They did what they had to do to have the most freedom while they lived in their parents' home.

I didn't really feel that left out with Loren and Jess usually—just like I was often second. "I mean, I'm lucky to have two best friends, yeah?" I wasn't sure if he quite believed me. Or, if I did either. Isn't that something I wanted? Not that you could run out of love. Yet, I wanted to be someone's first thought, not always and forever only part of a group chat. Maybe it was seeing how much two people could love each other, not just Jess and Loren, but my dad and mom too. Maybe that made me feel like I was missing something.

The other life we had was with my aunties on the Cherokee Reservation where, until a year ago, we used to visit once a month. Dad and Mom would hunt and fish when deer was in season. Sometimes I went with them. Often, I stayed and helped my aunts, tried to learn some Cherokee by listening to their conversations, went with them to forage in the woods, attempting to remember what was edible, what it was called in Tsalagi, what to stay away from. I showed Adam the sketches of wild onions and hickory nuts, a few recipes I'd jotted down. Detailed drawings of baskets and river cane and blowguns with darts fletched with rabbit fur.

I realized neither one of us was eating; he had just listened while I talked. Kept the flies out of the barbecue sauce.

I asked him about his life and took a bite of fatty brisket. Adam deflected, said his mother had died early and he had been raised by many "fathers and mothers." I hoped he really was Cherokee. I doubted we were cousins. Figured my mom would have known about him and his family, though, of course, the chances were never zero. But now, knowing his mother had passed, I didn't feel comfortable pressing. And the longer I looked at him too, I prayed we weren't.

"No real best friend either," he said, then turned it back to me. "Where are you happier?" he asked.

I took another bite. It gave me time to think. Finally, I swallowed and took a big drink of soda. The sweet, caffeinated drink may have been getting warm, but it felt refreshing in the heat. "I can't choose," I finally said. "Texas is where we work, go to school. Where I get to hang with Loren and Jess. The work life allows my family time and money for the other. The Reservation is where we spend time with family. Hunt, fish, cook at camp together, go to the stompgrounds. It's the only place I really hear my language in conversation. And that's the best way to learn Indigenous languages, you know. They have to be applied, be part of your life."

Adam nodded.

"And, well, Mom, Dad, and Levi are in both places, so . . ."

We were quiet a few minutes. A welcome breeze shook the invasive bamboo that grew along the river. I wondered how long ago river cane had thrived here too.

Finally, I spoke again. "I don't know, one feels like something we have to do, the other feels like a place we belong, but too special to be every day, you know?"

"That's too bad," he said. "Why do you feel guilty for being where you belong?"

I didn't know how to answer that. Instead, I leaned into the hard stuff, but also the stuff I was looking forward to doing. I told him about Levi's allergies and the different times he had ended up in the hospital. Then I began talking about my plans for next year, going to college with Loren and Jess. We had already reserved a dorm. Adam listened attentively.

Eventually, all out of words, I asked him what he would be doing after the museum. He'd had his hands clasped together, but now he rotated them out, like when you make the shadow puppet of a flying bird.

"The future is unwritten."

I laughed. "You stole that from Joe Strummer."

He smiled mysteriously. "Only borrowed."

Garageland

As part of Adam's internship, he had a warehouse space in which to live and work on his own projects. After lunch we drove over there.

Adam opened the garage door and pushed the motorcycle in, leaving the door open, allowing what breeze there was to flow across the concrete floor and out the windows along the roof that provided ventilation. The district the warehouse was in was mostly abandoned. The small office next to the open garage door was walled off in the corner and had been turned into a bedroom as cozy as you would expect being in a hundred-year-old corrugated metal warehouse. The office/bedroom door had wavy glass, which was impossible to see through. OFFICE was stenciled across it.

To get to the bathroom, you had to go through the office/bedroom, so I did. I washed my face and tried to untangle my hair using my fingers as a comb. Adam's bed was old and iron, a lean twin with starbursts decorating each thin rail between the larger posts. It was older than the warehouse, I guessed. On the wall next to the door inside the room was an old rolltop desk. That was at least as old as the warehouse. And on top of it sat an old fax machine. I picked up the phone's handset and listened. No dial tone. I hung up the phone and returned to the quiet of the cavernous space.

Adam was using a long pole with a hook on the end to open windows along the top of the tall warehouse walls.

"It's weird to live alone," Adam said. "I thought I would like it, after years of living in shared spaces." He paused, as if weighing each word. "But I miss the energy of other people. Even when no one is speaking, the comfort of people who are part of a community and care for each other in the same space. Like in the workshop. The rhythm of people making things. That hum, you know?"

I nodded. It was like that in my Aunt Geneva's house in Oklahoma, especially in the kitchen. Compared to that, our home was still, especially when it was just me and Levi.

Adam and I were each lost in our thoughts.

"How about some music?" I said, pulling out my phone. "Do you have a speaker?"

He shook his head. "But I have a record player."

"What? No way."

"There were boxes of vinyl when I moved in. Most of it's in good shape. If you wipe off the years of silence." Adam pointed to the wooden fruit box on the counter next to the sink.

I began to sort through. I pulled out Leon Bridges's first album. "This guy is from here. Super talented, super versatile." He was one of Mom and Dad's favorites and was still making incredible music, even as an old guy. They took me and Levi to shows when he was in town. Bridges had more range than anyone else I could think of. He could sound old school or contemporary, never seeming false.

"Which side are you playing?"

"The *A* side, of course. I'm not a monster."

Adam laughed. The song that came up was the title track. Without closing my eyes, my parents held each other in front of me, swaying, singing softly.

"That's nice," he said. Then Adam excused himself to get cleaned up, disappearing into the bedroom. I could hear the shower kick on. I sat down in a camp chair and texted Loren the warehouse address, not expecting to hear from her until her next break. Adam had offered to give me a ride home on the back of his motorcycle, but I wasn't ready to ride on the highway, and I knew Dad wasn't going to be happy if he saw us driving up to the house. The warehouse was fairly close to our neighborhood, so Loren wouldn't have to go out of her way.

I texted Jess a quick "Hello" too, but they texted me the emoji that meant they were busy at their parent's ice cream shop. So, I put my phone down and got my camera out of the saddlebags on the motorcycle. I took a few pictures of the motorcycle and the hand-tooled leather saddlebags. Then I began to wander around the rest of the building. Towards the back there was a long workbench on which lay a variety of carving tools and works finished or in progress. At lunch, Adam had told me he liked to reclaim wood that would be otherwise burned or end up in landfills, and various pieces of old fence and barns and floors were stacked on pegs in the wall, as well as other tools. To the side, another wall blocked off a large portion of the back of the warehouse, creating another separate space. I walked around the wall and saw it had larger pieces. Specifically, several sawhorses ran the length of the room. On top of them were several long pieces of wood, long poles that were rough and unworked. I wondered what Adam planned to do with those; what kind of wood it was. I photographed the long poles. They seemed oddly familiar.

"Stevie?" Adam called from the other side.

"Back here," I hollered back.

Adam was quickly in the space with me, his face a bit concerned, his hair loose and damp.

"Could you maybe not take pictures of this bit?" he asked.

I looked at him.

"I'm superstitious about this part of a project. I don't know what these pieces will be, yet." His lips twisted in what seemed a self-conscious smile. "This is when I—well—I talk to the wood. Ask it what it wants to be." He laughed. "I'm not embarrassed about that part, I just don't want people to see it beforehand."

"Oh, sorry." I started clicking through the photos I had taken, deleting them. "I should have asked first. Sorry." Suddenly, I was embarrassed, as if I were a peeping tom or a spy.

"I don't mean you," he clarified. "Just not for the museum, not for the shop."

"All gone," I said, smiling. "No problem." I nodded in understanding. I was superstitious and sensitive about my photographs, too. I wondered if he really meant it when he said I was an exception, or if he was just being polite, trying to make things less awkward.

"Ready to get to work?" I asked, holding up my camera, as if I'd suddenly remembered I was being paid to hang out with him.

"Let's do it."

We spent the next three hours talking while I shot a variety of portraits in various styles. Leibovitz, Arbus, Clark, and Weems. I thought of what Tex had said. So, I shot the final ones in what I considered "my style." I took some headshots for him too. Photos I thought he might be able to use in the future.

It was stupid hot outside, but not much worse than the warehouse's interior, in spite of the large, noisy fan. I took pictures of him on the motorcycle riding slowly around the warehouse, then on the long gravel road, the dust kicking up behind him, his hair loose and tangling in the wind without his helmet.

When we went back inside, his hair was a mess. "Let's do a few more formal ones," I suggested. "You have a nice button-up shirt? And a brush for that hair?"

He laughed and disappeared into his bedroom. He came back out a few minutes later carrying a brush and wearing a crisp white shirt, not quite buttoned up, hanging over a pair of black jeans. Everything was tight enough to communicate the muscles underneath. Christy was going to love these. "Is this okay?"

"Sure," I shrugged, as if I didn't notice.

We staged some photos as if he was carving, but his hair kept falling across his face, over his hands, blocking the camera's view of him and hiding his dark brown eyes.

I grabbed the brush and suggested he put it back in a braid like he'd had it earlier. He pulled it all back and then extended the brush and a rubber band to me. "I'm sorry, but would you mind? It takes me a while to get it even."

"Oh, of course." I put the camera on the workbench. I brushed his hair carefully, dividing it into three sections, but didn't pull tight enough to make a good braid, so I had to take it out and try again.

"I'm sorry. Want me to skip it?" I asked the third time I started over.

"Please, no." I felt him shiver as my fingers brushed the back of his neck. I blushed, marveling at how quickly we had become seemingly intimate. I was finally finishing the plait and sliding the black rubber band into place when I heard Loren say, "Knock-knock," and I turned to see her, Jess, and Levi walking in, Loren's eyebrows raised at me.

I immediately felt self-conscious. I always did when I was taking pictures with other people around, at least until I got in the zone, until the world outside of me and the camera disappeared. But this was next level.

Levi let go of Loren's hand and ran over. He was always happy to see me, which in turn always made me happy. I bent down and hugged him. He stared up at Adam, taking him in. "Is he Cherokee too?" he whispered. Not well. Little kids aren't great at whispering.

Adam dropped down to Levi's level. "Yeah, Levi, nice to meet another Cherokee." Adam held out his hand and Levi smiled wide and reached out and shook it.

Loren and Jess had hung back, watching.

"These are my friends Loren and Jess," I said, leading Levi and Adam back to where they waited.

"Nice to meet you," Adam announced, extending his hand to Loren. Jess was holding pints of ice cream and made a big deal about not being able to juggle and shake hands at the same time. Sometimes they were a goof.

"What time is it?" I asked, but then picked up my phone to check. I saw I had missed several text messages from Loren. "Oh, Loren, I'm sorry."

Loren waved my apology off. "No, we're early. The power went out in the arts district, so everything closed early. There were only a few kids whose parents couldn't come pick them up right away, so most of us got to go home. That's why Jess isn't still scooping ice cream."

"And why we have free pints! Not everything would fit in the emergency generator cooler."

"Since you didn't answer, we came straight over." Loren's eyes flicked between me and Adam. "Should we come back later?"

"No," I said quickly. "We're almost done."

Adam had gone to his fridge and gestured to Jess to put the ice cream within. They returned with several glass bottles and a bottle opener. "Don't worry," he said when he saw me, "the orange one is for little brother."

I laughed. I ignored the look on Loren's face.

Suddenly he looked sheepish. "I'm sorry, I should have asked first," he whispered. "Can Levi have a soda?"

"Yes, yes, that's fine. He's not allergic to anything in orange soda."

Adam opened the soda and gave it to Levi. He gave Loren a choice of the other sodas he had brought over. Jess had already grabbed a root beer and was making floats. Loren took a cola and opened it.

"You can use my office," he said, gesturing towards the door, "if you want to work while we finish up."

Loren cut her eyes at me. I widened my eyes and shook my head to let her know I hadn't blabbed about her projects. I added, "We'll only be a few more minutes taking pictures. Almost done."

"I'll just sit and read," Loren said, and pulled a worn copy of *Parable of the Sower* from her back pocket.

"Me too," Jess added, pulling out their e-reader.

"What are you reading?" I asked.

"*An Unkindness of Ghosts*," they said. "Again."

Jess kept all their books on an e-reader so their parents didn't see what they were reading. They were real book-banning types and would not have cared for Rivers Solomon, as much as we loved them.

I reached for a mineral water, suddenly aware of how thirsty I was. Adam went to the workbench and reached for something on a shelf. He had what appeared to be a cube of wood wrapped in ribbons, but when he held it up, I saw it stretched out and was made of six squares of wood attached to each other by ribbons. "May I give this to Levi?"

"What is it?"

"A toy . . . a magic ladder." He smiled.

I nodded and called Levi over. He showed my brother how to make it look like the top block was traveling back and forth down the ladder, clacking until it seemed to reach the bottom. Levi thought it was cool and ran to show Loren and Jess.

We took the drinks back to the workbench and I took a few more photos, staged, like Adam was working. His sharply braided hair hung across his shoulder now, contrasting with the white of his shirt. He sanded the gentle details on the round shape of a bird curled up in a ball, its head tucked back into its wing. It was the size of a nuthatch, small. Though abstracted, the tiny bird looked like it might take a breath. I photographed it in Adam's outstretched hands.

When we finished, I asked him if he wanted to look back through the photos.

He shook his head. "I trust you. If I look good, you look good." Then he smiled at me in a way that made me feel like he was flirting, saying something that had more than one meaning. Thank goodness it was so hot—my face was already red, so this time he wouldn't see me blush. If I had any game whatsoever I would have said, *You don't make it hard.* But I don't. I have zero game. I never really even wanted to play before. I struggled not to laugh out loud at the thought as I put my camera back into my camera bag.

Adam held the small bird he had been working on out to me.

"Here," he said.

I hesitated, but then accepted it. "Wado."

He smiled. "Hawa." He had learned at least three Cherokee words in one day. To share with me.

Good, I thought. "Osda," I said.

"Wado." *Make that four.* This time, though, I only smiled, otherwise we'd be "Wado"-ing and "Hawa"-ing all day.

My water was still sweating on the counter. I grabbed it. We walked back to where Loren sat reading. Levi had turned his attention to his orange soda. I took a drink of my water and it still tasted like the coldest, sweetest thing.

Loren closed her book and Adam began talking to her about the philosophy Butler had written about in her Parable series. Loren loved talking about two things most in the world: Octavia Butler and spiritual philosophy. Adam had somehow navigated to both. I sat on the floor with Levi and picked up the ladder. With a coin from my pocket, I showed him what happened when you slipped a coin behind the ribbon of the top block of wood. I kept handing him coins and he kept feeding them into the ladder. Adam and Loren were happily debating what Butler meant, and whether or not it was truly the author's opinion or merely the character that believed that "God is Change." When they started talking about energy and reincarnation, I started listening intently.

"But energy can't be destroyed, so it makes sense."

"Yes, it's the only thing I can think of that does."

"Not if you're my parents," Jess interjected.

My phone buzzed. I checked and saw I had a text from my mom that groceries were going to be delivered soon.

"Sorry to interrupt," I said. "But groceries will be at the house imminently." I didn't add that I had invited Jess and Loren over for dinner with us, because I felt like it would be rude not to extend the invitation to Adam as well, especially since it looked like his cooking facilities consisted of a microwave. But I had the feeling Loren would have some questions for me.

"See you tomorrow," Adam said.

"Yeah, for sure."

When we got to the car, the first thing Loren whispered to me was, "I want to know everything you told him." I saw Jess raise their eyebrows at me, like they felt sorry.

"I didn't say anything about the app," I hissed back, "I promise!"

From the back seat Levi hollered, "I like your new friend."

Loren raised her eyebrows at me. "Your new FRIEND seems nice." Then to me, quietly: "And for a man he's pretty beautiful." She shrugged. "If you like that sort of thing. I mean, I don't even like dudes, but . . ."

I blushed. I had pulled out my camera and was clicking through the images. Deleting the bad and blurry ones.

"Can't wait to see those photos," Jess said, giggling.

"I want to see," Levi said, reaching forward into the front seat for the camera in a futile effort. I was looking at one of the few I had taken with Adam's shirt unbuttoned to his waist, his muscular torso showing. Jess was already leaning over to see.

"Interesting . . ." they muttered.

I turned the screen towards Loren so she could take a look. She glanced at it from the road, raised an eyebrow, and returned her eyes to the road. I turned the camera off and put it away. "Maybe later," I said loudly. "Tell me about school today. What happened when the power went out?"

"Everyone screamed," Levi announced, matching his energy to what he was saying.

Loren gave me a conspiratorial look and laughed. I couldn't help but look embarrassed.

For that week and the next, Adam and I ran into each other early in the morning, hanging out together, sometimes sketching the *Ladder*. Sometimes I just wrote in my journal. We would end up talking. Then we'd see each other again at lunch in the break room. We never made plans or talked about it. He still didn't have a cell phone, which seemed wild to me. I didn't know anyone over twelve without one.

Heaven Sent

Jess and I both had that Monday off, so that was our day to hang out. Sometimes we went to movies Loren wasn't interested in, or we went hiking or kayaking. I always brought my camera. Because I always carried my camera.

That day we decided to take a canoe to the Nature Center early, hoping to catch a glimpse of the small bison herd. Mom and Dad had a truck they used mostly for moving stuff. They let Jess drive it when we wanted to go out on the water, if we promised to wear life vests. There was still enough water in the river to use the canoe, as long as the reservoir was managed.

Once during Indian Summer Camp, a Nature Center employee had showed us a photo of bison skins and skulls stacked taller than a man. Another man stood on top. The railroad made shipping the furs and bones back east easy. Until there were no more bison to exploit. The small herd we had now was a nice gesture towards reparations, but it would take a long time to grow the bison population. I had hopes that cloning would bring back the DNA of some of the long-gone herds, because we were still in danger of inbreeding, as most of the bison left descended from one herd. It was a problem. A man-made problem. The solution would be complicated and expensive and who knew what the long-term complications would be? We were still trying to figure out the long arm of cell phones for the last few generations. But ever man fools around and finds out, doesn't he?

I had brought a telephoto lens. It was a sunny day and I hoped to get some decent pictures of the wildlife of the Nature Center. "*Portraits of Critters*," I joked, my first gallery exhibition.

Jess laughed. We always had fun together. Someone you can count on and laugh with, how do you quantify how much that is worth? How do you even get a friend like that? I thought of the mushrooms that popped up after a certain amount of rain, their spores hanging out under pine needles, waiting for the right amount of shade, water, and perfect temperature. Sometimes friendships mushroomed. But it was impossible for me to make it happen on cue. I put my camera and lenses in a waterproof bag and we launched our canoe. We paddled upriver, towards the lake where Goatman, the star of local urban legend, was said to frequent. Once at the lake we drifted a bit, watching for eagles where we had heard they perched to hunt fish. Relaxing instead of paddling.

I was taking pictures of the different dragonflies flying around the lake's edge when Jess nudged me and directed my gaze to the trees. A large bald eagle was roosting above the water. I turned my camera towards the huge predator. Suddenly, he dove for the water, then pulled back up, as if he had used air brakes. From the trees I heard the alarm of crows. The eagle was flying, burdened with the large fish he had grabbed and trying to return to his nest, when the chasing crows overtook him, one harassing him from the side while the other snagged his catch.

Just as quickly, the crows were gone. The eagle turned back and took another perch above the water, resigned to trying again.

Jess laughed. "I love crows. They understand the importance of community. Eagles are too solitary. Makes life hard."

I agreed silently. I wondered if Jess was going to be a biologist now that they had a scholarship that would allow them to do what they wanted, instead of having to do what their parents demanded.

"Do you know what my parents gave me for graduation?" Jess asked.

I shook my head. I was surprised they gave them anything. Jess worked in their ice cream shop for nothing, ostensibly, except room and board.

"They donated to one of those Christian gay reeducation camps in my name."

"Well," I said, "that's pretty on brand."

"I guess I should be grateful they didn't send me," they mused. "Though, honestly, I think it's just because they would've had to hire someone to work my shifts, or do it themselves."

We both laughed. I tried to think of something to say. My parents wouldn't have cared who I loved or preferred for intimacy, as long as they were able to consent. They wouldn't have cared if I was non-binary or anything else. They wanted me to be a good person, to stand up for the oppressed, and take care of myself and my brother and friends. But as long as I had known Jess, their family had gone to increasingly conservative churches, each stricter than the last. Their mom still bought them things embroidered with "Jessie," as if that would reinforce their femininity. As if to say, "It's a girl!" When Dad coached soccer when we were little, Jess had come in skirts over their shorts and had to keep them on as long as they weren't on the field.

My extended family wasn't perfect, though. I told Jess about the year after Dad and Mom married and how one of Mom's great-uncles didn't like Dad because he was Black. It was something that always surprised me, when one brown person disliked another brown person because of prejudice.

"Isn't that weird?" I said.

Jess had picked up their paddle, working the water for both of us while I took pictures. We were headed back towards the mouth of the river. I switched lenses so I could shoot things closer to us.

"You know, it seems like prejudice can even trump blood too, you know?"

"What do you mean?"

"My grandmother had an older brother named James, beautiful man . . . this was back in the 1980s. I've only ever seen one photo of him. They always tell other people he died of cancer."

They looked up at me. "He was gay." Now they were tearing up. "And sensitive and kind and beautiful and artistic. My great-grandmother, his grandma, loved him anyway. He took care of her until she died. She left everything to him, but he would have rather kept her."

Jess sniffled. "I'm sure that didn't endear him to the family. Anyway, one of my older cousins told me that when he got sick, they filed a suit to take what she left him. He didn't have the energy to fight them, or even have the HIV treated. He was so tired. So, he just moved into the house of a friend. But when he went to the hospital my grandparents took over and wouldn't let anyone in to see him but family."

"The same family that hated him for being gay?"

"Hate the sin, love the sinner," Jess corrected. "Then when he died, they let his friends pay for the funeral and make the service decisions, on the condition they bring in his childhood preacher. Well, that guy came in to save souls. A real fire-and-brimstone man. He looked at James's friends and said that James had renounced his sinful lifestyle and friends and that James prayed his friends would do the same." Their voice was shaky.

The tears for this man I had never met flowed.

"Seems like the people who are supposed to love you and support you can be pretty conditional in dispensing love and kindness." Jess rarely sounded bitter. They always acted like everything was okay. "So, your Native great-uncle hating your dad just because he's Black? That doesn't surprise me at all. I wish it did."

It was impossible to go to Jess and hug them in the canoe, so instead I reached into my backpack and pulled out the fancy granola bars I had brought.

"Have a snack. I'll paddle." I picked up the paddle and moved us through the water. They knew I'd listen if they had anything else to say.

Ancestor
Song

Aunt Geneva's seventy-fifth birthday was that next weekend. Mom wanted us all to go, so I had taken off work and Dad was meeting us there. We left right after work Friday for the five-hour drive. It was pretty much dark by the time we were driving up the mountain.

I hadn't been where Mom called "home" in a year. Mom and Dad and Levi had gone up about once every two months since then. Seemed like we got busy with moving after my grandmother died, and then weekends just filled up with work for me. The weather had been bad that winter with ice storms shutting down roads during the usual holiday visiting time. I hadn't even talked to my aunt in the time since, except when I called to thank her for sending me money for graduation.

Mom had loaded the car with so much stuff to deliver home our bags barely fit. I picked up one box when we arrived and the taped-on lid slid to the side, so I could see it was filled with family photos and important documents. Mom noticed me noticing and demanded I hand it to her.

"What the heck, Mom?" I muttered.

"Fireproof safe in the storage building. Safer here."

"Safer than our house? Where we live?" I whispered back.

"Sissy!" hollered Aunt Geneva.

"Don't make your aunt stumble out here in the dark. Get."

I ran to my aunt and hugged her. She was a solid woman but she couldn't see well in the dark. She held on to me in a tight squeeze.

"You got to visit me more. Half the time people only see each other at funerals."

Ouch. "You're right, Auntie." I felt a pang of guilt thinking about how much less I might see her when I went to college, another four hours away.

"You haven't even seen the new house!"

I was confused. "What house?"

"The one your parents built for y'all."

I wondered if my aunt was confused.

She patted me. "Your uncle cleaned it up before he left for work. Get a flashlight. Let's go see it."

"Mom?"

Mom was still moving boxes to the storage building. Levi had fallen asleep in the back seat and was still there. "You can come back and get him once you're set up. Do what your aunt says." I grabbed a flashlight from the glove compartment. "And take those cots with you." In the trunk were two foldable camping cots and a double mattress pad. For once we wouldn't be sleeping on pallets on the floor of my aunt's living room. *Yes!* I thought. I slung both cots over my shoulder with their straps.

Behind my aunt's, it was dark and level. Just past the storage building was a field of corn. I could see it waving gently in the night breeze.

"What kind of corn are we planting this year?"

"Rainbow corn."

I smiled. Cherokee Colored Flour Corn was my favorite. The multicolored tones of blue and purple looked like gemstones. It was an heirloom crop, so we had to be careful with it. You couldn't plant a different type of corn close by, or they would cross-pollinate. Cross contamination would ruin your seed. We were lucky our land was far enough from the farms that produced GMO crops for the big companies. Though that corn was standard fare on this continent, it was illegal to even sell many GMO products to other countries.

Past the cornfield, I could see a small house with a light in a window. As we got closer to the house, a light came on over the door.

"Solar. With a motion detector," Auntie said proudly. I held my aunt's arm as we walked up the stairs; she gripped the handrail and pulled herself up. We opened the door and Auntie pointed the flashlight at the table next to the door. There were lanterns there. I set them around the small house.

"It's nice," I said. I meant it.

"It's well insulated too. Bound to get cold this winter. We're building me one next and I'm going to let some more family move into my house. Something more elder-friendly for your auntie. And quiet. I love those babies, but I also love my sleep. And my shows."

I laughed. But I was confused what she meant.

"Look at this. I made this. Here, give me a match." Auntie was holding a small triangle of wood with a candle on it. A piece of metal wire poked up over the candle.

She lit the candle and then picked up an aluminum can that was punctured all over.

"Now, go turn off all the lights," she said.

I did. When I was back at her side, she placed the can over the wire. It balanced precariously. All along the wall were birds. She had cut lots of little bird shapes out of the can. Then, the can began to spin and the walls were filled with murmuration. Birds swooped up and down along the walls.

"Oh, Auntie, I think that's the best part!"

Aunt Geneva laughed and we watched the birds in their endless flight.

I set up the cots in the small new home, walked Aunt Geneva back to the house, and returned to the car to get our blankets and pillows. Our cousins were asleep in the back bedrooms when I went to check in with Mom and Auntie. We tried to talk quietly. Mom would hang out in the kitchen with Auntie drinking coffee. She'd be there until Dad got in. We worried about him driving rural roads alone at night. For that matter, there were dashcams in all our family cars, for a reason. Sometimes just existing was a resistance that met with violence. Cell service didn't work out here, but there was a landline in the kitchen. Until he got in, there she'd stay. I went back to the car and carried Levi to bed.

The small cabin was like a studio apartment with a loft. I went and got the double mattress pad and set it up for Mom and Dad upstairs. I put the sheets and blankets on their bed and stretched out. I looked out the large window at the night sky. From there I could see a few more little houses in various stages of being built across the acreage. I wished Mom would come in alone so I could ask her what was going on. Were they all going to move back here when I went to college? There was a lot of new infrastructure on the allotment. It didn't seem like a normal amount of change, though I had been gone a year. Dad knew about this too, obviously. My brain hurt thinking about it. I just needed to get moved to Austin with Loren and Jess.

Outside the stars were brilliant. Light pollution was minimal and the air was cleaner than in town. It was a new moon. There would be dancing tomorrow night nearby. Maybe stickball in the afternoon. And a big meal. I wondered if we would all go.

I thought of the word for "Friday" in Cherokee. There were two of them. One referred to the fact that in boarding school, Fridays were wash days, all the kids forced to wash the many linens and sheets and blankets that kept a boarding school running. "Junhgilosdi" translates to "the day they wash their clothes." The other version of "Friday" simply meant "the fifth day." "Hisgine Iga." How messed up was it that it became such a part of life, it changed the very word for a day of the week in an entire tribe's language?

I thought of Loren and Jess and Adam. It was good to have friends, but it was sometimes good to disconnect, not have a conversation only a thumb swipe away. Adam didn't have a phone, so even back home, when I thought of something I wanted to share with him or ask him, I always had to wait, think about it. It gave me time to get what I wanted to say just right, or abandon completely, something I didn't need to do with Jess and Loren.

I was crushing, wasn't I? How wise was that? If crushes were wise, they would have a different name. We were positioned to go in completely different directions soon. He had focus, a plan, a career. I had things to figure out. Could you do that if you were in love? Wouldn't you always be thinking of yourself in relation to the one you loved? Was I in love?

And, anyway, wasn't I already doing that with Loren and Jess? I didn't think that was even a bad thing. You should plan your life to be near the people who were integral to your happiness.

I picked up my camera and shuttled through the portraits I had taken of Adam. I liked seeing him work, could feel his focus as he carved the wood. A piece that had been the knot of a broken tree branch became a nestling. His inner visions, outer beauty. I looked at the photo where he held the wooden bird he had given me. It was still in my camera bag. I took it out and set it next to the light Auntie had made for our little house. They seemed to belong together.

I got into my pajamas and then into my cot. I thought of the questions I had for my parents.

Dearly Departed

Somehow my parents managed to avoid being alone with me, and I didn't want to ask what was going on in front of Levi. Once back home all my questions seemed less pressing, forgotten.

The Monday after we came back late on Sunday from my auntie's, the third Monday I had known him, Adam didn't show up. He hadn't been at the *Ladder* that morning and didn't come to the lunch room either. I wondered if he was out or just, well . . . just not, just no longer . . .

I ate my slice of sourdough bread loaded with butter and honey. I took a bite of the apple. It was sweet and crisp, but the skin was like leather. I was suddenly too tired to eat it and put it back in my lunch box. I pulled out the book I hadn't been reading, only carrying it around since Adam and I had started having lunch together. It was *The Sentence* by Louise Erdrich, the story of a white pretendian ghost haunting a Native bookstore. I loved it. As I jumped back in, I read it nonstop, never taking my eyes off the page, even though I heard people coming into the lunch-room and leaving. I even finished it. So, I pulled out my copy of *Robopocalypse* by Dan Wilson to reread. Sometimes it's easier to revisit a satisfying story rather than be disappointed by a new one. But I just glanced at the clock, flipping through the book. There wasn't really time to start, so I put it away to return to the gift shop and work on a display of novels. There was that Bribri writer who would be coming for a members-only event on the new exhibit that month.

Le sigh, I thought.

Just before I got off, Tex came in and walked around the shop. He stopped at the display of Adam's work. Several pieces had sold, so Christy had suggested Adam raise the prices. He had told her to do what she thought best. As I was signing out of the register for the day, Tex called me over to where he stood.

"I have a note from your friend, little sister," he said.

"Who?" I asked.

Tex rolled his eyes and pointed towards the display with his lips. "He said he had to leave early and for you to give him a call before you left."

I took the note, thinking, *He got a phone?*

Tex nodded next towards the creatures, carved like water had sanded the wood. "I like these." Then he walked back to the museum's front doors.

I scanned my ID to clock out and went to the backroom to text Adam. The message bounced back saying it was a landline. I thought of the fax machine my mother had. I had seen one on Adam's desk too. A machine that printed and copied and, apparently, made phone calls . . . but couldn't accept a text. Weird.

I saved the number in my phone, then called him.

Adam answered on the third ring. "Stevie!"

"Hey," I tried to sound nonchalant. "You okay?"

"Yeah, yeah, I'm good. Can you come by after work? Bring Loren and Levi? I want you to meet someone, a girl. Can you come?"

I made a conscious effort to not sound too disappointed. It was stupid. We were just work friends—not even work husband and wife really, just two people who worked in the same building. I didn't even think about him that way. Sure, Loren and Jess had teased me, but I adamantly denied feeling anything. It was true, mostly. College awaited. A new life would begin, and yet . . .

"Let me check with Loren."

"Great! I have snacks, stuff little brother can eat."

I smiled. He remembered.

"Get a taxi or something if Loren can't. Bring Levi."

"Uh, okay." Bring Levi. To meet a girl. Great.

I texted Loren and she agreed we could go over when she picked me up. I texted back that he wanted us to meet a girl and she sent back a thumbs-down. I didn't respond, even though I wasn't feeling great about this development either. I hated this. If he was trying to make me jealous then gross. It wasn't like Adam was the only dude in the world I might find myself attracted to. Other women weren't my competition. That's something books and TV still sold and I wasn't buying. I just wished he had mentioned this girl when we had our first talk—when he told me he didn't really have a best friend. *Not cool, Adam*, I thought.

I sat and actually read Wilson while I waited for Loren and Levi to come pick me up. Levi was super excited about seeing Adam and his workshop again. Then I told him about the snacks and I thought he was going to lose his mind. I really hoped Adam didn't disappoint, at least on the food part.

Loren reached over and squeezed my shoulder once I had my seat belt on. "Buck up, little camper. There will be so many people into you at college."

I looked away. "That's why I was never interested in more than friendship, anyway," I whispered.

"Uh-huh," Loren said.

She put an album by The Runaways on. In the back, Levi piped up when the very singable "Cherry Bomb" came on. My parents were going to be thrilled about that.

When we got to the warehouse district we saw Adam walking through the tall, dry grass behind his home. He was carrying a tennis ball, juggling it from one hand to the other. Then he threw it toward where we had parked. Dashing out of the field right behind it was a floppy-eared Doberman puppy. Seeing us, she skidded to a stop, and turned around to run back to Adam, disappearing into the grass. She wasn't a puppy puppy; more like a young dog. But she was small enough that he picked her up and was carrying her to us. Levi ran and grabbed the abandoned tennis ball.

"Can I?" He looked back and forth between me and Loren, then at Adam, who stepped out of the grass.

"Let's meet her first," I said.

Loren looked at me and smiled really big. Then a laugh around the words: "You got ninety-nine problems."

I laughed, too.

Adam walked towards Loren and me.

"This is Princess."

Loren and I touched her, stroking her floppy ears. She couldn't decide who to lick first. Her fur was like warm velvet. She shoved her nose into our hair, licked us obnoxiously, and finally, Adam carried her over to where Levi stood with the ball. She licked him too, and leaped up in excitement when she saw he had the ball.

Levi threw the ball back into the grass and she ran. He followed right behind.

"My friend Brandon, he travels a lot. He asked me to take care of her. She's no trouble. Mostly trained."

Levi and Princess exploded from the grass. Levi let her lick his hand. Then he hugged her, but she kept her eyes on the ball, occasionally licking his face. We were all sweaty, hot, salty humans. It came with June. For that matter, it came in between the extreme cold throughout most of the year now. The change had been abrupt for me, but Levi didn't remember four distinct seasons.

We retreated to the garage. Adam had added a large fan to the sitting area that swept air over a large metal crate nested with a blanket and a water bottle. It looked like it was made for a giant hamster. On top of the crate were some chew toys that looked like they were made for wolves.

"Is she going to get as big as that crate?" Levi asked.

"I can't just let her run around the garage while I'm gone. It's not very secure and she might get into something dangerous for her. And she's already crate-trained, so she likes her little space." He raised his voice a little and turned towards me. "The only bad thing is I'll have to leave work at lunch to let her out."

I didn't say anything about eating alone.

"Levi, why don't you get her a bowl of water?" I was worried the two of them would get overheated before they stopped playing.

"I want a dog!" Levi called.

"Yeah, but do you want to take care of a dog?"

He was carefully carrying a bowl of water to set next to Princess's crate while she dogged his steps. "Sure," he said. He patted her head as she lapped up the water in the bowl. When she'd had enough, she wandered over to her crate and lay down with a decisive thump. I explained to Levi that the crate was her safe place, like his bed, and she needed a nap before she would be ready to play again.

Adam grabbed a tray of cheese and grapes and crackers from his fridge. "Tree nut–free," he said, handing me the box. I read the ingredients and nodded. Adam showed Levi how to build some creatures with the cheese and toothpicks.

"Maybe he should wash his hands first." I foresaw being handed various grape-cheese creatures to eat covered with Princess hair and saliva. Yuck.

Adam told us to get the sodas we wanted out of the fridge. I grabbed Levi something without caffeine and sat and watched him build a food tower. I hoped it wouldn't fall on the floor. Loren and Adam were soon talking about apps and computers and AI learning.

"AI chats are based on large language models. It needs to be taught the same way we teach critical thinking to children. The problem has been that it's had access to everything, the ocean of information is too wide, broad . . . You wouldn't exclusively use pulp novels on cheap paper to teach history. Garbage in, garbage out. We need to limit access to trusted sources first. Scaffold learning. Just like children are taught anchor beliefs based on their caregivers' politics, religion, and culture, the anchor beliefs should be accurate and with an eye towards preserving the planet. Once the cornerstone beliefs are there, they only change with overwhelming reliable evidence. AI needs to be taught to vet those sources, and even recognize context when there is biased language of hate."

Adam was staring intently at Loren. Almost like he wanted to take notes.

Levi handed me a dog-shaped creature to eat.

"What happens if someone hacks the system, teaches that certain people are evil or 'filth'?" I said, quoting a senator who had seemed to forget that democracy was supposed to be for everyone, not just those with the "right" religious outlook.

"Haven't they already? One of the early problems with AI was it was like kids being taught to test. Except it was willing to provide you any answer, rather than being concerned with the right answer. It learned from all the stuff on the internet. Garbage in, garbage out. Ideally, it should only provide answers that don't cause harm. There will be times it should say 'I don't know.'"

"Do you think people will keep using something that doesn't reinforce their own anchor beliefs?" I asked. I was trying to speak carefully. Loren's first, second, and third rule was "We don't talk about Soulcraft."

"That's where the games I'm making come in."

"What games?" Adam said.

"Games that teach cooperation, the greater good, and that life is not a zero-sum game. Games that translate real-life world history and scenarios into strategy and world-building and show how short-term strategies of exploitation are losing strategies in the end. Games that reward players who err on the side of compassion, but defend themselves and the oppressed. If you saw the long arc of history and were reborn into the same world time and time again, and saw that you could limit your own suffering by making choices in your first life that took the value of all life into account, wouldn't you choose best, if you could do it over?"

In the past, Loren had created games and asked Jess, Levi, and me to test them out. There wasn't a lot like her games on the market, but there were some. I hoped her work could compete with the perennially popular first-person shooters, where you only clearly won if you killed everyone.

"Haven't there been people who said this before . . . ?" I questioned. Not for the first time.

"And there probably will be again. Sometimes you have to try a new strategy. It's like with any teaching. You have to repeat yourself. This is what I can do."

"I guess it's like every time I read bell hooks, or James Baldwin, or that book *As We Have Always Done*. I find myself feeling like they figured out the answers long ago. If only people kept hearing . . ." I finished. Sort of.

"Or started listening. And that's it—we have to raise the vibe to have a better world to play in. One self-interested bully ruins it for everyone."

We were all quiet for a few minutes.

Adam looked over at me. "Can I get you anything else?"

I glanced at my phone. "No, Dad is home today. He's making dinner, so it's family meal night. Even Mom will be there."

Levi jumped up, remembering his dad would be home. He ran to Adam and asked if he could feed Princess some cheese and grapes.

"Call her to you and tell her to sit. Then give her a piece of cheese when she does. But grapes are bad for dogs, so no grapes. Or toothpicks."

Levi nodded very seriously and took apart the cheese man he had made. He may have given her more than a piece (or two) of cheese.

"See you in the morning," Adam said a little later, as we got ready to leave.

"Mañana," I replied.

"Sorry I wasn't there this morning. Kind of lost track of time with walking and feeding her and stuff." Adam looked really serious. "I'll get up early tomorrow."

Yeah, I was definitely crushing. Damn. "I'll be there . . ." I said as I turned to the car.

He and Princess stood outside and waved as we drove off.

"Hey," Loren said, pulling onto the highway, "I'd say he'd be a lot less likable if he stayed and talked to a pretty girl at lunch while his puppy paced in a crate at home."

"We're just friends." I sighed. "I can't be falling for someone when I'm about to start my new life two hundred miles away."

"I don't know. A little crush, a little pining . . . it's good for art. For soul building."

"Soul building? Are we talking about me or your future masses?" I glanced at Levi to make sure he wasn't listening. "Who needs heartbreak when I'll have an app to help me create art like my heart has been broken?" I touched her arm to let her know I was joking.

"I'm just saying, a little unrequited love never killed anyone," Loren muttered, before adding, "But yes. Some people need more empathy, through no fault of their own. Children come into the world adults manufacture."

I knew who we were both thinking about. Their parents worked full-time on building the child they wanted. Jess had a soul, but they were having to fight a constant war over it.

"Misery loves company," I said.

"I surely do."

"This will all change when we get away." Loren had pulled into our driveway, but she didn't turn off the car.

"You don't want to come in and have dinner?"

"The app calls. I have some new ideas. You and Adam got me thinking about how it could be exploited. Tell your dad hello for me."

I went to her side of the car and hugged her through the window. Feelings were hard. Love was hard. And, I was fairly sure unrequited love had killed a few people.

What's Going On

Mom and Dad were in the kitchen cooking together. They were taking turns covering the lasagna noodles with layers and layers of cheese and spinach.

"Where's Loren?" Dad said, looking up.

"She had to go write," Levi said, running in to put his arms around his father's legs. "And Adam has a dog."

I sighed. This was not a conversation I wanted to have. I would have liked dinner before the third degree. "Stevie's friend," Levi added. Mom raised an eyebrow at me. She and Dad had been to the gym and she still had her hair in a ponytail. She might have looked like she was ready for yoga, but underneath, I felt her inner attorney stepping onto the stage.

"And how do you know he has a dog?" Private Investigator Dad asked, kneeling down to Levi's level. My parents had run background checks on all our friends before sleepovers. They tried to make sure that only known suspects—I mean, relations—would be in the same space as me and Levi. And not without good reason.

Though, Levi had yet to be invited to a sleepover by any of his classmates.

"It's at his garage, where he lives." Now, I could tell, even Levi was wondering if he should keep talking. I smiled when he looked to me to check if he was doing okay. I nodded. But my parents were not going to let it go anymore without comment from me.

"New artist intern from Costa Rica. He works in the shop. They let him have a warehouse for a studio and place to live. It's not a *garage* garage."

"Does he know about Levi's allergies?" Mom asked.

"Yes, I explained."

"I don't want Levi going over there anymore until we meet him," Dad said. "See if he can come for dinner Wednesday. Ask Loren and Jess too. They haven't been over for dinner since graduation. And y'all are still going to the zoo tomorrow?"

Mom and Dad exchanged smiles. The kind of smiles between a couple—your parents—that made you feel uncomfortable. I mean, yeah, I was glad they still *loooooved* each other. I could almost forget about the faxes when they acted like this. But I didn't want to think too much about the date night they were planning while we went to the zoo.

"I called Susan. She'll be there tomorrow. Make sure y'all go by." Susan was my mom's cousin on the Wilson side. Cherokee. Had gone back to school to work with elephants after her kids moved on to college and out to Washington State.

"I'll text her when we get there," I said, hoping I could escape before the PDA got embarrassing.

Levi had already disappeared to his room. I walked into the living room and found Leon Bridges's album *Coming Home*. It was the kind of album that should spin with a needle crackling. As I headed to my room, Dad called, "Find out if he likes venison! For Wednesday."

"I'll ask him tomorrow." It seemed obnoxious to use his number for a second time in one day the first chance I had—too much, too extra and obvious. We'd just left his little charcuterie. I understood my parents were a bit overprotective, but on the flipside, having worked in Child Welfare and criminal investigations, I knew the things they worried about were much more than idle imaginings. They kept the home office locked because they didn't want us to accidentally see something we couldn't unsee.

In my room, I updated Loren and Jess.

"Wednesday! You know I have to work," Jess said.

"Come over afterwards. Bring ice cream," I responded.

"You know my parents make me pay for that ice cream, right?"

"We got you." Loren and I both typed that.

Then Loren threatened not to come so it would seem more like a date to meet my parents. A few panic emojis later and she rescinded: she really didn't want to be the cause of a panic attack. Which was a real possibility. Later that night, I took the anxiety medication that helped me sleep. I had been trying to wean myself off it since graduation. But by midnight, I gave up, frustrated with the tossing and turning. I couldn't decide if I was looking forward to or dreading dinner in a couple days.

Elephants

On Tuesday nights the zoo was open late. Jess picked us
up. All three of us took turns being Levi's main person.
Little kids are so much themselves: filter-less, energetic,
curious. It's kindest to be your best, most patient self with
them. So, we rotated roles, Jess or Loren being the best
aunties possible, playing to their strengths. Jess took over
at the playground. I texted Susan that we were headed her
way. Loren took over as Levi's companion at the elephant-
and giraffe-feeding area. My aunt told us to come back
later when she would be giving a talk about the exhibit's
expansion and we walked towards the aviary.

I loved birds. In the house where I grew up, I would go
out to the deck alone to read but end up just stopping to
listen to the various birdsongs, like my own piped-in avian
symphony. It didn't occur to me then, how many bird
voices were missing—like the Indigenous languages that
had been murdered. I didn't tell Levi how sad it made me
to see the nets and cages and clipped wings here. I thought
of the poem "All Nations," by Heid E. Erdrich, about the
one-third decline of the world's birds in less than fifty
years. At the parakeet house, I bought twenty dollars'
worth of feeding sticks. I gave some to Jess and Loren too,

and any little kid with a free hand. When a bird landed on Levi's seed-covered stick, I reminded him to stay still and calm so the bird would accept his offering. We both said the word for "bird" in Tsalagi: "jisqua." There were specific words for all the different kinds of birds the Cherokee Nation had always known, but I didn't know the word for "parakeet." We knew our colors though, so we took turns naming what we saw. Jisqua sakonige. Jisqua dalonige. Jisqua itse usdi. Blue and yellow and green birds. When one pooped on Levi he proudly told Loren and Jess and shared that it was good luck. Then we decided now that we had fed the birds, it was time to feed ourselves.

After our picnic dinner, we bought ice cream. Raspberry sorbet was a safe and delicious choice. At least in a cup. We all got cups, so Levi didn't have to feel like he was missing out. I checked my backpack again for his EpiPen and Benadryl, just in case. But all went well.

It was time for Susan's talk. We returned to the elephant stand in time to catch her spiel on the new expansions in the elephant area. When the rest of the guests left, we stood around talking with her about the herd. Susan got a faraway look in her eyes when she told us about visiting the homelands of the various elephants. "I feel so funny being a keeper of these beautiful beings who wander for miles there. I mean, they're safe, here . . . but . . ."

"But you wish it could be different," Loren finished.

"Yeah. I wish they didn't have to be caged to be protected."

"It's like being a girl, a woman, or non-binary," Jess said quietly. "We always have to think about where we're going, how we'll be safe. Hiking alone means carrying a taser and always being on guard."

"You have a taser?" I asked, taken by surprise. They were legal and, in theory, nonlethal, but there were some age restrictions.

"Your mom got them for both of us," Loren said.

Susan smiled. "That tracks. Y'all's mom is the best," she said, looking at me and over towards Levi, who had run off to play.

I shrugged. *Yeah*, I thought. *Except when she's not.*

I looked over at Levi climbing the small statue of the elephant goddess. *Mom would do anything for Levi*, I thought. The thought felt scary, rather than comforting.

But I knew I would too.

The Day
Texas Sank
to the Bottom
of the Sea

After work on Wednesday, Loren came home with me and Levi. She had offered to give Adam a ride, but he deferred because Princess. He needed to go home and spend an hour or so with her. I was nervous about him showing up now on a motorcycle. He may have been an adult my parents hadn't raised, but motorcycles were something they had opinions on. Before my wreck, Mom used to say, "At least a car protects you from the stupidity of others." I felt like the fact that she didn't say it anymore was both a kindness and an accusation.

She was in the office, but when I knocked on the door, Mom told me Dad was cooking ribs in the backyard. He was nowhere to be seen when I went outside, though, and fire was shooting out from the sides of the grill. He must have gotten distracted. His truck was gone. So I grabbed the leather fire gloves and opened the grill. These ribs were definitely going to be well-done. Loren got me foil and I covered them and set the charred, dry bones to the side.

Luckily, venison sausage was marinating in the fridge.

Dad pulled in the driveway and came in through the garage. He was carrying gallons of tea and coleslaw from Braum's. Whenever Dad offered Loren sweet tea she liked to tease him and say she'd have a soda, since it had less sugar. It was funny, because it was probably true.

"Um, does your mom know I burned the ribs?"

I shook my head.

"Okay, let's let that be our secret. An owl stole them off the grill, right? You mention an owl and she'll stop thinking about the ribs. Did you turn it off?"

I nodded.

"I sure hope this Adam likes venison."

Loren and I both looked at each other. We both knew that Dad would not judge him favorably otherwise.

"I don't know if they have deer in Costa Rica," Loren said, pulling out her phone. "They do," she answered.

Dad got distracted with sweetening the tea, so Loren and I excused ourselves to sit in the swing on the back porch.

"Should you tell Adam he better praise the venison, if he knows what's good for him?"

"If he doesn't, like, maybe that's a red flag."

"I have the feeling that if he were covered in red flags, you'd have a hard time seeing them."

"Whatever." I was blushing. I was definitely blushing.

Dad came out with tea for us. No sugar in Loren's.

"How was the last fishing trip?" she asked him. Dad taught both outdoor and foraging skills on his tours and gave his clients confidence to get out in the wild. He taught them where to find the information on where it was safest and most fruitful to forage.

"Well, my clients had lots of time to relax because there were fewer fish than ever. So, for me it was stressful. Thank

God for catfish, or they might have gone home with an empty ice chest." He paused; I could see he was still thinking about those ribs. Dad got distracted sometimes. He'd been diagnosed when he was an adult and tried medication for his ADHD for a while, but he and Mom both agreed it didn't work for him. "Should I have made catfish? They eat lots of fish in Costa Rica, don't they?"

"No, Dad, venison is awesome. Especially the way you make it."

He flashed a smile and continued, "I never saw so few trout. Waters are too warm. But fresh catfish breaded with good cornmeal, worth the ticket every time."

We were all quiet after that. I noticed less insect and bird noises in the woods behind our house, suddenly. I hoped it was because we were in the yard disrupting the environment. But I knew, even at night with the windows open, the summer was quieter than years past. It was a silence that felt like it was increasing exponentially. It was worth crying over, like the extinction of trees and birds we knew about, but it seemed to be ignored by people who could make the exponential changes necessary to slow it down. It seemed living things had no real right to life, the same way humans seemed to have no right to free and clean air and water.

Dad changed the subject, talking about a place he was going to take a group who wanted to see the northern lights. I offered to go get the corn and make the salad and left him and Loren to talk. We all heard the motorcycle coming down the street at the same time. I was taking the soaked corn, still in their husks, out to the grill when it sounded like the motorbike had stopped in our driveway. Dad turned and raised an eyebrow at me.

"Is that your friend?"

"Probably," I said, dropping the corn onto the grill.

"Have you been on the back of that bike?"

"Only once, just for a few minutes." I didn't add "twice."

"And?"

"It was scary."

Dad laughed.

"If you want to ride a motorcycle, I guess I'll teach you and you can get your own. Your mom will leave me, but, you know, anything for my daughter . . ."

I laughed. "You lie. Besides, that sounds scarier than driving a car."

He smiled in relief. "Exactly. Which you need to try again. A car gives you independence. I don't want you always having to pay for or ask for rides to do what you want to do. Once you start driving again, you'll understand. That kind of independence changes lives. It's a privilege I want you to have."

I shrugged, "I like my life and bumming rides from my friends and family." I winked at Loren and hugged my dad. "Glad you're home." Then I went to open the door for Adam.

My mother had gotten there first and Adam was handing her a bouquet of sunflowers. Levi was coming out of his room and was disappointed to see Princess was nowhere to be seen.

"I'm going to have to get a sidecar, I guess, so I can take her places," Adam said, stepping inside. Where he couldn't see, I widened my eyes at Mom, to let her know her thoughts were out loud on her face. She shrugged.

"What's a sidecar?" Levi asked.

I pulled out my phone and showed Levi a picture of an Indian Motorcycle with a sidecar.

"That's cool!" he said.

Now Mom shot me a dirty look. I was definitely no longer looking forward to dinner. "It's a way to kill two or three people on a motorcycle instead of one," she muttered, not loud enough for Levi and Adam to hear—just me. I returned her dirty look.

Adam had stooped down and was handing Levi a long piece of what looked like bamboo. From his pocket he pulled out several barbecue skewers, carved to a point with an end that looked topped with rabbit fur.

Now I noticed Mom was smiling.

"A blowgun!" Levi squealed. He had used them before when we went to Cherokee Holiday. It was one way Cherokees used to hunt small game.

"River cane," Mom said, slowly, happily. "Wado." She looked expectantly at Levi.

"Wado!" he said. "Can I go shoot it in the backyard?" he asked.

"No animals!" she yelled. In answer, the back screen door slammed.

Somehow, we got through dinner. Loren updated us on her mom who was getting her PhD in creative writing in Chicago. My parents asked about swimming lessons again, ostensibly for Levi. *If they could, they'd sign him up for driving lessons and make me accompany him,* I thought. Dad and Mom tag teamed questioning Adam about his history growing up in a commune in Costa Rica. I could see Dad ticking through a list of cults in his head, checking to see if his answers pointed towards any of them: *No savior figure, no polygamy, check, check.* They even asked for his mom and dad's family names. Mom was Maria Rogers; father, Dan Rickman, originally of England. But Adam said he used his mother's name. I was pretty sure when Dad excused himself to the kitchen, it was to plug their names into one of his many databases.

When he wasn't being questioned, Adam was effusive about the food. The venison bangers and mash were pretty incredible. They were one of my favorite comfort foods. With the brown beans, cornbread, salad, and corn, it was all too much. But they were each things Levi could safely eat. At home he never felt like he was missing out on anything. As we finished dinner, Adam gave Dad a carved fish in the shape of a trout.

"This is beautiful," Dad said. "Too bad I can't use it as a decoy, might help the next time I hit that part of the world. Thank you, Adam."

"Let's put these plates in the dishwasher and go for our walk," Mom said.

"I'm out," Loren announced. She left the table with her plates and returned from the kitchen with her keys and bag. "I'm picking up Jess from work. They send their regrets. I still have to get some work done tonight." Loren hated bugs, and after the one time she found a tick under her pant leg on a walk with us, she was done.

The best thing about Grandma's house was we could walk into the big prairie space behind it without going out onto the road. How strange that it had once all been sea-floor. We could just walk down into the backyard, out a gate, and into 160 acres of rehabilitated bluestem prairie. It allowed us to skip the small sign that declared it was the Atatiana Jefferson Tall Grass Prairie, which had been renamed after local activists continued to call attention to the murder of the young woman in her own home, while playing video games with her young nephew. It happened during a "wellness check." We didn't need to be reminded it wasn't safe to be a brown person in your own home, or that a visit by the police could get a person shot. It was dangerous enough walking while brown.

Dad had binoculars and Levi carried a flashlight and he held our parents' hands. For a few minutes, he came over and grabbed my left and Adam's right and walked between us. It was kind of nice. *Like holding Adam's hand by proxy,* I thought. I didn't look at my parents.

At the top of a hill, we sat down on the log benches a group of local students had placed for stargazing. If you looked away from downtown, you could see the stars better. It was hard with two big cities so close together, but the binoculars helped. Adam borrowed the binoculars and pointed out some constellations he was familiar with, along with three satellites that were too bright and didn't seem to move, and two space stations for rich people. He told me who owned each one, the country of origin, the corporation, what they did, which wealthy families had invested in them. It was their place to go the next time there was a big pandemic; a place to hang out and not be too inconvenienced by the end of the world.

"I think that is the weirdest set of facts I have ever heard," I said, handing back the binoculars, our hands briefly connecting. "And you've met my parents and best friends," I whispered.

Adam smiled. "Commit it to memory. It may come in useful. There are a lot of man-made objects out there. Those are just a small percent."

"That sounds more ominous than comforting." He handed me back the binoculars; again our hands touched, this time a little longer than necessary. Then I looked again at the various pieces of space junk taking attention away from the stars and planets.

"Okay," I said, "quiz me."

He did. I didn't get a 100 percent, but I passed.

"There's an app, you know. You can download it to your phone and point it at the sky and it will tell you what you're looking at."

"So, I just wasted brain cells on something I could let an app do? Ah, man . . ."

When I handed back the binoculars this time, our fingers linked. I glanced over to see my mom watching me, but Levi was in Dad's arms, falling asleep with his head on his shoulder.

"Time to get him in bed," I said.

Adam stood and held a hand out to pull me off the bench. I didn't let go once I was standing. Not at first. We were all quiet on the short walk down the hill. Instead of trekking up though the more overgrown path to the house, we caught the road that was easier to navigate in the dark and wound up in our driveway. Mom, Dad, Adam, and I all touched Atatiana's sign as we passed this time. When we got home, my parents and Levi went in the house. Adam and I talked a few minutes before he got on his motorcycle.

"Can you call? Let me know you made it home safe?"

Adam looked at me and smiled. "Always," he said quietly.

Once in the house, we heard the motorcycle start up.

"I don't want you riding on that thing," Mom started immediately. Dad gave me a look and I knew he hadn't told her. "A helmet won't protect you from a collision." She paused, "Well, maybe your face, so you can have an open casket funeral. Walter, didn't Tim have to have a closed casket funeral for his daughter?" I hadn't forgotten our neighbor's daughter and husband had been killed when a truck ran a light and crashed into them. But I tried not to think about it.

"Okay, I get it."

"A good motorcyclist can't control the people in the cars."

I felt my stomach turn, thinking about my own accident. My heart was starting to pound. In order not to say something I'd regret, I returned to the kitchen to help clean up. I put some happy music on to fill the conversation space. I was tired. Maybe my parents thought talking to me about this would keep me safe, but it just made me anxious; made me tell myself stories about how dangerous the roads were, how even in a car you weren't safe, from yourself or others. When we were done, I excused myself and went to bed. I was definitely going to need my meds.

When Adam called, we talked a long time. I sat down on my bed and closed my eyes, only hearing his voice. I told him about my anxiety. He asked if he could read me to sleep. I didn't say "always," though, I thought it.

Then I fell asleep, his voice the last thing I heard as I swam into the ocean of sleep.

ALie
Nation

I had completely forgotten about the event happening at the museum the next day. I came in at my usual time on Thursday, forgetting that I was not scheduled to work until later so I could be present to help with the reading and book signing. I found Adam at the usual spot, drawing detailed sketches of the portions of the *Ladder* where the rungs and rails met.

"I thought you were off today."

He smiled. "This isn't work. At least, not museum work."

"Guess what?" I said.

"What?"

"The author from Costa Rica is coming tonight."

Adam paused. "I'd forgotten about that."

"You're going to come, aren't you? The curator is doing a presentation on Costa Rica and the artisans and artists. I bet you'll recognize some of them! You might even be in there. Didn't you and the curator meet at one of the markets? The author is going to read from her book. You can meet her. I'll buy you her book and she can sign it. It's so good."

Adam took a deep breath. He put his pencil in his pocket, closing his sketchbook. "For sure."

"I've seen most of the curator's presentation. Costa Rica looks amazing. Oh, and they're going to serve small cups of cacao, made by a Costa Rican chef. I thought you might like that, at least."

Adam kept staring at the *Ladder*, not saying anything, which meant I kept babbling.

"Anyway, I don't work until this afternoon, so Dad is going to come get me now. Promise you're coming, please? Lots of people from the local Native and Indigenous community will be there. I want you to meet them. I want them to meet you." There would be people I had known most of my life. I was of two minds about Adam meeting them. On the one hand if he stayed local after his internship, it would be good for him to be introduced to the community. And, well, we had held hands last night and talked until I fell asleep, so maybe there were other reasons I wanted him to meet the community.

"For sure," he said. "I promise. I gotta start early this morning. I'll see you later."

Start what? I wondered.

I sold books at the beginning of the event. Tex came in and walked right over to me.

"Hey, little sister. Did your mom come?"

"She's saving you a seat," I said. "One for Adam, too, if you see him before I do."

"I didn't think he was coming tonight," Tex frowned. "Did he tell you he was?"

I shrugged. "Yeah, I don't know. I just assumed. Costa Rica and all."

Adam didn't show up for the curator's talk or the author's reading either. Tex sat by Mom. They gossiped and got caught up. I wished I knew what they were talking about. Tex had come back after he got off work and had dinner. Adam was nowhere to be seen.

I called his phone number and when the stupid fax machine kicked on, I swore and hung up. I looked up every time the door to the auditorium opened. I felt like I had the day I sat alone reading *The Sentence* in the lunchroom. But, I doubted he was going to produce another dog he had to take care of suddenly.

After the event, I took payments for books again and placed pieces of papers with the name meant to go in the dedication. I saw Native community people from all over the metroplex. There were kids I knew from American Indian Education's Summer Camp. When I told them Tex was there, each one sought him out to say hello. He had taught a lot of kids to paint. For some of them who had been disconnected from their tribal elders and homeland, he was the only older Native man they had to look to for advice. I realized he had been that for me, too, when I was away from home.

One organizer who focused on justice for Missing and Murdered Indigenous People asked the author about the impact of logging on Indigenous people in Costa Rica. So many problems we had were the same, though the way tribes were recognized by the various government entities varied.

While they were speaking, I heard someone call my name. I turned, expecting Adam or Tex, though the voice was wrong. A man who I had met at a training at the Chickasaw Cultural Center waved at me. I struggled to remember what few phrases I knew in Chickasaw.

"Chinchokma, Kabi'?"

"ii, ishnaako, Stevie?"

"Anchokma," I said.

"You're working here?"

"Just in the gift shop."

"It's good to see you. Let me know if you ever want to do some intern work in Ada." Years ago, Mom and I had attended a class on NAGPRA—the Native American Graves Protection and Repatriation Act—that Kabi' taught. I had been fascinated by the fact that the Chickasaw made reproductions of items that had been returned and then buried the originals in Ceremony. It was the kind of stuff that made anthropologists and some olds crazy, as well as the institutions who held on to our bones, carving away bits to test them and leaving them in cold storage far from their stolen homelands. The Chickasaw returned them to where they belonged. In our tribe, there had been a tradition of not messing with the dead once they had been buried. It was the responsibility of the person who had disturbed the graves to make it right. At one time, our people had been buried with their belongings and their houses burned. But that had been a long time ago. There was no one way to deal with the lingering effects of grave robbing on our dead, just as there was no one way to live as an Indian.

My mom was at the end of the signing line now with Tex and our neighbor Ida, who was Choctaw. Also in line with them was her granddaughter, Pakanli—Paka for short. Paka was two years older than me and carrying a tiny baby. Her Grandma Ida got out less than she used to. I suddenly felt intensely guilty for not going over to visit her more. I hadn't even known she was expecting a great-granddaughter. I hugged both of them.

"What have you been up to?" I gestured with my head towards the baby. "Other than . . ."

We laughed. It turned out Paka had moved back close to our house with her husband, Frank, and baby, Nihi. I saw Ida give my mother a look when Paka mentioned Frank. I knew all I needed to about him in that glance. So did Mom.

Tex said goodbye to all of us and Mom promised to have me bring him some yaupon holly tea she had made in the morning. It's the only plant with a good amount of caffeine native to North America. The plant looks great in the yard, has berries the birds share with the world, and the tea made from its roasted leaves tastes so good, especially iced in the summer. It was a drink Indigenous people had made for thousands of years. Along with our herb garden, it was a plant in the yard we kept watered.

When Mom was finished speaking to the author about all things Indigenous and women, she pulled me aside. "Dad looked into your friend."

"Adam."

"We can't find any records on him prior to arriving here. Nothing on his parents in Costa Rica. Not by the names he gave us. Does he go by another name?"

"Adawi?" I said.

"Are you sure? That means 'Adam' in Cherokee. And 'Ada' means 'wood.' But you know that."

I did know the word for wood. But not Adam.

"Look, don't take Levi over there anymore, not until Dad says it's okay."

"Yeah, sure. How weird." I felt shaky.

"And you be careful. I don't want anything to happen to you." Mom had leaned in close so no one else could hear what she said, but she was holding my arm gently.

"Etsi," I drew out.

"I'm serious. You think you're grown, but you'll always be my baby too. I would say it's okay to trust, but verify, but you know I think that's stupid. Verify first. Always."

I nodded.

"I'm going to walk them out. I'll be back when you're ready to go." Mom disappeared with Ida, Paka, and baby Nihi.

As the signing line finally drew to a close, I noticed the books were almost sold out. The author signed the last five books so we could sell them in the gift shop.

I spoke up before I lost my nerve. "I have a friend from Costa Rica," I told her.

"Really? Was he here tonight?"

Suddenly I felt stupid for bringing him up. "No, he couldn't. But I promised I would get him a book."

"Cool," she said. "Who do I make it out to?"

Good question, I thought. "To Adawi, I guess," I said with a laugh. A weird laugh that made my mom look at me worried.

The author smiled graciously and signed the book. I promised not to sell it and she laughed too.

"Did you like the cacao?" she asked.

"It was amazing. It was like tasting . . ." I struggled.

"Love? The earth and the sun?" I meant it. How could Adam not have come at least for a taste of home? Why had he promised me he would come, then ghosted me?

When I went home that night, Levi was still awake. He came to my room long after my parents were asleep. I welcomed his presence.

"What's up, kiddo? You have school tomorrow. What are you doing up so late?"

"I fell asleep right after school. I was having a headache, so Dad let me sleep."

Levi crawled in bed with me.

"How's your head now?" I said. "Will it hurt if I touch it?"

"No, it's better. But now I can't sleep."

"Want me to read you a story?"

"The Coyote and the Weasel?"

"I don't know where my copy of that is," I said.

"But you wrote it! Why do you even need a copy?"

I laughed. "Let me look on my phone. I may have it there."

Levi reached out and grabbed my phone. "I don't like the light. Keeps me awake. Just tell it. Like a storyteller."

"Okay." I plugged my phone in and put it on "Do Not Disturb." "But don't get mad if I forget parts."

"I know how it goes." Already his voice sounded sleepy.

"Well, back in the old days, when the animals still danced and talked like we do, Weasel found herself living alone with her little ones . . ."

When I went to work the next morning I hadn't called Adam and he hadn't called me. I had brought Tex the yaupon tea my mom made for him. In the security guard office, there was a new guy whose name tag said "Brandon," along with a guy who usually worked evenings.

"Hey," I said. "Where's Tex?"

The two men exchanged looks. I didn't like the look that passed between them. Then the new guy said, "He won't be in today. I'm sorry." His voice was soft and warm.

Something was off. I left and went back to the gift shop. I opened my phone and plugged in Tex's name into a search engine. Nothing. I went ahead and opened my work e-mail. That's when my heart broke.

"It is with deep regret that we share we have lost an employee who has been with us ten years. Martin (Tex) Kishketon suffered a fatal heart attack in his home last night. Funeral arrangements will be forthcoming from the family. He will be buried on family land with a view of the Wichita Mountains."

I burst into tears. Christy found me eventually. I called Dad then, and Christy gave me the day off. She asked me to please come in Sunday morning.

Instead of texting me to come out, Dad parked the car when he got there and came into the gift shop. Christy sent him back to the employee lounge. He found me there, curled up on the couch. I didn't care that people were coming in and seeing me that crushed. It didn't matter. Why did we have so little time with people we cared for? Why didn't we spend time in a meaningful way with people we admired? Our friends, our families, our elders?

I thought about my mom, talking about how she wished she had quit her job and school when her best friend had cancer, but she always assumed she and Cynthia would have more time. She'd get better. And then Cynthia was gone.

"I never thought I'd have another best friend," she would say. "But then I met Walter."

"Hey, kiddo. You want to go get some lunch?"

I sat up. I wanted to cry again.

I shook my head. I squinted back tears.

Dad looked at his watch. "Six hours until we go get Levi. Fishing or the gun range?"

I laughed. Despite everything, I laughed. "How about the archery range?" I stood up.

Dad picked my backpack off the floor and slung it over his shoulder. "That sounds like a challenge."

I laughed again. "Well, BarBQ on the River is on the way. So, if I beat you in archery, I'll let you buy me dinner."

"I hope you brought your money. I might surprise you."

"We'll see."

Archery was one of the things I'd started doing at Indian Summer Camp. Since Dad liked to bowhunt, he had been thrilled. I used to compete and everything. But I hadn't been out in a while. And, apparently, Dad had. Our scores were pretty close. I wasn't sure if he let me win in the last round or what, but we ended up going to get brisket by the river and talking. It was the place Adam and I first hung out. Dad didn't ask me about him. I knew he thought Adam had lied to me. But why?

That night when I got home, I called Adam. I didn't let him talk. "Tex died. Where were you last night?" I hung up after a too long pause.

He didn't return my call.

Landslide

E-mail from Stevie #2

TO: Angel Wilson (LawAngel@ICWA.law)
FROM: Stevie (stevie@hmail.com)

Auntie, I want to talk about Levi.

You know how much we all fell madly in love with Levi when he was born. Not just me and Dad and Mom, but Jess and Loren, and you too. I loved Levi more than I have ever loved anyone. I wanted to be able to be with him and protect him all the time. I couldn't be there with him at his preschool, but Loren was. She knew even better than I do that most people don't let you forget you're brown in this country. At least not for long. Not even if you're a little kid. Loren made sure Levi wasn't bullied for having a darker complexion than most of the other kids in the program, and all of the staff were super vigilant about allergies, the kind that kill little kids. There wasn't a lot she could do when he was the only kid who wasn't invited to the birthday parties outside of school, though. Cruel racist parents breed cruel racist kids sometimes.

I'm sorry.

You see now, if I opened my mouth, I would find out I am not yet all cried out.

Donadagohvi,

Stevie

Creep

When I went to work the next morning, I didn't go see if the new security guard would approve of me going to sit and sketch the *Ladder*. I wasn't going anymore. That was over. Tex was gone. I didn't need any new friends. Losing friends hurt too much. Besides, friends don't lie to you.

At lunchtime, Alan showed up in the gift shop. When he smiled at me, it was warmer than ever.

"Hey, Stevie, I brought some more photos to sell. We need to get together and look at those photos of yours, though. Your pieces are amazing."

"Wado," I said.

He picked up his camera and pointed it at me. I flushed. "I want to try out some new flash equipment I got for portraits. Would you mind helping me? I wouldn't charge for the photos. You could use them for headshots when you have your own show."

I blushed. I was used to being behind the camera. Still, Alan was a professional. He charged a lot for his work.

"I don't know." I suddenly remembered Tex and their last awkward conversation I had been privy to. I realized I hadn't seen Alan since.

"Did you hear about Tex?"

Alan looked solemn. "What a tragedy. Who could have foreseen that? I thought he would outlive this place." That seemed like a reach, but I thought maybe he was trying to make me smile.

Alan disappeared into the back of the gift shop with his work. He and Christy came out when it was time for her to give me a lunch break. I turned to go to the break room, but Alan called me over. "Let me buy you lunch. Plus, I still have to walk you through that camera like I promised. How about I pick you up after work and we go get that stuff? Maybe shoot those portraits?"

It was all a lot to parse at once. Too much. I said yes to lunch, not even thinking about after work—just wanting to avoid the break room. I had been dreading it. Tex wouldn't be there, and I would think about Adam too. He didn't work Saturdays. Why not let Alan buy me a nice lunch in the museum restaurant?

It was hard not to be dazzled by him. He was nice looking and pretty famous, by local standards.

At lunch, after we ordered, Alan handed me his camera. He showed me how to pull up a gallery on the large digital screen, toggle through the images. There were various photos from his travels. A giant garbage dump burning, an island of plastic recyclables growing in the ocean, houses in remote areas made of refuse and thrown-away bits of America, barely protecting their inhabitants from the elements.

"Wow, you make the tragic beautiful," I said. He took it as a compliment, but I wasn't sure. I thought about Tex and what he had said about the artists who made money off photos of poverty.

"Show me the portrait you used for your show."

I pulled out my phone and showed him the selfie I had blown up to go with the portraits I had in the senior art show.

He rolled his eyes. "Your photo should be as good as the portraits you were showing. Not a selfie." He practically sneered. "Seriously, no one will take you seriously if that's how you portray yourself, as an artist."

I took my phone back, embarrassed.

"Anyway, I just got paid quite a bit for the photos in the gift shop. I can pay you to model."

I laughed. "Yeah, no, I don't think so."

"You sure? I'll give you free prints and send you a digital file so you can use them, free of charge. How often are you going to get a deal like that?"

I laughed. "I'll think about it," I said. We talked some more. I was shy eating in front of him. He offered to buy me a glass of wine. I laughed again. "They know I'm not twenty-one here."

"It's legal if you're over eighteen and an adult buys it."

I didn't say out loud that that bit of knowledge, whether true or not, was creepy. Still, he disappeared and came back with two glasses of prosecco at the end of lunch.

He toasted me and wouldn't pay until I finished the bubbly booze. Then he walked me back to the gift shop. "I'll see you after work," he said, before I could argue.

Fine, I thought. He would be a distraction. A handsome, slightly famous distraction. An artist who could help me with my career. I texted my parents that I would be home later than usual. Then I texted Loren and Jess that I was going over to Alan's apartment. They were hanging out together and sent me all kinds of very confused emojis. I hadn't told them about the reading or Adam maybe not being what he said he was. Only that Tex, my friend, had died suddenly, and I was really sad.

After work, Alan was waiting for me in the parking lot in his red Charger. When he started it, it was loud. Too loud to talk. Almost too loud to think. That was a bit of luck, I thought. His condominium was close to the museum, a modern gray-scale apartment with lots of porcelain and marble and north facing windows. As soon as we walked in, he said, "I'll make us a drink. Something lemony. You open your gift." He handed me a heavy box he had sitting by the door.

I stood, stupidly, watching as he chopped up lemons and juiced them over ice. From under the counter, he grabbed bottles of simple syrup and tequila.

"Oh, no, I better not," I said.

"Have you ever had professional portraits done?" he asked. He poured the liquor into a measuring glass that looked like a shot glass.

"No."

"Trust me, this will loosen you up. If you don't relax it'll show up in the photos. Open your gift."

I set the box on the counter and tore the shiny paper. It was the kind of camera that took photos with film. I knew it was Alan's old camera, the one he had learned to take photos on in high school.

"Oh, gosh, I can't. This is too special."

Alan shrugged. He handed me the drink. "It was just gathering dust. Might as well get used, by an artist. It's already loaded with film for you."

I blushed. I pointed the camera at Alan. He smiled. It made me smile, too. I pressed the button.

I set the camera down and took a drink. It was like a lemonade. At first. As I walked around the apartment looking at the art pieces he had picked up from his travels, I started to feel the drink quickly, a loosening of muscles that started in my abdomen and rushed downwards.

Woozy, I thought, and sat down.

I sipped slowly.

Alan excused himself upstairs for a few minutes. To get the studio prepped, he said.

I got up and looked at the huge photos on the wall. I felt floaty. I wondered if I would fail a cop walk. "Good thing I don't drive," I said aloud, laughing. I pulled out my phone to text Adam and then remembered he only had a landline. I called it and let it ring, but hung up when he answered.

"Never drink and dial," I told myself, before adding, "No regerts." I laughed out loud, then hoped Alan hadn't heard me.

I wandered around the apartment. On both walls were giant portraits he had taken, some of which had been made into billboards for projects about climate change or copies of which hung in museums all over the world. He seemed to appear as soon as I finished my drink. He handed me another and said, "Let's hit the studio, happy girl." He reached out and brushed my hair back from my warm cheeks. They flushed.

The studio was on the top floor of his apartment. I had seen photos of it in magazines and presentations. It was more beautiful in person. On one wall there were bookshelves with portfolios organized by subject matter or country.

"I didn't bring makeup or anything," I said, sipping at my drink.

"A little lipstick wouldn't hurt. I have some if we need it. Otherwise, you don't need any. Youth is natural beauty." He picked up his camera and pointed it at me.

I laughed. He took a few pictures. He directed me to sit on a chair with the lights pointed towards it. He put on some music. It reminded me of the stuff my parents put on when they were slow dancing after dinner.

He was looking in the camera's display, frowning. "That top isn't working though." He turned the camera display towards me. "It's the wrong color for your skin."

"Even in black and white?"

"Especially in black and white," he said. "Let me see what else I have in the closet." He handed me his refreshed drink before he disappeared.

I sipped at it. I thought about dumping it in a plant but finished it anyway. It was sweet and non-threatening, but it was enough for me. I hadn't had a lot of alcohol, ever. My parents didn't keep much around the house, and what they had smelled and tasted not great. I had never had so much in one afternoon.

Alan came back carrying a white sheet. "Now, hear me out, how about you wrap this around you? The white will offset your skin, otherwise the picture will be all grays and blacks, except for the whites of your eyes."

He didn't mention I would have to take off my shirt and bra, but I knew that was what he meant.

"Um, okay." I looked at him. "But we're not taking anything topless, right?"

"Nude," he corrected. "No, of course not. Maybe a few that make it seem like you're nude, we can adjust the sheet, but it would just be an illusion."

I took a deep breath. He handed me the sheet. I went into the little bathroom off the studio. I took off my top and stared at myself in the mirror. I took off my bra and quickly wrapped myself in the towel. I looked like I was going to a toga party. *Really classy*, I thought.

"You okay in there?" he asked.

"Yup." I tightened the sheet around me.

"Let's see."

I opened the door and he came in. He turned me to face the mirror and picked up a brush. He began to brush my hair. It felt wonderful and terrible. He parted my hair into two sections and began to put it in braids. From a drawer he pulled out a pair of long beaded earrings, the kind that would brush my now-bare shoulders; the kind made in sweatshops.

"Do you have any lipstick?"

I did. But I shook my head. I was feeling dizzy.

"I have some in this drawer, I think." He pulled out a tin of lip and cheek stain and brushed it on my lips. In another circumstance I might have liked it.

"Beautiful," he said. He led me back to the area in front of the camera lights. "Sit here. Lean back." It wasn't a comfortable position. He stepped back behind the camera he had on a tripod, then stooped over and adjusted the flash. I thought of the paintings of women posed on display for painters, for men. Young women. Muses. Targets. Objects.

"Try to smile," he said, stepping back behind the camera. *Click flash click flash.*

From downstairs the doorbell rang.

The smile from his face disappeared.

"Don't go anywhere," he said.

I nodded. I tightened the sheet around me.

As soon as he had turned to go downstairs, I took my phone out of my jeans pocket. I checked my location on Google Maps and sent it to Jess and Loren.

"Please come get me. ASAP," I typed. "The black door with the red Charger in the driveway."

I could hear him speaking downstairs, his voice getting louder. He sounded like he was getting mad. I stood up and walked over to the camera. I wanted to see what the photos looked like. I started clicking through the photos he had taken of me. Already there were a lot. But then, suddenly, I was looking at photos that weren't me. An earlier photo shoot on the camera's memory card.

There was a young girl on the screen. I felt sick. She looked familiar. One of the young artists from a class Alan taught at the museum. A sixth grader. I wanted to puke. No one should photograph a child this way.

Acid burned at the back of my throat. I pushed the button that ejected the SD card from the camera and slipped it in my back pocket. I took a deep breath. I set the timer so it would take a few photos once I sat down. Enough pictures to override the message that there was no SD card. I didn't want him to realize it was missing before Loren and Jess got there.

My heart raced as I positioned myself. The camera clicked and shot ten photos triggered by the timer.

I heard him shut the front door. Prayed the camera would stop clicking. Stop flashing. But then I heard him opening and closing his refrigerator, making yet another drink. I realized that I had no idea what the ingredients were. I knew better than to drink a drink someone else handed me. How had I forgotten so many rules of self-preservation?

"That was weird," he said as he came in the room.

"Yeah?" I wasn't really listening. I was taking the drink he handed me while he held his own in another hand. "Cheers!" I announced, catching him off guard.

He pivoted the glass back towards me and I knocked them together, then let my own glass drop from my hand, spilling on both my sheet and the floor, splattering his khakis. He clicked his teeth, hard, as if he were trying not to let something out of his mouth. Then he took a large step back and a deep breath.

I jumped up. "Oh, no! I'm so sorry."

His face reflected anger for a brief moment.

"No, no, it's okay."

I leaned down to pick up the glass.

This time he raised his voice, "Sit down. I'll get it. You can have mine."

I stood up. "I got the sheet all wet. I should go take it off."

Alan handed me his intact glass. "Please sit. It doesn't matter. We're going to lose the golden hour."

I sat down as he unhooked the lights.

"So," I said. "What was weird?"

He turned and opened the curtains that covered the floor-to-ceiling windows facing the sunset. "Kid on a motorcycle claimed he lives on a street with a similar name and wanted to know if I got a package addressed to him. Wanted to come in and look around. I thought he wasn't going to leave."

"That is weird," I said.

He took a photo. I needed him to take a few more. I needed a few minutes escape time. He walked over to me and started to undo my braids. "Let's try this," he said.

Then the doorbell rang again. At the same time, the phone in my pocket buzzed.

"For Christ's sakes, this kid." Once more, he seemed ready to explode. As soon as he turned away, I ran into the bathroom and pulled my bra and shirt back on. I slipped quickly and quietly down the stairs, standing as close behind him as I could and remain unseen.

He had pulled open the door and Loren was standing on the portico.

"Here to pick up Stevie. We have a date tonight."

Alan looked perplexed. I wondered if he was remembering her face from the portraits I had done for the show. I slipped out between them.

"I totally forgot. We'll have to do this another time."
I was backing towards the car and watching him and waving. He was no longer trying to hide his annoyance. Jess had the engine going, still. I opened the back door and slid in. Loren hopped in the passenger seat and I screamed, "Go!"

"Go where?" Loren said.

"Home. Police department. I don't know what to do."
I was about to start crying, lose the ability to make decisions. My heart was pounding.

"What happened?" Loren was turned around; Jess was navigating the car downtown to the main station.

"Did he hurt you?" Jess yelled back at me.

I was crying. "No, no, not really. No. Just drive, please."

Jess got onto the highway. "Oh, crap," they said a few minutes later.

"What?" Loren asked.

"Is that his red Charger behind us?"

Loren turned around. "Crap. Maybe. Stevie, what happened?"

I blubbered. I told her what I had in my pocket. I told them what I had seen, though it made me sick. Loren went pale.

Jess took our exit and the Charger sped up behind us, its roar a threat. We were right in front of the police station when he clipped Jess's compact, causing it to spin into an electric pole. Jess's scream was cut short by their airbag. The pole was the breakaway kind, and it went up and over Jess's car. It bounced on the road and then bounced again, coming down into the front portion of the

Charger's top. All the world stopped. When I could take stock of my surroundings again, I heard the sirens.

The safest place in a car wreck is the back seat. You think airbags will be like pillows, but it's like being punched by a beach ball. There is a smell of gunpowder. Everything stops for a moment. It's like waking up from dental surgery. While you were out, the world continued around you. But you are not the same.

Loren and I spoke to each other at the same time. Then I panicked, remembering Alan. Someone came to the window and asked if we were okay and said an ambulance had been called. Jess was moaning. We couldn't tell how badly hurt they were. There was a cut on the back of their head and it was bleeding profusely. From what? A hair clip? A flaw in the headrest? Loren handed me a piece of T-shirt to hold on the cut on Jess's head and got out of the car and disappeared for a minute. A bystander popped the airbag that blocked my window and asked if I could open the door. I squeezed the handle and threw my weight against it and it crunched open.

A EMT stopped me from going any further and had me sit back down in the car.

"Let's have a look at you."

"What about the car that hit us? Where's Loren?" I was panicking.

Loren was back within earshot. "It's okay Stevie. Everything is going to be okay." She was back in the front seat. "That guy who hit us? Lost cause," she whispered as the other EMT cut the seat belt and airbags spiderwebbing Jess.

I took a deep breath. The EMT looked at my eyes, asked me about pain, had me turn my head and, finally, stand up and walk. He asked if I wanted to go to the hospital and I said "No." By the time my parents were there, Loren and Jess were long gone, in the ambulance.

Loren texted me a little later that Jess had a head injury and possibly some joint sprains, if not actual breaks. Alan had been taken away beneath a cadaver blanket.

When Dad and Mom got to me, I told them what happened. Dad went to the responding officers and told them what I'd said. I got into my parents' car and we were escorted to the police station where I turned over the SD card and sat through a lot of questions. I gave them the name of the girl in the photos. Then Dad and I sat in a hallway while they located her and her family.

Mom left for a bit and returned with my antianxiety meds. I called the therapist I hadn't been seeing for the last few months and left a message with the answering service. Later, when I saw his number pop up on my phone, I couldn't answer it. Didn't want to answer it. Didn't want to talk about it. The drinks. Being flattered by Alan's attention, being malleable. Being stupid.

At some point we saw the girl and her family walk in. Her mom had her arms protectively around her while a female detective took her down the hallway. The girl glanced at me. She looked so afraid. I smiled at her. She smiled back a little. Once they had disappeared, I leaned over and whispered to Dad, "I want to go home."

Dad got up and went to the desk. A few minutes later the female detective came back out.

"Here's my card. If anything comes up, give me a call."

I nodded. Dad reached out and took it.

"Mom's outside. Levi's with Ida."

Afterwards we went by the hospital and found Loren in the waiting room. She seemed okay, but Jess was unconscious and in surgery. Loren hugged me. I told her what had happened at the station. She said she wasn't going anywhere until she had information about Jess.

"You go home," she said. "I'll call you."

I hugged her again. I felt terrible.

"It's my fault."

"Your fault? You didn't do anything wrong. Did you ram the car we were in? No. Now go home and do whatever it is you do spiritually for people in the hospital."

I nodded. Mom and Dad hugged Loren. "Have you called your mom?"

"Yeah. She wanted to come home, but I told her to stay. She's doing a short film. I promised to go see her when Jess gets out of here."

"Do you want to come stay with us tonight?" Mom again.

Loren shook her head. "Naw. I'm where I need to be."

My parents hadn't told Levi anything. They took me home. Before I got out of the car, Mom asked me if I wanted to see anyone, my counselor, or something. She said she could take off work and get me there whenever I wanted. Or I could do a video visit.

"Nope," I said, my mind made up. "I don't want to talk about this anymore. Not unless I have to." I didn't say: *not until Jess is out of the hospital.* No point in processing something that wasn't over yet. Mom gave me a look like she wanted to say something else. I didn't want her to remind me how she didn't think I should move far away. If she had said that, I might have screamed. Instead, she just nodded and let me go in the house. She and Dad went to Ida's to get Levi.

When I got inside, I plugged in my phone. It had died at the hospital. There was another message from Loren. She said Jess's parents had gotten there, and were sharing information with her, but they wouldn't know anything until later. She said she would call me.

I saw I had a voice mail. I never got voice mails. I checked it.

"I just wanted to make sure you're okay." It was Adam. He sounded emotional, like he had been crying. "Loren called me. She told me about the wreck. I can explain. I have a good reason. A good, unbelievable reason. Anyway, I hope you will let me explain. But most of all, I want you to be okay." He paused again, very definitely crying. "I hope I didn't ruin everything. I broke the rules, but I didn't think . . ." He took a deep breath. "Call me. Whenever. Bye, Stevie."

I wasn't going to call.

One lie invalidates all your truths.

Heartaches
and Pain

I didn't normally work Sundays or Mondays, but I had already asked Christy if I could be off for Tex's funeral the next week and agreed to work a long day on Sunday. The museum was having a summer's celebration and Levi had been looking forward to it. Mom and Dad weren't crazy about leaving us alone. At the same time, Mom was anxious to do another run to Oklahoma that weekend, before she had to take off for Tex's funeral. Moving court hearings is a big deal and had a real impact on the young children she worked for and their families. Dad had a freezer full of fish from his last two trips and Mom wanted to put some of our furniture in the little house. I still hadn't talked to them about that.

I was a little sore from the wreck, but it was the kind of sore that would only get worse the more I didn't move. Jess was still in a lot of pain and in and out from the drugs. Loren had stayed in the hospital waiting room all night. She wasn't going anywhere until she had to. Levi and I caught a bus to the museum.

On the lawn next to the museum there were tents and bounce houses. I was assigned face painting. Levi let me paint his face with the marks of a monarch butterfly before the event started. It wasn't bad, but I had a limited repertoire; my lifeline was a cheat sheet complete with patterns that would limit the choices the kids made. From where I sat, I could watch most of the lawn, keeping an eye on Levi. I made him promise to check in with me between activities.

Loren had planned to come to hang out while Levi played, but that was off the table thanks to me. My coworkers from the museum knew Levi, though, so I felt like he was pretty safe. I saw Adam from a distance. He was posted up near the temporary playground. Before him was a table with a display about river cane, the giant grass native to the area and often confused with invasive bamboo. He was making flutes. Once a family listened to his talk on the benefits of river cane and seemed to understand why it was an important and endangered part of our ecosystem, he would give the kids a river cane flute.

When I looked his way, he smiled. I turned and looked away. Levi had already brought me a flute to hold on to for him. I felt numb. I had needed Adam as a friend, and I'd thought maybe we were becoming more than that. I had expected him at the event on Costa Rica—his home—and he had just gone missing without explanation. And now Tex was gone too. Strangely, I kind of blamed Adam for everything over the last few days. He couldn't be counted on, could he? He was unreliable. A waste of energy when people I loved needed me. Maybe he just wasn't ever really into me, was he?

The rest of the morning was uneventful. At lunch, I took a break and Levi and I went and had the food I had brought from home. I wondered if it bothered me more than it did him, that he could normally only eat safe food, food from home or that had been checked by his parents or me. So many times we had had to turn away proffered goodies, because the risk wasn't worth it. Levi never really said anything to us, though. He ate his sandwich quickly. I gave him the extra water bottle I'd brought for him, since he'd emptied the first one before we finished lunch.

"When I take a break later, we'll get snow cones."

"Great." Levi jumped up. "Can I go back to the playground?"

I put away our lunch things. "Sure, let me walk you over."

Adam was sitting in the shade on a blanket. Levi ran over to him again to say hello.

"Osiyo, oginali."

"Siyo, Adam," replied Levi.

I stood to the side, letting them talk. Then a little boy ran up and asked Levi if he wanted to play tag. The two of them took off running. I turned to go back to face painting.

"Hey, Stevie."

I turned back around.

"Are you going to Tex's funeral?"

"Yeah."

"How are you getting there?"

"Mom's taking me." She had been pretty devastated by his passing too.

"Okay, well, if something comes up, I can take you." Then we were interrupted by a woman screaming.

We both turned and saw Levi clutching at his throat, his face a wordless terror. I think I screamed too. Adam and I ran; Adam reached him before me.

I dropped down next to my brother. The little boy he had been playing with stood helpless, looking terrified.

"What happened?" I asked him. The little boy was crying. His words were unintelligible.

Levi's breathing was ragged, fraught. "Can't—breathe," he gasped, and grabbed on to me. His nails cut half-moons into my arm.

My bag. Had I packed an EpiPen that morning? I hadn't brought my camera bag for once. I usually stuck one in there. I had been so focused on snacks and lunch and drinks. I didn't remember getting it out of his school backpack. And we hadn't brought either.

I was sure my heart was going to explode as I looked around helplessly.

Then Adam pulled an EpiPen from his jacket pocket. He rolled up Levi's shorts and jabbed the needle into his leg. I held Levi, speaking to him as calmly as I could. Adam capped the used pen and handed it to me. Then he went to make sure the emergency personnel could find us.

Levi was soon able to breathe well enough to cry.

"Sweetheart, what happened?" I asked desperately.

Levi reached into his short pockets and then held out the remains of a Rice Krispies Treat. "My friend gave it to me." I looked around. The little boy he had been playing with was nowhere in sight.

I took the treat from him. Though it shouldn't have caused him problems, it must have been contaminated with tree nuts. I wrapped it in the torn plastic wrapper. I washed Levi's hands with a bottle of water. We heard the ambulance before we saw it. In a few minutes paramedics arrived with a gurney. They asked me if I wanted to ride to the hospital with him, so I grabbed my stuff from the painting table.

Adam said he'd take my spot painting kids' faces and for me to call him later. I didn't say anything. I hoped we would get out of the hospital before my parents came home. I was dreading calling them, but I assumed the hospital would want to get in contact. I couldn't believe we were headed to the medical district again. We would be going to Children's, a few blocks from where Loren sat waiting with Jess.

We had gone through this with Levi a few times before. It was scary, but they would check him out thoroughly to make sure he was okay. This was just part of what life was like for us. There was, also, the chance that he would have a second episode, so we were probably looking at spending the rest of the day in the hospital.

As soon as we got to the hospital and got him checked in, I called my parents. Their phones both went to voice mail, so I figured they were in a no service area. I called my auntie's house.

Aunt Geneva answered on the fourth ring.

"Stevie!" I hated how I felt as I heard her voice. Aunt Geneva sounded so happy to hear me. I didn't call enough. And this wasn't a happy occasion.

"Auntie, I'm sorry. I need to talk to my parents. It's an emergency."

"They're in the storage building." I heard her call someone else to go get them. "I'll have them call you right back. Are you okay, Stevie?"

"Yeah, it's Levi. He's had an allergic reaction.."

"Oh, Lord. I'll start praying, dear, I love you. Donadagohvi. Tell Levi we love him."

"Gohvi, Auntie."

While we were still waiting, Mom called. They had already gotten on the road to come home. Just as she rang, the orderlies called us over, so I told her I would call her back as soon as possible. I followed them as they rolled Levi's gurney to our own room in the Emergency wing. Levi's primary doctor had already been called as well.

Someone came and took samples of Levi's blood for tests. As soon as they were done, I turned on the television for him. He was in bed and looked exhausted. I stepped outside and called Mom back and told her what had happened. I was pretty sure we would still be there for observation by the time they made the five-hour drive back.

My phone dinged right after I hung up. It was a message from Loren that Jess was awake but would need to stay in the hospital a little longer. There was a break in their arm that needed to be operated on now that they were stabilized. Their leg was sprained—bruised really bad.

Loren sent a picture of her and Jess. I almost cried. Jess's hair was cut short. Not the shoulder-length cut their mother insisted get no shorter. I assumed it was because of surgery. I was so happy they were awake. I showed the picture to Levi. "Woohoo!" he hollered. I typed his response back to the two of them. I updated them on our new situation and promised to let them know when we went home.

We had been there about four hours, still waiting for Mom and Dad, when Levi's doctor showed up to talk with us. He called me into the hallway and had me get my parents on the phone. This time I spoke to Dad; they were about two hours away, he said, as I put the phone on speaker. I handed the phone to the doctor who assured them it was precautionary, but he was concerned about Levi's blood cell counts and wanted to run some more tests. He asked if any childhood cancers ran in the family. I started to feel panicky then but tried to breathe. I didn't want to scare Levi when I went back in the room. It was bad enough he was going to have to have more blood taken. I texted Loren. She told me that when Jess's parents got back from church to sit with them, she would come over, if we were still there.

I went back and sat with Levi. He was drowsy but had stayed awake waiting for me. I came in and he rolled over and I rubbed his back. "My sweet baby," I whispered, making sure I didn't sound emotional. The last thing he needed was his big sister to start crying. I could wait until he was asleep for that.

By the time my parents got to the hospital, we had been moved to a room upstairs, both for continued observation and to run the additional tests. It was Levi's white blood cell count that was off. Mom and Dad took turns sleeping next to Levi or on the folding chair for visitors in the room. When Loren got there, she gave me a ride so I could sleep at home, instead of the waiting room. We both had work in the morning, so Loren said she would see me in a few hours.

The house was quiet. I went in and stretched out on Levi's bed. I didn't mean to fall asleep there, but I did. I heard my parents come in around dawn. I sat up when they flipped on the light in Levi's room. I got out of his bed and Dad put him in. Mom drew the cover over him.

When we left the room, Mom grabbed me and started crying. I could tell Dad was trying not to cry as well. What they knew wasn't a whole lot. Levi was going to need even more tests, but they hadn't ruled out leukemia or another form of cancer—yet. If it was leukemia, they were catching it early, which was good. There was no evidence of metastasization. Levi hadn't had any symptoms, and if he hadn't had the blood test, nothing would have been suspected. We agreed to not let him know, yet. Because of his allergies, he was more used to blood tests and hospital visits than some other kids.

I went to lie in my own bed. Two of the people I loved were not well. I didn't know if either of them were going to be okay. Tex was gone, suddenly. It was too much. I began to cry, but didn't want my parents to hear. At least I would see Loren soon. At least I had Loren and my parents. What would it feel like to have no one? How did one endure? I couldn't imagine. I was grateful for what I had, the people who loved me. I was grateful for Adam having an EpiPen when Levi needed it.

I sat up in bed a little.

Why in the world had Adam been carrying an EpiPen?

Judadatla Tsisqwa (Spotted Bird)

The next day was a blur. Adam came by the gift shop and asked about Levi. I couldn't talk about him without crying, so I simply said he was fine. I didn't go to sit at the *Ladder*. I stayed busy. I worked or I was with Loren or at one hospital or another the next two days, or with my family.

Loren said Jess's parents had kept their phone and had the nurses turn off the phone in their room, under the guise of helping them heal. Loren had to get permission to bring me to visit. I tried to think of something I could bring them. Until high school, Jess had loved to draw. Something happened between them and their parents at some point and they had stopped. I asked Mom to take me to the art supply store and I picked up a few coloring books, crayons, color pencils, a small portable watercolor set, and a multimedia sketchbook. I put them in a backpack with books by Stephen Graham Jones, Darcie Little Badger, and copies of *When the Angels Left the Old Country* and *Good Omens*. Then Mom and I went to visit. Mom went in with me and offered to take Jess's parents to dinner while I visited with Jess. Mom promised to text me when they were headed back.

As soon as they were gone, I said, "I like your new 'do." They turned their head so I could see their stitches. "Ouch. But, seriously, your short hair is cute."

Jess laughed and winced. "Mom was mad. They only had to shave a spot and I asked them to shear the whole thing."

I laughed louder than I meant to. Their face was lit up with their inner joy at this resistance. "If they kick you out, you can live with one of us."

"I know. How is Levi?"

I told them I didn't know. They asked about Tex.

"You should go to the funeral, if you can."

I shrugged. I didn't think that would be possible now that Levi was an unknown. Jess had decided, though. "I'll ask Loren to take you," they said.

"Let me think about it."

"It will be important to his family to see he was loved."

I didn't know why this mattered to Jess so much. But it did. I wondered if they were thinking about their own scare; our brush with evil, death.

I sat close to their bed but talked quietly. They had a headache. I felt bad, guilty.

They thanked me for the art supplies and books but said they could only keep the coloring book in the hospital room. It was birds and flowers, a field guide to flora and fauna in the Cherokee Nation. I had relatives who had done some of the research and art for the book. They decided to risk keeping the big set of color pencils too. "Save me the rest. For when we move." Jess leaned back against the back of the bed and winced as they lowered the head support a bit, as if everything hurt. They weren't the kind of person who had ever seemed physically fragile before. I stuffed down tears.

"What else do you want to do? When we get to college?"

Jess looked at me in a sneaky way, casting their eyes about as if their parents might be listening. "I have a list."

"Tell me."

"Well, I want to get back into soccer."

"Why did you quit?"

Jess gave me a look.

"Too unladylike?"

Jess snorted. Then winced. "Don't make me laugh. Seriously. Hurts. Not the best medicine: I have a concussion. No, that was my parent's decision. Sports for their 'daughter' was a waste of time when we should be at church or doing door-to-door witnessing. Can't spend the day at a soccer field when there are souls on the line."

I felt so bad. I knew their parents were controlling, but there was a lot they hadn't told us.

"What else?"

"Art. Thanks for the supplies. I want to get back into it."

"You're really good."

Jess shrugged.

"And I'm going to read every book that's ever been banned."

I laughed. "I thought you already were doing that on your phone."

"What? You mean I can find things on my phone or computer my parents would prefer I remain ignorant to?"

We both laughed. As long as there was a World Wide Web, kids were going to play on it. And the way I saw it, it was a far more dangerous space than the pages of a book. Books were about conversations. You didn't have to agree with everything you read, but shouldn't a child get practice thinking critically? I thought of the creepy dead artist taking advantage of girls. I tried to think about something else.

"I want to start a print collection, books, you know. Maybe one day own a bookstore," they said.

"You can start a little library with the books I brought. They're all duplicates from my house."

Jess seemed happier. I asked if they needed something for their headache.

"Naw. I'm tired, though. Can you read me *Mongrels* while I try to fall asleep?"

Tex's funeral was set for tomorrow. I couldn't ask my parents or Loren to take me now. A few people from the museum and from the American Indian Ed program were going, and I was trying to decide whether to reach out to one of the security guards for a ride, but that felt weird. The woman who ran the Indian Ed program was going down early with a few other parents to help cook.

Later that night, my phone rang. I saw it was Adam.

"Hey," he said.

"Yeah?"

"I can give you a ride to the funeral tomorrow, if you need one."

"I can't ride on the motorcycle. My parents would—" I didn't know what to say they would do at that point. They were both trying to keep happy faces on around Levi, even though I thought he was starting to understand there was something serious going on. They had no time for any foolishness from me right then.

"A friend is staying with me; he's loaning me his car. Brandon, you may have met him." Then he added softly, "So I can take you. And Brandon will take care of Princess."

"Oh." The guard I had met the morning I found out Tex was gone. The friend who had given Adam Princess in the first place. Weird. What a strange thing for one of them not to share with me, before now.

"It's a three-and-a-half-hour drive, starts at one. Want to leave about nine, to give us plenty of time?"

I thought of Jess in her hospital bed telling me to go. I thought of Tex's family. *If it were the other way around*, I thought morbidly . . . "How about eight? To be on the safe side."

"I'll see you at eight, then."

Loren already knew about the funeral, so I didn't bother her. I knew she'd text or call later, after she saw Jess after work and got an update from their parents. I poked my head into the living room where my parents and little brother were curled up on the couch, watching a cartoon, and told them I had a ride to the funeral.

"With?" Mom asked.

"Adam."

"On the motorcycle?"

"Car."

Mom and Dad exchanged a look, but just nodded. Their bandwidth for care was strained. Adam was the reason Levi was alive. Though that didn't mean they ever stopped being wary. Mom had gotten me a taser too.

Levi was going to school the next day as if everything was normal. He'd missed Monday after getting home late from the emergency room. He'd had doctors' appointments today, and would maybe have more Friday, or as soon as they got back test results. My parents thought routine would help everyone spend less time worrying. The death of The Artist had been overshadowed by an investigation that included a search of his studio and interviews with former students. It was dark. It was ugly. I didn't even want to know how terrible it really was. I'd been warned I could be called back in for questioning at any time. Whenever I thought about it, I felt ill. I didn't want to talk to anyone. I didn't want to think about Alan braiding my hair or taking my picture. I wished Tex were still alive. But I was pretty sure I wouldn't have talked to him about any of that either.

I went in the kitchen and made some chicken and dumplings to take to the dinner I was pretty sure they would have after Tex's service. That's what we did when we grieved. We made sure people ate. I made extra for my family for dinner the next day. When I finished, I went back to my room and tried to read, but that wasn't helping me sleep, so I went back to the front room and squeezed onto the couch with them. There, finally, I was able to relax and laugh and forget about all the stuff I wanted to forget about.

In the morning, I woke up groggy and listened to my parents and Levi leave for the day. I should have gotten up. I should have said, "Later. Donadagohvi." But I just couldn't. It felt like bad luck to talk to them on my way to a funeral. I felt like I was contagious and didn't want to get anything bad on Levi like I had Jess and Loren.

Finally, I got up and made mint tea for myself. I drank it slowly. It was supposed to be calming. I needed more than mint and sugar, though. I packed the chicken and dumplings into an ice chest for the road.

Everyone else had left the house, though Dad would be back, but maybe not until after Adam picked me up. "If he picks me up," I said aloud, because I no longer trusted anything he said. Still, I took a quick shower and put on black. I brushed my damp hair into a ponytail and wore a pair of beaded earrings my auntie made.

I used the last of the coffee Dad and Mom had brewed to make iced coffees to take with us. They were more cream and sugar than coffee, but they were good. Adam still didn't have a cell phone, but I heard a car in the driveway and met him at the door.

He was holding a bag of donuts from the shop a few blocks away.

"Uh, thanks." I took one out and walked back into the kitchen to get a paper towel. "You want some coffee?" I asked, then added, snidely, "It's Costa Rican."

Adam gulped. "Sure," he said. I handed him the travel mug and we stood in the kitchen awkwardly eating donuts and drinking coffee. There was a giant lying elephant in the room, but, despite my snideness, I really hoped we didn't have to acknowledge it before the funeral. *One trouble at a time*, I thought.

I went to my room and grabbed my backpack. I realized it was heavy because I still had my camera in it. I took the camera out and put it on my dresser before leaving.

When Adam started the car, no music came on. I took my phone and charging cable out of my bag and plugged it in. I shuffled my favorites, and we didn't talk. Adam finally mentioned he hadn't been to this part of the States before. Then he mentioned the topography a couple times. He was super excited about crossing the Red River, the geographical boundary between Texas and Oklahoma. He seemed to be trying to memorize the landscape. He was, actually, using a map to navigate.

"It really is red," he said of the dirt and the river.

"Well, duh," I muttered. He glanced at me, hurt, then returned his eyes to the road.

I had taken a pill for anxiety, and it made me sleepy. I leaned my head against the car door and slept a little. Sleeping made my feelings about riding in a car go away for the most part. The worry had increased again since The Artist had clipped Jess. I tried not to think about it. Adam stopped the car at a gas station, and I jolted awake. When he opened the door, the cool air inside the car traded places with the outside heat. I reached up and rubbed my sleepy face. Oh, lord, drool. I checked to make sure Adam wasn't looking at me. He wasn't.

When he got back inside the car, I excused myself for the restroom. I went inside and bought us two cold waters and four fried pies: one peach and one pizza each. I always felt guilty when I used the facilities and didn't buy anything. In the summertime heat, the waters weren't going to go to waste, and I figured Adam had never had these famous fried pies. I handed him a pizza and a peach. It should have been special. But I didn't have the energy to announce, "Here are the world-famous fried pies."

He immediately unwrapped one and before I could warn him took a large bite.

"No!" I hollered, "they're super hot!" Too late. He was spitting the molten cheese and tomato sauce back into his napkin and chugging ice water.

I couldn't help but laugh, while I mumbled apologies, but added, "They're FRIED Pies! As in, fresh and hot and cooked in boiling oil."

Adam dabbed at his burned tongue, mumbling, "Wiv and wurn."

"More like bite and burn," I replied.

Suddenly, I didn't feel angry at him anymore. I handed him my cold water to make up, but he waved it away.

"They're really good, though. But maybe you could hold on to them until they are less dangerous."

"Will do," I said.

I broke the pies open so they could cool and handed him halves when they were safe.

Adam said it looked like we were making good time and we would be in Anadarko an hour early. "Mind if we stop somewhere?"

I shrugged. "I didn't even finish my pies. And there will be food after the service."

"Not food," he said.

I shrugged again. I handed him half of a peach pie and drank from my water bottle.

I put the music back on and sat up watching the landscape. Adam exited where the signs pointed out a national park. What had once been Fort Sill, a military base, had been turned into a public land whose main attractions were the grave of Geronimo, a military museum, and a bison herd owned by the local Kiowa, Apache, Caddo, and Wichita tribes. I had never been there before.

Adam paid at the park gate for a day pass. I wondered what he was interested in at the Fort. "You have your camera?" he asked. I thought about how my standard response for years had been, "I always have my camera." But that morning, I had left it at home. Again.

"Nope," I said. He looked perplexed. He checked the watch he wore. It was one that actually had to be wound and didn't keep track of anything but the date and time. Went well with his landline and fax machine.

"There's a bison herd here. This park extends to the Wichita Mountains."

"Cool." I was interested. I was always interested in seeing bison.

"If we don't see them now, is it okay if we come back? After the service?"

"After dinner? Sure."

"Cool," he said.

"I want to show you something."

"I thought you had never been here," I remarked.

He paused. "Geronimo is famous. Timeless. His tomb, even I know about that."

I nodded.

He parked and we took the trail that led to the place where Geronimo was supposed to be interred. It was a mound of round rocks, with an eagle at the top of a pyramid shape.

"You know the story?" he asked.

"Skull and Bones? White, affluent teens raiding his tomb while they went to school here to train to kill people? They acted like it was war plunder. But really it was just grave robbing. Then the cowards put it on display in their secret society tomb."

He nodded. "Pretty much."

We stood silently. Adam started picking up the stupid things people had left for luck. Not tobacco or anything sacred, but coins with dead white presidents and other garbage. He had a shopping bag in his pocket. He filled it with litter, garbage, on the tomb of a warrior who fought for his people to keep the life they had. And his bones may not even be here. Another stolen Native body, pillaged graves, as if that would break us.

"The reason I am here is to fix stuff like this," he said quietly.

"What? Here? At the fort?"

He shook his head. "No, in this time. I'm from 2201. I traveled a hundred and fifty years back in time to steal art that's important. Art that is necessary for the future. Art that communicates the insanity of hate and racism, particularly the hate human beings engender against each other using religion, race, borders, gender, and ethnicity as an excuse."

I stared at him.

"Whoa," I finally said. "I'm gonna need you to—repeat that?" I took a step away.

"I'm a time traveler. I'm from the future. Your world is about to implode. Three months of sickness and anarchy and people dying who shouldn't, because they needed to go to the hospital for emergency care at the worst possible time this decade. And people dying from another pandemic, a sickness that it will take a while to end. Ninety days to be exact."

I handed him the mostly empty bottle of whiskey I had picked up, tucked behind Geronimo's grave. "Give me the keys," I said. He did.

I turned and walked back towards the car. I unlocked it and got into the passenger seat. He sounded like my mother. Except my mom wasn't this specific. I was surrounded by people who kept telling me the world was about to end.

Adam got into the driver's seat. I had already started the car, so the air conditioning was on, the windows down to blow out the heat that had built up in the short time it was parked in the sun. Always and forever, the cars were parked in the sun.

"When it happens, there will be chaos. Places will be looted, sacred places and museums and anyplace with things of value. And some of those places will burn. I'm here to make sure the *Ladder* survives." He shifted uneasily.

"You know how you prefer vinyl to digital? How it feels warmer? It's kind of the same way with art touched by the artist's hands. Their atoms are on it . . . their DNA. It matters. Human capacity for creation matters. Otherwise, we could just 3-D print stuff like the *Ladder*. There would be no reason, but even the act of saving it is Ceremony, kind of. You know?"

"So, how are you going to fix Geronimo's grave? His tribe and his heirs have differing feelings about his bones." *Was this a bit?* He seemed as serious as ever.

"I'm not. It's an example. I mean, there are people I'm working with who are returning funerary objects and remains where they belong. But, yes, some tribes don't believe in touching the dead at all, so—like everything else—it's complicated, but ultimately should be left up to the tribe."

"Sovereignty."

"Sovereignty. But there are art pieces that would be a tragedy to lose, full stop. We are trying to move these pieces to a safe place, so they will still be seen by future humans, the actual pieces created and touched by the artist. There will be buildings designed specifically for these pieces: places to visit, make pilgrimages to, meditate on living intentionally. Kindly. In the future, there will be a building with the *Ladder* at its center, like a wheel. And around that axis, there will be other rooms: libraries and displays where people can read about the social constructs that made it relevant, the long arm of history that birthed the artist and the piece, the fiction and film those times spawned. Dubois and Booker T. Segregation and integration; how the world and people were shaped by a world that constructed race and racial hatred. And greed. And fear. They can listen to the voices of the people who were impacted by the time, and the people who constructed the time and world. They can read the books and watch the films that stirred both hate and love."

"Will there be vinyl?"

He laughed. "Of course."

I was watching him, looking for tells that he was making this up. I didn't see any. In a way, that was scarier than if he was weaving together a fantasy. And to what end? "We should go."

"Give me a day, to convince you."

I didn't say anything.

"Twelve hours," he said.

"How are you going to do that?"

"Ask me questions. About my world. Our traditions."

"First of all, this is pretty unbelievable. Second, how do I know you aren't lying to me? I mean, a woman comes from the country you spent eighteen years in to talk about the art and culture and history, which you are now telling me you are all about, and you just skip? There was cacao, for God's sake!"

He was quiet for a moment.

"Stevie, I'm not from there. I spent a few months there to have a backstory for the curator who was coming."

He put up the windows, backed up the car.

"So, what tribe are you really?"

"Tsitsalagi," he said quietly. "From seven generations in the future."

I turned and stared out the window. He was quiet. People have dreamed about time travel forever. In the movies, weren't there rules about telling people about this kind of thing? Couldn't you throw the world into chaos by the smallest action? I turned and looked back at him. "I have a lot of questions. You can't just drop this on me and expect me to believe you. I mean, if this is true, how much have you told me that's a lie"

"That's a fair question." He had turned the car to drive back towards the road. "But I promise to never lie to you again. I'm sorry. I may not tell you everything, because I can't. Costa Rica was part of the backstory we gave the museum, the curator. It explained why I was there in the commune, though I was really only there a few months. I am a mix of many cultures, but Cherokee mostly. I'm also Black, Scottish, Indigenous from Mexico, Eastern European, English. I'm an Ancestry.com dream. Or nightmare. I knew when I told you a Cherokee family name, it wouldn't take long for you to figure out I have an unproveable claim. Your dad and mom probably already did. My parents haven't even been born, yet. Neither have my grandparents. I will be the seventh generation from now."

I didn't say anything.

"I wanted to get to know you. I wasn't supposed to. But I knew about you. When we trained—when we studied this time—we learned all about the place we were going, the people who worked there, so we could figure out who to trust, who would help us, so we would know what would happen to them. They sent me here because of the *Ladder*, but that's not the only thing here that's important."

"Okay, that's creepy."

"I know."

"But how many of you are there?"

"A lot. Some have already come and gone. Time travel is the most important technology there is. There are rules. Do you remember the League of Nations that almost existed, after World War I?"

I shrugged.

"It's as if the League of Nations had a baby with the people in charge of World Heritage Sites. They vote on what should be addressed, what art will teach lessons that will maintain peace. Cooperation. That time, my time, it's not a utopia. But there is cooperation on the big things. Because the planet is about to let us know, if we don't live with it, it will live without us. There are places where dictators still decide what's best for their people, holy men, councils of all women, councils of all men, and places like my country. But a consensus has to be reached between all of the Nations before time travel can be used. Not a majority. Consensus. Do you know how hard it is to get consensus?"

Consensus. A fail-safe. Otherwise people would abuse it. I could already think of a ten things I would move through time to fix or change, if I could.

"All over the world are these chapels, like medicine for the world, that remind people what a world of self-interested politics and economics and governments and laws fueled by judging and hatred and greed have done. To disregard the earth and all humans is to create a hell on earth."

He swallowed. I could tell he was about to tell me something next that maybe he didn't want to. "Some travelers have departed from the original mission. Some want to save the world and some can't wait to watch it burn. My friend, Brandon . . . he's invested in this time. He's fallen in love with a girl, and he hardly sleeps for all that he's doing to save as many people as he can."

"Your roommate?"

He nodded.

"So, why did you know about me?"

Tears were running down his cheeks now. Adam sniffled. "You need to understand this is more science than art. I mean, people have studied this time and the people here a long time, trying to figure out how to intercede without interfering. They run algorithm after algorithm. 'If this, then that.'" I reached up and brushed the tears from his cheek. "I was supposed to befriend you only after . . . well, you were supposed to experience a couple of tragedies. Trauma."

I turned and looked at him. His eyes didn't leave the road. "Wow," I said.

We were both quiet. I felt numb. "You were supposed to use me?"

He shrugged, nodded, his lips pinched together. He was holding his breath. He was very near ugly crying.

"What traumas?"

He didn't answer.

"What fucking traumas?" I screamed.

He still didn't speak.

My mind raced. Tex. Alan. (Bastard.) If Jess and Loren hadn't come? Photos? Rape? Self-destruction? Where would it have ended? Jess in the hospital, even now.

"You knew all this terrible shit was going to happen to me?"

"I knew about Tex. And I'm sorry. But Jess . . . that was not on the timeline. That was my fault, though. I didn't follow the rules. I broke the rules. I shifted things around by acting when I wasn't supposed to."

"How is it your fault Jess is in the hospital?" I remembered Alan coming back from downstairs, after I had called and hung up on Adam, tipsily, then texted Loren and Jess, frantically, put them on their fateful journey. Suddenly I understood. "That was you? At Alan's door, the kid who wanted to come in and look for a package?"

He nodded. "It gave you time to plan, to escape, to get away. To see the other pictures."

"To lead Jess and Loren into danger."

"You saved others. I'm sorry about Jess, but he was a really bad person. Those photos of that kid, that middle schooler? There would have been more. Though one was bad enough."

I let that sink in. The terribleness. The predator ruining life after life. "So, what other tragedy is going to happen?"

Adam didn't say anything.

"What else is supposed to happen? How do I stop it?"

"It was Levi."

"What?"

"I wasn't supposed to be at the playground."

I felt like the wind had been knocked out of me. "So you don't always carry an EpiPen?"

He laughed. "I do now. For Levi."

"So, he was supposed to die?"

Adam nodded.

I stared out the window. I picked up my phone and put the music back on. I checked my phone, no messages. Tears began to stream down my cheeks. I hoped Levi was having a good day at school. I texted Loren, who should have been on lunch, and asked how things were. She sent me back a photo of Levi painting a violet dog. "From this morning," she wrote. His expression was full of concentration, so serious. The dog looked happy. Everything looked the opposite of the way I was feeling. The picture was replaced by the words "Mom calling."

Can't
Take It

Adam pulled the car over to the side of the road. I hit the button as quick as I could. "Mom?"

"Stevie? Are you somewhere you can talk?" Mom's voice was quiet but urgent.

I glanced over at Adam.

"I can talk."

"Levi does have cancer. But it's treatable." Mom sounded confident. Like Levi was already all better. I wanted to believe her.

"What does that mean? Treatable how?"

Adam scooted over closer to me. I felt him lean his head in between my shoulders. He was breathing deeply, slowly.

Mom hesitated. "Well, there will be more tests tomorrow. But it can be treated."

"What do you mean when you say 'treated'?" I thought of chemo. I thought of his hair falling out. I thought of nausea and dizziness and vomiting and loss of appetite. Is that what she meant by "treatable"?

"Stevie, don't go there. Most of what you worry about never happens."

And some of what never occurs to me, does, I thought.

"I need you to keep treating Levi like you always have. We let him have a normal childhood, as normal as we have managed for him so far. He is the one who needs care. Don't make this about you."

Ouch. I didn't say anything. We were both quiet. I heard a voice in the background, Dad, speaking to her, low, quiet.

"I'm sorry," Mom said. "That's not what I meant." She sighed. "Look I just know everything is going to be okay." Then her voice lifted at the end in a way that didn't sound quite right. Almost threatening hysteria. "We love Levi. We would do anything for him, wouldn't we?"

I nodded.

"We just have to keep doing that." I heard Dad behind her again, low.

"Your dad wants to talk to you."

They changed places.

"Hey, Stevie. Where are you at?"

I told him.

"You're not on a motorcycle, right?"

I laughed; Dad could do that with a tense situation. He knew I wasn't. We had cameras over the front of the house. He would have seen it. "No, Dad."

"Good deal. I'm going to send you some money in case you have car trouble or something. Or if you need to get TWO hotel rooms because it gets too late to drive. You know how dangerous it is after midnight. If he gets sleepy, find a hotel. Levi and one of us will be spending the night here."

"Wado, Dad," I said.

"We love you," he said. "Be careful. Your mom wants to ask you something."

She told me they were coming up with a treatment plan and asked if I could be available whenever that would happen, probably the next Monday.

"Sure, Mom. Absolutely. How are you and Dad?"

Mom took a deep breath, "Walter asked Jeff to guide the trips he has scheduled. It's one of his busier times, but obviously he's going to be here. We have to stay positive for Levi." Jeff was one of my mom's aunt's sons.

"Of course." I didn't charge her with not answering the question. If she needed to deflect, I would let her have that.

"Be careful, sweetie."

"I will."

"Where are you?" *Verify then trust, Mom, I get it.*

"Just left Geronimo's grave."

"Try to see the bison while you're there. And after dark, the stars are amazing. So you should stick around and look up."

"Okay, Mom. I love you."

"I love you too, baby."

I hung up. I crossed my arms around myself and ducked my head down.

"Is Levi going to be okay now?"

Adam looked off. He tightened his jaw.

"Look, I can tell it's not good by your body language. But you promised not to lie to me anymore."

Adam bit his lip and shook his head. He took a deep breath. "It's an aggressive cancer. Rare. Barely treatable, forty percent chance of survival under normal conditions." His voice was shaky.

"What do you mean by normal conditions?"

"Not during a plague, not during a pandemic, not when the power grid is failing and supply chains are disrupted." Adam's face looked as if he had seen terrible things; as if closing his eyes could never erase it.

"Why are you telling me all of this? I don't even know if it's true, but . . . why? Why Levi? He's never done anything—" I knew my words made no sense. Of course he didn't do anything to get cancer. Of course he was worthy of more time and less pain. All kids were.

I balled my hands into fists and leaned my head into them in my lap. I howled like a dying animal. My car door opened and Adam was standing there. He reached in and pulled me out, into his arms. He held me while I cried.

Levi dying, it was wrong. It was terrible and awful and none of us deserved that. Especially not Levi, my sweet baby brother. "Why?" I cried. "Why?" I moaned.

"You made me promise not to lie anymore," he whispered.

"No," I screamed. "Why is this happening to my baby brother?" Adam held me until I couldn't cry anymore. Until I was exhausted. When I had no more tears he opened the passenger door and I slid back into my seat.

He got in and started the car. When it chimed, because my seat belt wasn't fastened, like a robot I clipped myself in, because that's what you do.

For the rest of the ride, I was numb. I picked up the map that sat between us. I watched the roads and the landscape. We found the funeral home but had to park a few blocks away. I was glad to see so many people had turned out for Tex's family. His children lived in the area.

His daughter was a doctor at the local Indian Health Services facility and his son was an art teacher at Riverside Indian school. Tex had talked about them to me a few times, nothing but pride in his voice. The room was full of people from the area, some of whom resembled Tex, which was a little disorienting. I had only met his kids briefly, so when the head of the museum, Mark, and another curator waved us over, Adam started to go sit with the two of them. I saw the people from the American Indian Education program had seats towards the back on the other side and went to sit over there. Adam realized I was not following him. I watched him look around, confused. It took him a few minutes to spot me.

"Here you are," he said, when he got to our row.

"You didn't see that coming, did you?" I laughed wickedly. A few people turned and gave me, the unstable stranger, a concerned look. They made room for Adam to squeeze in next to me.

I would describe the look on Adam's face as sheepish. I had read the term in books, but here it was on Adam. It was a good word choice.

The service opened with Tex's grandchildren singing "Amazing Grace" in Kiowa. I thought about what Adam had said. I thought about my family and Levi.

I wept.

Red
Dirt
Boogie,
Brother

It was odd to walk past the open casket. I had only ever seen Tex solid, intentional, thoughtful. It was like seeing him asleep. I felt like it was something I shouldn't have seen. Wrong. I made a conscious effort not to think any more about people I loved while we were there. It felt like wishing for things to turn out differently than I feared they might. I would only be positive. I would only think good things around them, I told myself. I was in a daze when we left the chapel, joined the line of cars to drive towards the Wichita Mountains. I was glad this was where Tex was going. It was beautiful. I had seen his paintings of the area. It was home. A cemetery in the shadow of the mountains. After the final handshake, it was back on the road to follow the line of cars to a nearby church for the dinner the family and church had prepared.

At the entrance to the church were several paintings, some by Tex and some by his son. The landscapes by Tex caught the spirit of the area, the land. Then there was a portrait by Tex of his family, his wife, Jewell, and his young son and daughter. It was them, but it was in Tex's style, the way he saw them, the way he felt about them. It reminded me of T. C. Cannon's kinder, gentler works, painting with love for the subjects, warm colors, and blue-violet shadows, the background meticulous in a fine detail that made it disappear in deference to the human subjects. Finally, there was a painting of Jewell and Tex by his son, also painted with love and care but in a completely different style and tone, like a colorized black-and-white photo. Tex's arm around a strong older beauty, their hands touching, his left hand crossing his body to touch her veined and knuckled hand with the matching wedding rings, shiny, tiny metal stars punched all around their circumference.

We visited with various members of the family and community. Both his daughter and son were sad they hadn't lived closer, seen him more, taken time off from jobs to just be with him more. Mom had told me it was a common refrain from adult children who lost a parent suddenly. His daughter took my hand in hers and said, "Don't let geography define your relationship with your family, with people you love. Be intentional about where you go, what you choose to do, how you spend your time." Then she hugged me. *It's like my mother got to her*, I thought.

More of the museum employees had shown up, people who had worked with Tex for the last ten years, liked him, been impacted by him. He was a book of stories lost, an album of songs unsung, visions unpainted. He had made the world a better place and his sudden absence was a shock. There were a lot of good things to say about him.

Adam and I stayed long enough to help clean up. Put away chairs and tables. Removed tablecloths to be laundered. I was handed back the empty pot of chicken and dumplings, along with a few covered plates to take with us. The park didn't close until sundown, so we left in plenty of time to drive back there.

We drove towards the range where the bison were kept. The sun was dropping behind the mountains, the world a blaze of gold and yellow light. We passed through Medicine Park with all its buildings made of round stones, like natural cannon balls, just like Geronimo's grave. We found the gate that took us through the bison range owned by the tribes. They grazed occasionally on national park land. We drove slowly, enjoying the beauty of the tall, dry grasses, the rocks that made the red-brown mountains; we put the windows down and let the heat and the noise of the natural world in.

We kept driving until we found a large group of mommas and babies resting in the shade. It was wild that you were allowed to get out of the vehicle. I, suddenly, wished I had brought my camera. My phone was charged and it was the camera I had with me, so I took pictures anyway. The large, awe-inspiring creatures lumbered. Their long, flowing hair, muscular bodies, the care they took with their babies—keeping their eyes on us, watching the young ones play, warning them away when they were too rambunctious. Mothers and young. The babies, careless and carefree, but the mommas ever watchful. Eventually, the herd stood up, turned away from us, maybe headed to water, but then they ran. Have you ever seen a baby bison hop? Nothing like it. What would it have been like to live in a world where the massive, seemingly endless bison herds roamed the prairies and could cross the world at will? How is it anyone thought killing them all would make the world better? When their trail was nothing but dust, breathless, I got back into the car. I got out one of the plates Tex's daughter had made for us, tore the frybread in half, and handed part of it to Adam. "Honey or meat and beans?" I asked.

"Something sweet."

The honey tasted like the prairie, like the air, the scent of the edges of the wind and dust. It was lovely. How can honey taste like warm sandstone, but in a good way? *I will always think of this sun, this world*, I thought, *in the future when I eat honey*. Then I remembered I was with a boy who claimed he was from a much farther future than one I might see. And I had questions.

"So, are you even from this planet?" Was I really starting to believe him? Or was it just easier to make believe while we were hanging out?

Adam kind of choked on his frybread.

"Guess you didn't see that coming either," I remarked. "You're not very good at this seeing-the-future thing."

That only made it worse. I handed him a can of Pepsi. He popped it open and took a deep drink.

"No stuff like this in the future."

"No Pepsi?"

"Not like this. Tastes different. Tastes healthy in the future." He took another big drink.

I shuddered. "That sounds terrible."

He turned the can and pointed at ingredients that sounded like chemistry vocabulary.

"You know how, for the most part, you can buy things that have been found to be detrimental to your body? Stuff that is acknowledged to cause cancer in California?"

"Good thing I'm a resident of another state," I joked.

"How in France and Canada there are things you can't even buy there? But unless you grew up elsewhere, you would never miss them? That's my time. Companies self-regulate, for seven generations. Humans learned the hard way to respect the planet. But it could be unlearned. That's where our work comes in."

I couldn't imagine a world where people considered the negative impact of the short-term bottom line. It was a world that hadn't existed in recent memory.

"There is a mandated human right to clean air and water all over the world in my time."

"Why?"

"Because the planet is about to communicate pretty loudly that what is happening now is untenable. And—"
He paused.

"And what?"

He was obviously hesitating.

"What?" I said. I realized I was invested now, as if I believed him, even as I tested his world-building, his fabulism.

"Well, four things will happen soon. The first is that combination of pandemics and natural disasters, all related to rising temperatures and earth exploitation. It will more than decimate the world's population. It's happened before. Suddenly, everyone will have enough, too much, even, but at a terrible cost. Housing will be affordable for everyone. Health care will no longer cost individuals.

People will have work options that are humane. But only after a lot of protests."

"So, the survivors will have survivor's guilt and lots more to feel guilty about? Great."

"The second is an escalation of the not-so-secret cyber war between governments all over the world and climate activists and terrorist organizations. The impact of that many shadow operations on current communications and digital and energy technology is unfathomable, unpredictable. Even now, there are more people moving off-world while they can afford it."

"So, will all student loans be canceled?"

"That and, well, let's just say I hope you have hard copies of all the books, music, and movies you love."

"You know I love my vinyl."

He nodded. His pause was long, like he was reconsidering what he was telling me. "The third thing is an app called *Soulcraft* that will impact society and people. It will be the first thing many people who are lost will find that brings them comfort and answers in their grief. Somehow, it will survive the erasure, the Big Blip. It will help society and some governments become anchored in acting in the best interest of the planet and future generations. And that will spread."

I looked at him. I didn't say anything about Loren. I just stared.

"Yeah," he said. I think we both knew what we thought we knew. But I wasn't going to say anything. I had promised her. We kept each other's secrets. And . . . wow, was I going to tell her?

He answered that for me. "You can't tell her. We're not supposed to interfere. When we do, it's never predictable what could happen, how things could change. Even now, I have no idea the impact of saving Levi. Or of telling you all this, trusting you. Hoping you'll trust me."

"Wish I didn't know now what I didn't know then," I said. My mom loved Bob Seger.

Adam nodded.

"I thought I was going to tell you as soon as I met you. Then I met your family and I knew. But, you can't talk to your parents. Your dad, he can't know, yet. That's a directive. Even I don't know how all this works."

I looked at him. "I never thanked you for saving Levi. I should have. I've replayed that day in my head. How I should have had an EpiPen—I just was so distracted. The incident, the wreck, Jess . . ." If I hadn't felt all cried out from earlier, I would have started weeping again. "Thank you. Thank you for not letting him die."

"I haven't saved him, though. I wish I could."

"Can't you? Is there no way? You can't look in your crystal ball and find a way to get him what he needs? What if we went to another country?"

He sighed. "The problem is, the technology he needs just doesn't exist yet. All I have is a plastic fax machine; crystal balls can't carry analog information. Occasionally, I get messages bounced into my fax machine from my time. They're like radio waves that have reversed. The sound waves travel through telephone wires and end up printed on our machines. It doesn't require the same amount of energy as physically sending a human back in time, but the message has to be really important, because it still has to be in support of the agreed-upon missions. We can't send back things, or something like our secret to the energy dilemma. Sending stuff back would effectively erase them, because the conditions needed to create them would never exist.

Adam looked at me; held my eyes. "If Levi was in my time, he could be cured. But here, there's just not enough known and not enough energy. It's a rare cancer. To the pharmacy companies—the people who write the checks—it's not worth the money and time to research."

Money. Always money. Wellness should be a right, not something determined by disposable income; not something an insurance benefit manager somewhere heartlessly decided.

"What about something that would slow it down until this next lockdown is over? Bring it back here?" I was starting to get desperate.

"I wish I could. Not just for Levi, but all the others. But there are too many other things that need to come about, need to be invented, before a cure can be discovered let alone used. And part of that is related to the fourth thing. A source of clean and free energy. It will disrupt everything. Economies built around polluting energy industries will collapse. But entire new industries will arise around distribution and cleanup. What happens when you don't have to worry about buying gas or paying to get water and electricity? When there is a surplus of energy, even? It is what enables us to time travel.

It takes a significant burst of energy to move backwards in time. A bit less to move forward to return, to the future our pod came from. Little enough that it can be stored and generated in this time. Like a rubber band snapping back to its beginning, a bow's drawstring? We can bounce back to where we came from, return to our lives as if we never left."

Was I really believing him?

"Do you have the same holidays, traditions, religions in your time?"

"In our nation? Some. We have history, just another seven generations more than you. People pick and choose based on their affinities and families. Other nations have their own traditions, much like here." He paused.

"What?"

"Well, in my country we use a lunar calendar. So, during the first rain of each new moon cycle, you spend it with the person you want to spend the rest of your life with." He seemed to be blushing. "Ideally, that's the first time you kiss, but then each time it happens after that, you commemorate it with a kiss."

"So, have you?" I asked.

"No," he rushed. "No, I don't have, haven't met—well, haven't kissed—the one. Not yet."

"Well, good luck. Never rains here anymore."

Adam turned his head away from me. "No. But it will." I couldn't figure out his delivery. It seemed intentionally flat. Was he sad? Worried? Warning? Trying to keep me from reading anything into his words?

Adam started the car; it was getting dark. We were in danger of being in the park later than we were supposed to be.

"You up for a hike?"

I was wearing Doc Martens with my black dress. The dress wasn't ideal, but I had a pair of black jeans and a T-shirt in my bag. I had intended to change after the service but had forgotten.

"Sure," I said.

"I knew you'd say that," he laughed.

"Sure you did," I replied drily.

Satellite

We were able to drive to the summit of Mount Scott. It was twelve feet shorter than Mount Pinchot, but Mount Pinchot was closed. All of the land had once been part of the reservation that belonged to the Kiowa, Comanche, and Apache Nations. Inevitably, what the Native people preserved was taken by the federal government and turned into a park. Even though it was the summer, it was a weekday and there were no cars parked at the top of the mountain. I pulled my jeans on beneath my dress and then slipped it off and quickly pulled my T-shirt on over my sports bra while Adam was gathering things from the trunk of the car. "Chairs or blanket?" he asked.

"Blanket," I suggested. "Or two."

When he had the backpack loaded, he put it on. He handed me a flashlight and a hiking pole. "You need water?"

"Not yet." But even in the dark it was hot. I would need water soon.

"Let me know."

I was worried about snakes. I tried not to let on, but I was glad for the flashlight and hiking stick.

Already the stars were out, brighter than in the city, multiplied by the dark, the lack of streetlights. We walked without talking. Adam led the way, holding branches back from the path, warning about unsteady footing, frightening away any possibility of snakes. In the scrub and cactus, rabbits jumped, darting away. I occasionally caught the gleam of their eyes from the brush. *Nighttime in the summer is the best time to be on the move*, I thought.

We walked until we found a good place to stop from where we couldn't see the parking lot. He spread out the blanket and we sat down on the hard ground. The moon was bright, lighting the landscape below. It reflected off the water—three distant lakes reflecting the moon as if there were three different ones. I tried to capture the scene, but my phone wasn't quite up to the task, the moons disappearing, refusing to let me capture it in more than one place at a time. The rugged landscape was cast in black and white and gray. Now and then I asked him random questions, questions that tested the abilities of a world-builder, checking for inconsistencies in his stories, his ability to repeat the same information. He was patient. He didn't get annoyed at my fact-checking. Or at least he didn't show it.

"I'm sorry I had to lie to you. I didn't foresee that." He laughed. "We were supposed to be friendly," he explained. "But not friends, at least not at first. But once I met you, I was impatient. And you are so smart. So invested in the truth and authenticity and—" He paused. "So serious, so intentional, so thoughtful about your choices . . .

"I found myself having to answer questions I wouldn't have had to answer, if I hadn't wanted to be with you all the time." He took a breath. "I couldn't foresee that. Once we met . . ." He finished his bottle of water and returned it to the pack. I didn't know how to respond. So, I didn't.

"Once we met, I felt like I had never really talked to anyone before." He laughed again. "And I couldn't shut up. But, I'm sorry I lied. I tried to do it as little as possible." He looked like he felt incredibly guilty about something.

"I feel like you need to confess to something. Was there a big lie? Bigger than 'my mom is dead'?"

"Ouch. But yeah, that's actually not untrue. Our world isn't perfect. Not all chronic illnesses have been cured."

"Oh, I'm sorry." Now I felt guilty. How did Adam keep doing this? Still, it was confession time. "You were saying?"

Adam took a deep breath. "All that vinyl at the warehouse? I didn't find it there. I curated that collection to impress you."

Alarm bells went off. "Wait, did somebody write you a guide to seducing me?"

"No! No, that was all me. I like the sound of a record playing too. It's the closest thing to being in the same room with the singer, the artist, the musician."

I still had no words. So much of what he said, it was similar to the way I had felt about him too. But now I didn't know. Lying was one thing. But this—these other stories. What were they? Were they true? But how else to explain him saving my brother? Interrupting The Artist? I couldn't have been more grateful for both. What else could have explained those two things? I was tired, so I stretched out on what I thought of as my half of the blanket. Lying on my back, watching the stars, I felt the world turn slowly. It was a feeling that sometimes made me want to grab the earth, as if we could tilt off if gravity forgot us. Instead, I grabbed Adam's hand. We stayed like that for a long time.

I pointed out the satellites he had shown me when we took that first walk with my family—the space stations for the one percent who had nothing they were attached to, on the planet that had made them wealthy.

Adam looked sad. "One hundred percent," he said. "You've been practicing."

"I may have downloaded that app you told me about."

The wind had picked up and I sat up and moved closer to Adam. "Cold," I explained. Adam handed me a blanket and let me wrap us in it. The breeze gave me a chill when it hit the sweat on my body, evaporating it into the air, cooling me. It had blown a cloud in over us, the only cloud I saw for miles.

"I feel like Eeyore," I muttered, using my head to nod towards the cloud. Then I explained it in case he didn't know. He didn't seem to.

We were sitting close together when the first raindrops fell. "Can I kiss you?" he asked.

I looked at him.

"Did you know it was going to rain?" I hadn't seen rain in years, not even a few sporadic drops.

"It helps to be up high," he replied, smiling.

"Is that a yes?"

Adam nodded. I thought about what that meant. "Is this a future kiss?" I asked.

He leaned in close to me, spoke quietly, "If, by future, you mean forever? I hope so." Then he kissed me gently on the lips. Too gently, before pulling away.

"You sure we're not cousins?" I said.

He laughed. "No, no, we're not related. At least not too close."

"Because that kiss felt pretty platonic," I remarked. Then I leaned forward, pulled him closer, and I kissed him with an energy I didn't know I had. It began to rain harder, a cloudburst. But, still, we kissed. It was only lightning that brought it to a sudden end. We both jumped up, fleeing the thunderclap. We grabbed our stuff, put blankets over our heads, and hiked quickly and carefully to the car. I hoped I wouldn't step on a snake surprised by the cloudburst.

Once we were in the car I started laughing. The week had been one of super highs and super lows. Something bad would happen, then something good would seem to balance it out. It's what kept the world on its axis, I supposed. So much good, so much bad, but once there was too much bad, it was all out of whack. Adam looked at me. He wasn't laughing, but he was smiling, big, the kind that makes your cheeks hurt. It was late. We weren't going to get home until maybe one in the morning. I thought about whether or not to get a hotel for us. I put on Leon Bridges and we sang "Texas Sun" together. When it was over, I turned off the music. We listened to the rain hit the metal roof of the car. When it stopped, he started the car.

We had driven about twenty miles before I finally spoke again.

"So, what else you got?"

"What do you mean?" He glanced over at me, but then turned back towards the road.

"Proof. How do I know you're from the future? How do I know you're not here to bring about the end of the world? Or making it all up so I'll help you steal some priceless artwork and abscond to Costa Rica or something?"

He was quiet. He drove. I watched the road. We saw signs for a roadside rest stop, complete with a playground, Wi-Fi, and vending machines. He pulled over into it. He checked his watch, though the car had a digital clock.

Once he parked he said, "I was kind of hoping you wouldn't ask. I sent you an e-mail earlier about it. Just so you would know I wasn't making it up after the fact."

I reached for my phone.

He stayed my hand.

"Please don't. Let's get out of the car."

I followed him into the building with the vending machines. He bought some peanut butter cups. I loved peanut butter cups, but I never ate them because of Levi. Though he wasn't allergic to peanuts, sometimes the same facilities processed tree nuts. I would have to make sure I washed my hands, brushed my teeth before I was near him. Levi was that sensitive. I followed Adam back out of the building to the playground. According to the signs, we were too old to be on the swings. The same signs warned us to watch out for rattlesnakes. I used my flashlight liberally.

We sat on the swings. The stars were still bright out here. The heat emanated from the rubber mulch under the swings. It was impossible to even play in the heat of the day anymore for long, so nighttime was the right time. Some states were passing laws that all manual labor jobs had to have a few hours in the middle of the day for siesta, otherwise more workers would drop dead from the heat.

Adam handed me the chocolate peanut butter cups. They were already melting, so I ate them quickly, licking the chocolate off my fingers. Adam was watching the stars with his binoculars, swinging back and forth gently, then he stopped. He checked his watch again, then looked through the binoculars. He stood up from the swing's seat and handed them to me. Then he stood behind me and gestured with his head towards the sky, towards the satellites and space stations I had memorized.

I looked up. They were like a long, extended constellation of unblinking lights, but one of the space stations was now missing. I squinted.

"Am I looking in the right place?"

I had to turn to see Adam nodding.

"One of the space stations is off. The lights are off."

Adam had his lips pursed. He just nodded again.

The second station seemed to be moving, seemed to not be in the spot I had memorized. And the satellite closest to it seemed to be in its path.

"Adam, what is happening?"

"Sabotage."

"What?"

"Someone hacked the system; this is the beginning. One of those satellites is for GPS, another for cell phones, another for military surveillance."

"But the space stations?"

"One for research. It's the one without lights. It's there. The people are there. A rescue attempt will be launched. Most of the scientists will make it."

I handed him the binoculars. I didn't want to see anything else.

"But the other one?"

"It will collide with the satellite close to it. There will be no survivors."

I felt scared, afraid, freaked out. "Who is doing it? Is it your people? Why didn't you stop it?" I couldn't help it, I reached for the binoculars again. From far away, two more lights moved closer. Soon it would be sparks and space junk, falling and burning up in the atmosphere.

"We aren't supposed to interfere. Think of it as a controlled skid. We know the earth is in danger, and we know which way it's going to fall. For the greatest good, we have to control our response to the fall."

I thought of the car wreck I'd had the day I pivoted the wrong way, been where I shouldn't have been, shattered glass and crunched metal.

"What makes y'all think it can be controlled?"

"It can't. This was always going to happen. We just have to control how we prepare for it, how we respond to it."

Already the satellite and space station seemed to be pulling themselves together. They were too close. I thought of the people there. I hoped most of them were asleep.

I hoped they weren't watching their world end. I handed back the binoculars. I stood up.

"I need to get home."

We walked back to the car in silence. By the time I looked at the sky again, there were five less artificial lights, but the stars pulsed, brighter than ever, lighting up the dark.

When I got home, Dad was there and still up though it was after midnight. He was sitting at the dining table, tying flies. I was confused because he wasn't supposed to be guiding trips while they were taking Levi to and from the doctor over the next few days.

"Was worried about you, couldn't sleep, might as well be productive. And there was only a small cot at the hospital, so I let your mom have it." I liked watching him make the fishing flies, tying the thin line around bits of feather; it was an art.

"Who are those for?"

"I have to ship them to your uncle. He's taking over my trips for the time being."

"That's right," I said, remembering. That conversation seemed so long ago.

"How were things? The chicken and dumplings were good. Thank you."

I nodded. "It was sad. Got to meet Tex's family. Room was filled with love. Couldn't ask for a better celebration of his life."

Dad nodded.

I wanted to ask if he had seen the news, but then I didn't want to watch it myself. I didn't even want to read the e-mail Adam had sent, though, by the time I went to bed, I would.

Instead, I sat and watched him finish the fly he was tying. It was salmon-colored, like a little egg with tiny hairs exploding with red threads from its center. Dad was good. His flies brought the fish.

As he finished, he packed up his gear. "Levi has more tests tomorrow." I nodded. "I don't know, Stevie," he paused. "I don't know how to do this." His voice broke.

I stepped in and hugged him. "You just have to keep being his dad. You're good at it. As you always say, love is an action."

He smiled.

"See you in the morning," he said quietly, then disappeared into his own room. I couldn't tell him Levi wouldn't be saved, that Adam had said the world wouldn't allow him to survive this. I wasn't going to cry anymore. I wasn't going to accept that as Levi's ending. I went to my room determined to see what I could do to rewrite the future. Adam may have had rules to go by; had to let the future steamroll ahead.

But I was going to add another chapter.

Oh,
Spaceman

Dad and Mom and Levi spent most of the next day at the hospital. They had confirmed their appointment for next Monday to update our family on a treatment plan. After work on Thursday and Friday, I hung out with Adam at his workshop while Loren went up to Jess's hospital. Brandon rode the motorcycle and let Adam have the car. Adam even got a basic cell phone.

Jess was getting better and we hoped they'd go home soon. Jess's parents, at first reluctant, had began to appreciate Loren being there, since they had to cover Jess's shifts at their shop. Loren wanted to watch over Jess, sit in the waiting room in case she was needed, help them with rehab. Bring favorite foods. Sneak in books.

A few times Adam and I went by, but didn't stay long. Jess was only allowed visitors briefly. Since the last pandemic, the hospitals had become strict again about limiting time and wanderings of visitors. The concussion limited the time Jess could be on screens or read, so Loren would read to her, but she couldn't do video calls. The headaches they'd been having since the wreck were made worse by noise, light, and screens.

Adam hadn't told me much more about Brandon since the night of Tex's funeral. I had the feeling there were things he didn't want to talk about with me, because he had promised not to lie to me again, in which case I would learn more than maybe I needed or even really wanted, or have information he thought I couldn't keep secret. Brandon was rarely at the studio when I was there. I didn't ask and Adam didn't volunteer. Until, finally, he did.

We had gone to the warehouse. Adam seemed nervous. I put on a record. I hadn't meant to choose one that would encourage slow dancing. Well, maybe I had. And there we were. The warehouse was always gray without the overheads and lamps on. It was hot, we were sweaty. I took his hand and pulled him close and we danced. We waltzed. We spun around the room. We kissed. I laid my head on his chest. His heart was pounding. I let him lead. He moved us counterclockwise through the dark warehouse until we were close to the large curtained-off area in the back. The room he had asked me not to photograph. As the song ended, he stepped back and looked me in the eyes.

"I need to show you something."

He kept hold of one hand and led me into the back room. And there, hanging from the ceiling, was the *Ladder*.

I pulled my hand from his and covered my mouth.

"What? How?" I was stunned. More than thirty feet long, swaying slightly—the most important piece I had ever seen in person. At least, it sure looked like it.

"It's mine. It's a forgery. We're going to switch it out. Make sure the real one survives the interruption; the almost end of the world."

I swayed. Adam supported me. We sat down together on the floor.

"You're serious. This is real. The Big Blip. This is why you're here."

Adam wrapped his arms around me and lightly squeezed me. I leaned back into his embrace. I wished Loren was there to see this. I hadn't told her about the third condition of the world, how her app would change it, make the world more livable. I had told her other things, though. And I had told Adam I would. She understood science and physics and wormholes and dark matter in ways that I knew would allow her to believe.

"When?" I said.

"We switch it out in a week."

"You and Brandon?"

"Yes."

"Why did you show me this?"

"We have a favor to ask."

"You want me to do something? At the museum?" I felt nauseous.

"No. Somewhere else. It's something else."

I breathed. "Where?"

"In the Northeast. A family wants their great-great-great-grandfather's headdress back. It was taken off him in a massacre. It's been on display for nearly two hundred years. They want to bury it. If you are willing, you would meet with a curator, donate another forgery—a piece with Cherokee provenance, ties to Chief Bowles and his son and Sam Houston—and help switch the headdress out for another."

"That sounds complicated. And like I will get arrested."

"Brandon has the plane tickets and can get the fake identification for you."

I felt drunk. And I had only ever felt drunk one time before.

"What happens to the ladder?"

"We switch it out, and a few days later, we take it to the caverns."

"The caverns? What are the caverns?"

"It's where the traveling equipment and the art storage is."

"Who is 'we'?"

Adam leaned forward and held me tight. "I was hoping me and you. The piece goes into safe storage for a while. And, possibly . . . you and I go forward in time?"

"Forward in time? Back to your home?"

"Yes." He rushed on. "The way it works is one person in, one out. But since Brandon's not returning, you could go in his place."

Suddenly the sounds of the fans and music were just a buzz in my ears.

I felt unsteady. I realized my breathing was too shallow.

"You want me to go with you? Into the future?"

"Yes."

In the main room the record was over. I pulled out my phone. My music playlist shuffled to a cover of "Wichita Lineman" by Smokey Robinson and the Miracles. I reached out and took Adam's hand and pulled him to me. He started to speak, but I shook my head. "Just dance with me." He pulled me tighter. We slow danced through the warehouse.

We slow danced through Springsteen's "Thunder Road" and Patti Smith's "Dancing Barefoot" and "Swamp Thing" by the Chameleons. We slow danced until we reached the small, old iron bed in his room. He laid down and I was next to him, my head on his chest, listening to his heart.

"I can't answer you now. I don't know what to say. This is too big. This is—"

"It's too much. I know. We have two weeks. If you'll help exchange the hcaddress next weekend, when you get back, we go. And if you don't want to go, we say goodbye."

"I would have to leave my family, my friends, my aunties." Inside I felt the way I had when Tex died. How could I go? The world was ending. It was going to be terrible. My little brother was going to suffer and die and my parents were going to have their hearts broken. How could I not stay? How could I leave them? Jess and Loren were my ride or dies. You didn't ditch people like that. They were hard to come by.

He nodded into the back of my neck. He kissed the nape of my neck.

I pulled away. "Stop," I said. "That's not fair."

He pulled me back towards him and kissed my lips. "I know."

I buried my head in his neck. I cried silently. He rubbed my back, his movements only comforting now. If I had no one, the decision would have been easy.

"I want to go home."

He stood up. He held his hand out and I took it and stood up. We held hands. Adam let Princess out and she ran to the car. We got in the car and she jumped in the front seat, turning and licking the tears from my face. I laughed. I couldn't help it. Princess didn't want me to be sad. It's hard to be sad when a dog is comforting you.

We pulled into the driveway just ahead of my mom and Levi. Levi jumped out and ran to the car to see Princess. She licked him like crazy too.

Mom said Dad had to go meet with the clients he'd been helping out and would be gone most of the weekend. "He'll be back for our meeting over the treatment plan Monday," she told me quietly as we met. My mom invited Adam and Princess into the house. We went directly outside with Levi and Princess. Princess raced around the boundaries of the yard and then chased the tennis balls Levi had found in the house for her. How could Levi be dying? How could this happy child be fated to suffer so much in his short life?

Adam stayed for dinner and the starlight walk through the Atatiana Jefferson park. The satellites and the two space stations had left the sky as it had always been. When a star falls, what does it leave behind? Mom was quiet. I let Adam and Levi hold up the conversations. I was barely aware of what was said. Princess and I let our actions communicate for us. She was happy, thrilled to be included, thrilled to be with people. I was content, but sad. That is how life is though. Without sorrow, happiness is unappreciated. To love is to build the foundation for heartbreak. To avoid the latter, you would have to give up the former. And what is a family or a world without love?

Retribution

On my day off, we had an afternoon appointment with the team putting together the treatment plan for Levi. That morning, Brandon called and asked if I was in or out. I said I was and he picked me up and we went back to the workshop to go over the plans. He wasn't exactly chatty. More wary about what he said than Adam was with me. Whereas Adam avoided subjects that might make me ask questions, Brandon just said, "I can't answer that. Purely need to know." He wasn't unkind, and he smiled. Occasionally, he reached up and scratched at his short, shorn hair. He looked like a young Vin Diesel.

"How many of you are there?"

"I can't say. Did Adam tell you I do a shortwave radio broadcast?" Adam wrote down some numbers. I was pretty sure Mom had a radio stored away that I could use to find it. "It's random days. Seven in the evening, Texas time."

"Adam asked me to go with him, into the future. He said you're staying. How many others are?"

"I don't know. We're in cells. Interconnected only to the extent we need to be to help each other. But no one else in our cell is staying. There is one free spot."

Take it or leave it, I thought.

"Does it matter who goes? How old? That kind of thing?"

Brandon smiled. "No. It could even be a dog."

The weekend Brandon and Adam were going to switch the ladders, I was going to go out of town. Unbeknownst to her, Christy would soon be suffering so badly from tonsillitis she would need her tonsils removed. And she was going to ask me to step in for her to go to Philadelphia and pick up a delivery of glass art by Robert Willson to be sold in the gift shop. I wished I could tell her to stock up on ice cream, though not sure how I would have managed that without sounding suspicious.

I felt like a character in a play by Shakespeare, a pawn, but a pawn who was being looked after. Somewhere some committee knew how to make sure I had an alibi and so, suddenly, I was going to Philadelphia to inventory, pack, and ship glass art that ranged in value from $500 to $10,000 an object. This meant I would be nowhere in the vicinity when the switch of the ladders happened. While there, I would help with the liberation of another piece.

Brandon and I didn't have much to talk about after that. He would get the fake IDs and the fake Sam Houston hunting jacket for me just before I left. He took a picture of me in a blond wig with some makeup to use on the student ID he was going to make. Afterwards, he dropped me off at the house and then I waited for one of my parents to come get me for the visit with the oncology team.

When we went to the hospital, Levi stayed in the children's waiting room and met with an art therapy counselor while we met with the pediatric oncologist. Treatment would start in three weeks. The counselor suggested we go ahead and tell Levi soon, perhaps even that evening. They also suggested we shave Levi's head in order to avoid the stress of losing his hair in the future. They said it would help him feel a little empowered, assert control over the uncontrollable. That was what broke me. Imagining shaving my baby brother's hair, which had never been more than trimmed. Listening to the doctor describe the effects of the treatment, the things we would need to be aware of, the necessity of not interrupting treatment, not letting him be exposed to germs, bacteria, sickness. Even though the seeds of this aggressive cancer were in Levi, he wasn't, yet, experiencing symptoms other than headaches. The cure would be the first serious discomfort. The nurse gave us a list of the foods and drugs we should stockpile for the inevitable nausea and the pain. It would all be painful. But he would need to eat, even though he might not feel like it. Mom and I weren't stingy with our tears, with Levi elsewhere. But Dad was all stoic, as if all would be well, as if it was simply a matter of getting through. He held Mom and reached out and touched my back, a steady, strong hand, a man who had only treated me with kindness and love. We were lucky he and Mom had found each other.

The doctor told my parents that they could donate some of their bone marrow in order to formulate a better treatment for Levi, but they would have to go to Kansas City to do it. It was a serious procedure. Appointments had already been made for two weeks from now. My parents knew about this, but it was news to me. They wanted Levi to stay and go to school. Have another normal week, before the focus on survival started. I said, "Yes, whatever you need. But can we wait to cut his hair? Please?" I didn't really mean "whatever you need." I guess what I meant was, "whatever won't hurt Levi."

We had planned to go home and cook outside. We decided we would tell him on our evening walk. Levi played in the yard while Dad cooked. Mom disappeared into her office. I realized that since all this had started, I hadn't heard the fax machine once, had almost forgotten that she had been prepping for the end of the world too. The sort of end Adam had warned me about; an inevitable apocalypse that would interrupt and change everything. I stood in the hallway and waited for her to come out. She was startled when she opened the door.

"What are you working on?" I asked.

She looked at me. Then, she lied. I could see it in her tells. The way she turned away before she spoke. "Sending all my files to Angel, so she can take over my caseload. I'm taking a leave of absence."

She turned back around. We stared at each other. Then I heard the fax machine make the jarring noise it used to always make, like screaming telephone lines, or missives from space. Or hell. She went back into the office and shut the door behind her. I heard the lock click into place.

That night our walk was somber. Even Levi was less boisterous than usual, perhaps sensing trouble, probably aware that all the doctor's visits were not more of the usual. We made it to the top of the hill behind our house, crossed the stream, now seemingly dead. It was muck, more dry than wet, stinking of rot and sour. We all watched the stars from atop the blankets we had brought. The light from the stars takes years to get to earth. When you look at it, you see it as it was years earlier. Even the light from the sun is over eight minutes old by the time it gets here. When we look into the skies, we are always looking at the past.

My parents told Levi that the doctors knew why he was having the headaches and soon they would need to start treating him for them. They told him he had a rare brain cancer, that he hadn't done anything to cause it, that it was no one's fault. But it was treatable and they would start working on it soon. I wondered what Levi was thinking as he looked at the stars. Suddenly, he turned and looked at me, as if he was checking to see what I thought. I smiled, in spite of how I felt on the inside. He smiled back. He reached a hand out to take mine, slipping into my arms, wanting/needing to be held. I wanted that, too.

He turned back to Mom and Dad. "Will it hurt?" his voice was soft.

They told him it might, but that they would do all they could to keep him from hurting. That the doctors didn't want him to be in pain when he didn't have to be.

"Will I die?"

I wanted to scream "No!" and I sucked in a breath in spite of myself.

"Sweetheart, the doctors have come up with a really good plan. We'll be with you through all of it."

Levi looked tired and sad.

"We can make a list of questions for the doctor and give him a call. He said we could call tonight, if we need to," Mom said.

Levi shook his head. "Naw. I'm tired. I want to go home."

Dad picked Levi up and put him on his shoulders. Levi watched the sky.

"Look," he shouted, when we were almost home. We all looked up to see him pointing towards a star streaking through the sky. We all made the same wish with all our hearts.

One
Piece
at a Time

When I went back to work the next day, Christy said her throat was hurting. I suggested she go get some sorbet in the museum restaurant. She did. When she got back she asked if it was okay if she left. She was trying to get an appointment with her doctor. She was pretty sure she had a fever. "Of course," I said.

My anxiety was through the roof. So, I stayed busy. Christy had been planning to leave on Thursday morning for the museum in Philadelphia. By that evening, she had an emergency tonsillectomy scheduled for the next morning, Wednesday. No trip. After e-mailing the museum administrators and getting their approval, she e-mailed to see if I would step in for her. I called my parents and they thought it was a good idea. I had never been to that museum before or even to that city in the Northeast. I didn't tell them my bags were pretty much already packed.

On Thursday afternoon, I checked into the Akwaaba Philadelphia's Bed and Breakfast Blue Note room. It was luxurious, with a king-size bed and indigo décor. I walked around and found an authentic cheesesteak place. Meh. I walked more and then went back to the hotel and took a hot bath. Finally, I called Adam and asked him to talk me down, my anxiety pulsing.

"Want me to read you something?"

I felt kind of silly, but my anxiety meds were helpless against whatever crime I was going to be committing over the next few days, and being away while my brother was getting ready to start treatment. "Yes, please."

I heard Adam walk around the cavernous warehouse and could tell by his footsteps and the other ambient noise that he had sat on his old iron bed.

"How about *The Devil in Silver*?"

It was a book I had loaned him, a book my mother and I loved. One with a large portrait of a bison on the front. "I never say 'no' to reading LaValle," I replied.

I was asleep before the second chapter ended. I woke up briefly when my phone made a hang-up beep. I rolled over and plugged it in to charge and went back to sleep.

In two days, I would start my mission. The weekend was museum gift shop work. I would inventory and pack Willson's glass pieces for delivery to the museum in Texas. Currently, they were in a small gallery. I was paying for the extra days myself—well, Brandon was—in service of the real mission, with the justification that I had never been out here. And Christy had reserved those days off and the hotel anyway.

In my non-working hours I could both reconnoiter and sightsee. Produce a presence on social media for my alibi.

On Saturday morning I wandered the museum. The Native American exhibit wasn't bad, but it was all smoke and mirrors, wasn't it? I felt funny. Hadn't I always loved museums? Didn't I, too, enjoy looking at all the pretty things? Once more I was grateful not to work in a place that had ceremonial objects or bones or funerary items, which should have remained with tribes in the first place.

I turned out of the Native American gallery and into the African exhibit. I decided to check out the gift shop, which was just past the African gallery. In that gallery, too, were things that had been taken from tribes in massacres and put on display. I stopped in front of a sign before exiting the gallery.

A small sign near the exit acknowledged that much of the exhibit was the product of the looting and burning of a African village. "We're working with the current government to collaborate on future exhibits," the sign finished.

There it was. That was the most honest thing I had seen so far. On the National Mall, the war department was right next to the Smithsonian.

I felt eyes on me. I turned and saw a Black security guard watching, with a name tag that said "Octavia." I wondered if her mother also loved Butler, or if she had renamed herself? I smiled at her, but the woman's face went unchanged. Suddenly, I felt embarrassed, remembering the sign I had just read. I couldn't know what it was like for her, to walk by this sign every day; to be charged with protecting the trophies of colonization. Or maybe she didn't think about it at all. I knew myself that a museum job was a lot nicer than some other places you could work.

Here, though, I hoped that someone was coming soon to take the bloodstained cradle. A descendant coming to reclaim what belonged to their ancestral village. I wondered if someone would liberate these objects, place them in a place of honor to remind the future people of crimes past, man's inhumanity to man, the price of racial and religious exploitation and greed?

Suddenly, I was flustered, emotional. I went on to the gift shop and dropped my fake student ID card where it would be found, so I could return on Monday for the switch of the headdress boxes. I tried not to worry. I knew it would be successful. This was a task, a box to check off. The big job was back in Fort Worth. I would be successful here, because *already the headdress is buried a hundred years in the future with the warrior it belonged to,* Brandon's voice echoed in my head. Sometimes the spiral of time has already slipped into a well-worn rut. Some things can't be changed. But Strummer was right: other futures are unwritten.

On Monday the museum was closed. I opened my carry-on luggage with the white shipping box inside. I opened the box. The fake smelled old. It was good. There was old-style Cherokee beadwork, loose in the places you would expect from a piece that had been worn in battle. There was even the faint scent of old, dry blood. I wondered whose. I put everything back. I took my medication. Though anxiety was the most normal response ever to this mission.

It was the day that the deinstallation and reinstallation of the Native American gallery would begin. I didn't have an appointment. Brandon had a provided me with a tight schedule. Everything hinged on a predestined order of events.

My fake identity included a wig that looked like poorly bleached-blonde hair with dark roots. I wore huge sunglasses and well-placed beauty marks. I went to the delivery area, pressed the button for the intercom, and asked for the curator. Then I waited.

When they called back to me I said, "I have some old Cherokee clothes."

The woman sighed. I could tell she was used to sending people away with these kinds of stories. "One of them was given by my ancestor to Sam Houston, and then Sam Houston returned it to his son. Chief Bowles's son. My grandma sent it to me from Mexico."

"I'll be right down." She was hooked now.

When she met me, she would find the provenance impeccable. Down to the fake ancestry loaded to an ancestry website years earlier.

Nervously, I reached into my pocket for the phone that wasn't there while I waited. I had dropped it off in temporary storage over a deli near my bed-and-breakfast. Someone I might never meet—another time traveler or designee—would pick up my phone and take it with them to visit Poe's various haunts and post about them from my social media. (I did resent not getting to see those places myself.) Then they would return my phone and I would pick it up on my way to the airport. Cue the *Mission Impossible* soundtrack.

I was both a distraction and a mule. I occupied the curator with small talk. Back in the exhibit space someone was packing away the headdress and switching it into a box that was headed for the gift shop, while an empty box went to storage.

"So, how much do you think y'all would pay for this?"

"Oh, I'm sorry. Most of our objects are donations or from the various historical institutions that are federally run."

"And the war department?" I couldn't help it.

She didn't flinch. "Let me go get one of my colleagues to weigh in." The curator disappeared.

I looked around for a clock. Remembered the old windup watch I had worn for this very reason. Four minutes. In four minutes I needed to act offended and leave.

The room seemed more storage than office. I stood up and wandered over to a shelf with the label "Found in collection." Interesting . . .

I saw a note typed on an old label on one small rectangular box buried among other items. "Chickasaw ceremonial object." I hoped I had time. I checked my watch. I did. Two minutes. I pulled the box out. The paper around the object was falling apart. It had writing in pencil that was hard to decipher. It seemed to read, "Chickasaw delegate died in hospital on visit to D.C. 18—. This was in his luggage. Dr.—."

Wow. That didn't belong here. I didn't know where it belonged, but not here. Maybe in the earth with the dead delegate, or at a ceremonial grounds. I pulled out the paper but didn't open it. I felt something through protective natural cotton that held it. I didn't want to touch it. I shoved it into my blazer pocket and sat down. I took a long deep breath. The door opened.

"We might be able to find a donor who will purchase it. If you wouldn't mind leaving it."

It was time to act offended, take the box, and go.

"Well, I can't do that. I guess I wasted my time. And money," I said sourly.

"I'll have a guard escort you, Miss Bowles." I stood to go. "Please keep us in mind. It would be a shame for that to go into a private collection."

"What's more private than the federal government?" I drawled. "Once y'all have things you don't let go." I saw her tap her pen on the desk without a sound. She smiled a smile she didn't mean. That was fair.

I was surprised to see Octavia once more outside, in her guard uniform. We took the elevator down to the gift shop. Without speaking she unlocked the door and went to the register to get the student ID I had dropped on Saturday. Once behind the register, she spoke. "Hand me your luggage. I need to check it before you leave."

I handed her the suitcase, felt my heavy pocket. I had gone off script. It felt good.

Octavia disappeared below the register. I heard her unzip my suitcase and then open the box. I only knew what she was doing because of what Brandon had told me.

"All good," she announced, standing up. She rolled the suitcase around the counter to me. I had expected it to be heavier. It was.

Octavia escorted me out the nearest exit. At the door, she leaned out and whispered.

"Tell Brandon 'Halito.' Have a safe trip home."

"Wado," I said. "Or Yakoke. Chi pisa la chike." It was like saying "thank you" and "until we meet again," but in Choctaw. I turned away, overwhelmed with all I had to think about.

Black Is
the Color
of My True
Love's Hair

When I got back home, I didn't hang out with Adam that week, though we talked on the phone. I mostly stayed close to our house, wanting to be around for my parents or Levi. When I could, I visited Jess in the hospital and read stories to them. Loren was no longer allowed to come visit. Jess's parents had started to have concerns about the closeness of their friendship. My heart hurt for the two of them. Jess's parents had refused to give back their cell phone.

"They told me they'd rather have a dead child than an unrepentant sinner." Jess's voice was grave, sad.

I gave Jess my phone after they told me and left the room so they could call Loren. Jess was over eighteen, but for now their parents were still in control. Jess had needed to leave for college even more than I had previously wanted to. I couldn't even remember now why I wanted to so badly.

When I returned, Jess was laughing, talking to Loren. They told Loren goodbye. This time, their "I love you too" was clearly something different. We had always told each other "I love you." But this was not the way Jess or Loren would have said it to me. I tried not to wonder when I would hear those words in that way.

"Has Loren told you . . ."

"About your time traveling art thief?"

I laughed. "I guess you're all caught up then."

"I am. And maybe it's the head injury and the great meds, but I know it's going to be okay."

I didn't press. Jess had been through enough without worrying about the end of the world and the big blip today. They handed me back the phone. "It's going to be okay," they repeated. I was sorry I couldn't say the same words to them in a reassuring way. Why couldn't I comfort them? Because I didn't really know if things would be okay. What did that even mean? As many have said before me, *no one gets out of here alive*. Living was just postponing the inevitable. If you were lucky, life was more love and living than pain and suffering. How many of us were lucky? How many of us never appreciated it until our luck ended?

That next weekend my parents were going to Kansas City to do the bone marrow donations for Levi. We talked about the specifics of their trip, where they were staying, how I would need to be around for Levi all weekend. The words to explain the impossible stuck in my throat.

Levi was tired, so Mom and Dad skipped our after-dinner walk. I texted Adam to meet me in the park. I sat by myself and looked at the stars. I pulled out the app and checked to see what constellations were there. In the moon, I saw a rabbit. Tsisdu. The Cherokee trickster. I thought about Adam asking me to go with him into the future and then I thought of Levi, Loren, Jess, Mom, Dad, Aunt Geneva. I couldn't leave them to face the ninety days of chaos on their own. I didn't know how much help I could be. I didn't know if I could even *be* with all of them, or any of them. I didn't think I had any useful skills to bring to an apocalypse. But I couldn't give up what time I had left.

Princess came running through the tall grasses ahead of Adam and greeted me with the joy of a long-missing friend. I told Adam everything on my mind and heart. He put a blanket on the ground. I fell into his arms and lay on his chest and I wept. He held me. I made him tell me about the future. What would happen to a boy like Levi in the future? Would he be safe in his own home? Would he be able to walk places without being harassed or killed? Was there a legal system that would never allow the killing of brown children in the name of law and order by those with the right skin tone? Had people stopped calling each other ugly, racist names, even in their heads? Was the history of brown people no longer taught in relation to their conquerors, enslavers, and colonizers? Were people like Jess allowed to just be? Did all humans have rights? What about water and air? Were they cared for as the valuable entities they were? Not to mention animals? How could we say we were the caregivers of the earth's creatures while they vanished from the planet?

"Yes," he said, over and over.

"Is there really a cure for Levi in the future? One that won't hurt?"

"Yes," he whispered.

"Take Levi," I cried. "Please, take Levi."

Adam kissed my face. He was crying now too.

"I will," he promised.

And then we made the plan that once my parents were in Kansas City, he and Levi and the *Ladder* would disappear.

You Always Hurt the One You Love

The night Adam was set to leave town, I helped Levi pack a small backpack of his favorite things. He knew when Mom and Dad got back they would be going with him to another hospital out of state for a series of treatments. After packing snacks and toys, we stayed up all night watching movies. I cried during *Puss in Boots: The Last Wish*. I had tried to plan a fun evening. One he would always remember, one without pain, one where nothing sad happened. I think I was successful for him.

I sat on the floor in front of the projector screen and held him, tried to memorize the way he breathed, the way he said, "I love you, Stevie," the way he held my hand, holding on, how sweet and without malice or hatred our Levi was. I suddenly wished that instead of sending him away, hurting Mom and Dad, frightening him, letting him feel alone, I could instead die in his place. How many other humans had prayed for this? For a moment I felt in touch with the world's pain.

"Is this your favorite movie?" Levi asked.

I shook my head.

"What is?" Levi turned to ask me these questions, but then turned back to watch the screen.

"I don't know," I replied. Then hugged him. "Anything I can watch with you, I guess."

Levi laughed. "I love you too, Stevie. You'll always live in my heart." He squeezed the hands I had wrapped around him.

I sat there watching the cartoon and weeping silently. I was so careful not to let him know I was crying. I wished I drank. I wished there was something in the house that would take away the bone-deep pain I had. If I had been alone, I would have screamed the way an animal who has lost its baby cries.

When Adam called to say he was parked on the street near the park gate, I suggested he walk over and bring Princess. I turned off all of our security cameras. Adam had already planned to leave Princess with me when he left. Loren said she'd take her if my parents had a problem with it. I figured they'd be too distracted once Levi was gone to care. I grabbed my bag in which I had tucked Levi's smaller backpack of personal items. Adam knocked on the door and my brother threw it open, greeting Princess first.

"When we get to the park, can we let her run?" he asked with so much hope, what was left of my heart broke. How would it ever heal? How would I love anyone else? To love was to be insane, to ignore the reality that loving eventually means losing, to open your front door and say, "Yes, please come in grief and live with me, so you can sucker punch me after years of emotional invest-ment." It was begging the vampire to come live with you and be your love. I never wanted to have this pain in my life again. If the raw wound of these loves scabbed over, I would pick at them and remind myself that it wasn't worth it.

As we walked, Levi held the flashlight to make sure I was safe and grabbed my hand when I stumbled and I knew that if love showed up at the door again, I would let it in.

I would always let it in.

I would open the door and patiently wait and it would be the center of my world.

Every single time.

Waltz Across Texas

We sat on the highest hilltop on the prairie. It was the place where we had first sat together with my family and watched the stars. It was the place where I had asked him to take Levi instead of me. It strangely seemed so long ago.

I had thought so long about this moment, when I would have to both say goodbye forever and explain to Levi why he was going with a veritable stranger. It seemed so wrong to trick my baby brother. Even to save his life. But how could I tell him the truth? I had brought a powwow blanket and covered the picnic table near the benches. Adam lifted Princess up and she and Levi curled up together and watched the stars. I could see he was getting sleepy. Princess snored softly.

Adam sat next to me. I leaned against him. He was tall enough that my head was on his shoulder. He leaned his head down against mine. With his right hand, he reached over and touched my damp cheeks.

"I can't do this," I whispered.

"It's okay."

"Maybe you and I could talk to my mom? Maybe you could explain the way you have to me?"

"I can't do that."

"Why not?"

"Let's just say there are implied rules and specific directives. For whatever reason the powers that be have, being the one to initiate telling your mom was something I was told I could not do."

"But I could?"

"I'm sorry. I couldn't be part of it. I'm sorry."

"WTF?" I hissed.

"I honestly don't know why I can't tell your mom. Of course, I wasn't supposed to tell you, either. But I guess they didn't see that coming . . ."

"You have to leave tonight?"

"Yes, in order to get to the art storage and evacuate in my window, I have to go tonight."

"Could you tell me the location?"

"No."

"Send me a pin?"

Adam didn't answer. He turned his body towards mine and pulled me against him and kissed me. It was long and tender and made me cry more. When he pulled away, I involuntarily laughed. He looked at me quizzically.

I sniffled. Wiped my wet face and eyes.

"Well, one, if we're cousins that kiss was criminal, and two, it's not even raining."

He laughed, but this time I leaned towards him and kissed him.

For the last time.

I didn't say, "I'm going to miss you." He knew. More than two hundred years in the future, he would be reading the letters I would soon start writing. I would start writing as soon as I could hold a pen and not cry. That wouldn't be tonight, though.

We looked up and saw a falling star.

"Did you plan that?" I whispered.

He laughed. "I wish."

We were quiet a while. I noticed Levi was sleepily watching us.

"I can't send him with you."

"I know."

"You do?"

Adam shrugged.

"This was nice, though."

Adam nodded. Then my phone rang. We both jumped. I pulled it out of my backpack. Levi had been startled enough to wake back up. Princess was on alert now too. It was the ringtone I had assigned to Mom.

"Mom?"

"Let me talk to Adam."

I didn't even question her. My life had become so not what it used to be, I felt like every day was "Okay, this is new, I guess this is one of the rules of the game called life now." I handed him the phone.

He was silent a long time. Nodding, as if she could see. Then, finally, he said, "Sounds good. He's right here. I'm putting you on speaker." Adam stood and walked close to Levi, who was now sitting up on the picnic bench, Princess licking the perspiration from his face. I followed him.

"Mom?"

"Hey, sweetie."

"Where are you?"

"Kansas City. Dad's asleep, but we had a meeting with the doctor a while ago. There is someplace you can go where they can treat you. New procedures. Better. But you have to go tonight. Adam is going to take you." Levi looked at Adam.

"Will you and Dad be there?"

"Dad and I will meet you. Stevie has to stay at home a little longer. Maybe soon."

My heart was pounding. Levi looked as confused as I felt.

"Well, okay," Levi said. "I miss you."

I heard Mom's side go silent. Like her phone was muted. When she came back on, she sounded strained. More so than the whole phone call so far. "I miss you too, baby. But we want you to get better as quickly as possible. No more of those headaches. I love you, Levi. Give the phone to your sister, baby."

"Love you too, Mommy."

I took the phone, not knowing what to say. Not knowing anything anymore.

"Hey, sweetie. Take me off speaker." I did.

"What's going on, Mom?"

"I'm sorry about this. I can't tell you much yet, but we'll talk. Soon."

I turned away from Levi and walked away, talking as quietly as possible.

"I don't understand."

"I know, baby. I know. There is so much I wish I could say to you. And your dad. I'm sorry. Now tell Adam to get that truck and my other baby on the road. Time-traveling trains run on time, Sissy."

Then she hung up. I tried to call her back, but it went to voice mail. I texted Adam, since I couldn't talk with Levi there.

"WTF. Did you tell my mom?!?" I typed.

"Not me. Was told not to."

I thought of the faxes and felt stupid. All this time, Mom had known. How had I not put this together? Was Adam faxing from the future? Someone else? Levi? I almost shook with all I could not say.

"Who?" I texted.

"Not me," he typed again.

"That's not what I'm asking." I was trying to stay calm; not combust in front of Levi.

I sent similar messages to my mom, but her phone was on silent. And eventually I realized I didn't want to do this, have my last few minutes with Levi distracted by a puzzle that had just made the thing I hoped for, a cure for him, possible. I needed to focus on that. And breathe.

I put on a happy face for my brother.

"Well, Levi, looks like you and Adam get to go on a road trip!"

Levi began to ask Adam questions about where they were going as we walked to the semi parked at the end of the cul-de-sac. I listened, trying to remember everything he said, forgetting that we were walking to the truck, that Levi was leaving, jumping hundreds of years away. Once we could see the truck from the park, it hit. Would he even remember me years from now? I thought of people I had met in kindergarten. How they were a blur if I'd stopped seeing them. Aunties and grandparents who had passed—they were more ideas than people. Scents and sounds, with memories easily colored by what other people said. Would I be a ghost to Levi?

When we reached the truck, we all climbed in.

"I'll drive you and Princess home," Adam said. There was so much we weren't saying with Levi there between us. I nodded. I couldn't talk. My heart and mouth were not to be trusted.

Levi climbed into the bunk in the back and I turned and tucked him in.

"See you soon, sweet boy."

"But I want you to come too," he said sleepily. "And Princess."

"When you're all better," I replied.

"Princess is going to keep Stevie company. We can't leave her all alone."

My throat caught. I had read that phrase before. I had never lived it quite like this.

Levi frowned and lay back down. It was late. Much later than he ever stayed up. He was asleep before we reached the house.

We didn't talk in the semi anyway. Adam parked the truck in front and came around to help me climb down. I leaned over and nudged Levi awake. "I love you, baby."

Levi sat up sleepily and hugged me. "I love you, Sissy." He gave me a sweet kiss. He was back asleep nearly as soon as he lay back down.

I held my tears until Adam had walked me to the door. We let Princess in the house.

"Did you know?" I asked as I unlocked the door.

Adam looked away.

"You can't tell me? Won't tell me? How did my mom know?" I demanded.

Adam still didn't speak.

"So that's another directive? You can't tell me that all along my own mother has known about you? That when we thought she was being unnecessarily paranoid it was, actually, necessarily paranoid?"

Adam looked up at the stars. "I can't talk about it. You asked me not to lie to you." He looked back down at me, slipped his arms around me. "I don't want this to be the last thing we say to each other, Stevie. All I can say is you can't know more than you already know. I know you. It will be too much. It will screw things up in a huge way."

"It's already too much," I whispered.

"I have to go."

"Everything is already too much."

"I love you," he said. I wished he hadn't. I was grateful he had.

"I know," I answered, kind of laughing. I was supposed to be the one leaving at the end of the summer. Maybe that was why I hadn't let myself admit I felt anything when we met. Off to college and the rest of my life. But now what? Now that the doomsday clock was the one keeping time in my world, in my house, where would my life begin? Or was it beginning to end? Neither one of us said anything. He knew. He had always known.

"I'll miss you."

"I love you too." I sighed.

Adam laughed and reached out and hugged me one more time, then turned and went back to the street while I went into the house. I locked the door behind me and watched him drive away with my little brother. I reminded myself that Levi would be in a better place.

But, it still hurt.

I'm
Sorry

There were complications with the bone marrow harvesting my dad went through, so my parents were going to be gone several extra days. In the meantime, the school called each day to see about Levi. I avoided their calls. Loren had quit her job there after the accident, so I no longer had her to run interference for me. I was nervous as time ticked ever nearer to when Adam and Levi were supposed to leave the caverns. Adam wouldn't tell me where the caverns were, but had implied it would take three or four days to get there in the eighteen-wheeler he was driving. He had bought a burner cell and Levi talked to me and Mom and Dad every night. I didn't think Dad suspected anything. Mom would tell me what was going on there in Kansas City, but nothing else. I went to work and home and to the hospital where Jess and Loren were, but that was it.

The news was not great in the world, neither globally or locally. Fires had destroyed a large swath of land on the southwest of our city, taking out million-dollar homes, businesses, and small homes overnight. Immediately, the residents with no place to go were offered low-interest-rate loans to go off-world. According to the news, some of the poor had no homeowner's insurance and were being offered a pittance of their land value by real estate developers. It was like the tiny percentage Native people had been paid for their stolen improvements, goods, livestock, and land over two hundred years earlier, while the government charged them for their food and the coffins they needed because of the forced removal. In the meantime, states that had seized Native people's property had auctioned it off to white settlers for pennies on the dollar. Corporations now were buying up anything that seemed valuable, either outright for very little, or through quiet titles, stealing everything from those who had the least to steal.

Some saw the fire as a blessing, like winning the lottery. For others it was one more battle added to their already difficult lives. Not to mention the significant loss of life.

One evening, Dad called me directly from his cell.

"Hey kid, how are things?"

I was nervous. Attuned to his voice and the question.

"Okay," I said. "Did you see the fires?"

"I'll bet the air quality is terrible. Hey, I called because I keep getting phone calls and e-mails from the school. They say Levi isn't there. Why not?"

"Uh, he's not been feeling great. Headaches, you know."

"I just talked to him. He said he felt great. Let me talk to him again."

I froze. "Um, he's asleep."

"Stevie, I just got off the phone with him. Put him back on."

"Well, he's kind of busy."

Dad was silent.

I was quiet.

"Stevie, where is Levi?"

"He's with Adam."

"What? Where? Where is my son?"

"Talk to Mom."

"Stevie." The anxiety was building in Dad's voice, though I could tell he was trying to stay calm. "The school has called the police. They're on their way to the house for a wellness check. The cops are going to want to see Levi. I told them I didn't think it was necessary, but they didn't seem willing to listen."

I started to cry. "He's not here."

"Stevie, where is he? I've talked to him every night. Where is he calling from?"

"I told you, he's with Adam."

"Adam? Adam who lied to us about who his parents are? You let him go somewhere with this guy? How long has he been gone?"

At that moment, the doorbell rang.

"I have to go," I said.

"No! Stevie! Don't hang up. Let me stay on the line while they're there. I need to—"

I hung up the phone. On the porch were two cops. I put Princess in the backyard. I turned my phone off and threw it into one of the many Faraday boxes stashed around the house. It was one of the smarter things I've ever done. Then I answered the door.

Side B

Summer's End

Anyone Who Knows What Love Is (Will Understand)

E-mail from Stevie #3

TO: Angel Wilson (LawAngel@ICWA.law)
FROM: Stevie (stevie@hmail.com)

Dear Auntie,

By now, you and my parents know that Adam was not
who he said he was. He obtained a work visa and a job
by showing up in Costa Rica at a hippie commune a few
months before the curator visited. I met him at the museum;
he had come from two hundred years in the future to steal a
piece of art. We became friends. In exchange for
my help, he took my little brother out of this terrible world,
along with the art he had come to save.

Museums can be wonderful places and museum jobs
can be dream jobs. In spite of predatory artists and grave
robbing, neither of which is okay, but would probably exist
without museums. The human desire to see beauty and
truth and connect with art and artists—a space for the
creations of artists to speak. They provide an otherworldly
conversation space. By interacting with creation, I
understand creation.

Like holy spaces, museums can beautiful and clean, the objects they are decorated with imbued with meaning, chosen, the best of the world. If you have ever been to a certain theme park you know what a spell can be cast by attention to the little details. Museums are like that. The people around you believe in the power of art. They come to work in a place with high ceilings and a manicured lawn every day, surrounded by lovely people and artfully made things. Classical music is piped in. It's relaxing and there is a sense of calm no matter what else is going on outside the doors. It's my happy place. Museums are the chapels of the future.

Stevie

Solo

The ankle monitor buzzed, waking me. The world was dark. After I had been released, some privatized power grids in other parts of the state had failed. That's what happens when a heat wave crashes into an unseasonable cold front, multiple wildfires spread into cities, straight-line winds, and the system is hacked by a thousand computers looking to accelerate the end times. Not to mention the scattered tornadoes.

See, it was never going to be a single apocalyptic event. But whisper after whisper. Like a bad faith game of telephone. The world was beginning to fall apart. It happened faster than you might think. Take away people's access to entertainment, food, water, information, and the world will spin out of control quickly.

Princess looked at me. Her tongue lolled, a constant smile I could count on, her floppy ears belying the sharp teeth that shone in the moonlight and strong muscles that rippled under her smooth coat. It was quiet; the quiet of a world without electricity. Except for the stupid ankle monitor that would hold a charge for at least another week.

Early that morning I had been awakened by a sleet storm that brought down power line after power line, lighting up the night like mini lightning strikes until the local grid was shut down. Fires were an ever-present threat before due to drought. But now? Countless blazes had started before the electric company flipped the switches off to give them time to assess the damage. There were over 100,000 homes without electricity before my phone stopped connecting. The number was escalating, not decreasing last I read.

My ankle vibrated again. I fished out the flashlight in the old nightstand next to my bed. A pang of loneliness hit me. Adam and Levi gone to the future. Dad angry with me, heartbroken. Mom knowing more than she let on. Throwing me under the bookmobile. WTH? Maybe Dad wouldn't come back because he was looking for Levi; wouldn't give up until he found them, so maybe wouldn't come back at all, if Adam's memories—no, stories—about the future were accurate. My parents were supposed to come home from Kansas City sore, but heartened. Ready to shave Levi's head before he started treatment. Dad had shaved his already so they would match.

He had called asking to speak to the son he loved more than anything, yeah? I mean, when you're a parent, you have one job. All hell broke loose when the wellness check was made, and when I couldn't produce Levi, investigators showed up. The neighbor's camera footage showed me coming home with him and a semi out front that night. Eventually, they checked Adam's studio and found him and Brandon gone. There were questions, suspicions. Ankle monitor time for me.

That morning, the swell of guilt I felt waking in the dark after separating Dad from his son almost took me to my knees, even while the power going out meant I could check off one more accurate "prediction" of Adam's and his fellow travelers'.

I looked in the drawer with the flashlight hoping the paperwork about the ankle monitor was in there, too. If Mom had been home, she would have known exactly where it was. I felt the presence of her absence in all the things she used to take care of that I never before noticed.

But the paperwork wasn't there. I couldn't remember what I had done with it. Maybe it was in the kitchen or office.

Princess hopped off the bed, happy to get up and eat and potty early. In the kitchen, I let her out the back door. She hesitated a moment, the backyard an unfamiliar land—a sheet of melting hail. There were no power lines over the cold, white backyard, that centuries-old technology that should have given way to buried cables to avoid life-threatening electrical snakes arcing through the air, insisting on being grounded, killing for a way to burn.

I watched her, not needing the flashlight, the moon and ice a frigid light table, silhouetting my dog. When did I start thinking of her as my dog, not Adam's—and never really Brandon's? I realized I didn't even know if that story was true. I had never thought to ask. And now, I could ask in a letter to Adam, but would never get an answer.

When Princess came back in, I fed her and started making coffee for myself. Grandma's old stove was gas, so I could still cook things, boil, as long as there was still food that wasn't rotten and running water. The sun would be up before long and the ice would melt as quickly as it had come. The water made a funny noise in the pipes, something I might not have even noticed if the electricity had been on, humming, buzzing, an unnoticed, ever-present decibel. I ran some water into a glass and hit it with the flashlight's beam, smelling the algae and earth before I saw it. Time to retrieve a water jug from the garage. I wondered if I should go ahead and empty the fridge.

I had just put the water on to boil when Princess startled me by dashing to the front door and barking furiously. Once I got to a window with a view of the porch, she stopped. I saw someone carrying a large trash bag and wielding something like a tire iron. They had turned and gone back down the steps. I froze. Watched surreptitiously. They stopped and a second figure joined them, coming from the back of my house. The blood in my ears nearly covered the sound of the teapot's whistle.

"Just shopping," I told myself. "Looking for easy supplies," I told Princess. She cocked her head.

I thought of the hybrid truck in the garage and the cans of gas packed into its bed. I'd never driven it, not that I was allowed to leave the house right now anyway, ankle monitor thanks so much you snitch.

We returned to the kitchen. I poured hot water over the ground coffee and let it brew.

While it steeped, I used the flashlight, still looking for the buzzing ankle monitor's instruction book, paperwork about who to call—not that the last time I checked I could make or take calls. Nada. I held on to the tiny screwdrivers and various *L*-keys I came across while I looked, hoping I could break into Mom's office with one of them.

I put more sugar in my coffee than I needed. I wasn't sorry. It was the illusion of happy as I drank the warmth, the house relatively cool from the freak sleet storm. The heat was a comfort. I felt embraced from within. Then, I went to break in.

The small flathead screwdriver twisted, freeing the locked knob effortlessly. That gave me pause. All this time, it was that easy. I took a deep breath before turning the doorknob.

Princess went in ahead of me, immediately climbing up to lay on the old, comfortable couch my grandmother had kept for guests. I explored the room with the flashlight, my whole excuse for breaking in delayed. Most of Grandma's posters and workbooks from teaching reading were gone. In the place of the posters were road maps between here and what Mom had come to call home the longer she had been away from it, a place her own grandparents had farmed and held on to, a place Aunt Geneva lived with our cousins, a getaway, a few family cabins on a small mountain in what was once Indian Territory, but still Cherokee Nation. Otherwise, the walls were bare.

The desk was cleared off but for a fax machine and a slim, white three-ring binder. I opened it. Faxes. Faxes Mom had hole-punched filled the binder. The first was a facsimile of a hand-drawn map and a list of steps, routes, county roads and highways, turnoffs, and landmarks. Colorado. Who did Mom know in Colorado besides my "estranged" father? At the bottom it said, "Failure of power grid inevitable. Leave for Kansas City today. Kiss Stevie bye for me. I'm sorry we have to leave her." Then it was just signed with a symbol. I tilted the page, trying to figure it out. It looked like two hearts, conjoined as a kind of infinity sign.

I closed the binder, shaky. I didn't want to read these private missives, but there were answers, too, buried in there. Of that, I was sure. I needed a minute. Hell, I was under house arrest. I had lots of minutes to burn.

It is said that magic is simply something which science has yet to explain, while magic shows are simply tricks and illusions.

The sound of the last fax, whirring into the locked and abandoned room as the police escorted me out of my home in handcuffs, echoed in my head. I shined the flashlight on the fax machine. Facedown was a piece of paper. I picked it up and read the words by the light of my torch.

Stevie, I love you. You're the best daughter and sister in the world. But don't leave yet. You'll know when you have to go. See you on the mountain.

Love,
Dad

Once, I played soccer. It was how I met Jess. Dad was our coach. We were in elementary school and a girl from the other team slid into the back of my legs to steal the ball. One moment I was grounded, the next I was falling backwards over her, body completely out of control. And Jess was all over her while I lay on the ground winded, afraid I would never breathe again.

This was the emotional equivalent of that. I somehow made it to the couch and sat down. I read that fax over and over. What did it mean? Had Dad been the one faxing from the future all along? It couldn't be; he would never leave Levi. Was he faxing right now from Kansas City? Had I messed everything up by not going into the future, asking Adam to take Levi? In my head was the whirr of that last message. We were on the phone just before the last fax came in. He wasn't lying to me when he wanted to know where his son was. I had heard the anxiety in his voice. I picked up the handset of the fax machine. No dial tone. I looked at the phone number of origination, wished I could call it, wished I could write back. I had so many questions. There was so much unsaid.

Suddenly, Princess jarred me out of my head, running out of the room to the front door and barking once more. I stuffed Dad's message into my pocket and followed her into the front room.

World
Burns

Despite Princess's barking, I moved as quietly as possible to the front window. A car was parked in the street. A woman stepped out into the light of dawn carrying what looked like a child wrapped in a blanket. For a moment, my heart thought/wished it was Mom carrying Levi. Then I realized neither shape was quite right.

By the time she had reached the porch, I realized it was my auntie, Mom's friend, my lawyer Angel. I opened the door. She hurried in.

"Things are falling apart out there, Stevie."

I nodded my head. I had told her they would.

"Everyone who can leave the city is. Jane and I are going too. We have to get to my mom in Kansas City, then get us all back to Oklahoma." Classic Indian Relocation Cherokee diaspora. Kansas City, Dallas, Los Angeles, Denver. They moved us everywhere. Some of us stayed. Some of us were headed back. Some of us stayed lost.

I nodded. "It's going to get worse before it gets better." Adam hadn't lied about that.

Jane was groggy. Angel set her down on the couch and she curled up in a ball. I grabbed Princess's collar before she licked Jane's face. That would have woken her up.

"Let's go in your mom's office."

"You want a coffee?"

"Oh, my God, yes."

I went to the kitchen and reheated the water enough to pour it over grounds and make Angel a big coffee. She looked like she needed the caffeine. She had a long drive planned.

By the time Princess and I got to the office, the white binder was no longer on the desk. In its place were tools, much like the ones the sheriff had used to previously put on the ankle monitor.

Angel handed me a paper. "Stevie, you are no longer a person of interest in the disappearance of Levi Jones."

"What?"

"Levi and Adam are meeting your parents now. You are no longer a suspect in his disappearance because he's no longer missing. Your parents. . ." she paused, "well, they're on the road."

". . . How? Is Dad okay? I mean, the surgery, the bone marrow stuff?"

"He's been released. He has Levi."

"But how?" I asked again.

"Adam called him."

"But Dad—"

Angel stopped me. "Yeah, he's pissed. At everyone."

"Where is Adam?"

"You mom said he went home. Where is that? Costa Rica?"

I wondered if Angel never got the e-mails I sent, or simply didn't believe me. I couldn't even nod; my eyes burned. Levi and Dad were coming home. It was wonderful. But it was also terrible. It was more terrible than wonderful.

"I'm here to remove the ankle monitor, then we're leaving town. Here"—Angel patted the desk—"hop up so I can take that thing off."

Then, that's what she did.

As soon as she was done, Angel scooped up Jane and headed for the door. Jane woke up long enough to smile at me. I remembered her asthma. Asthma that the flu might trigger.

"Wait." I ran to the garage and grabbed a hundred-count box of masks made for kids. The best masks you could wear and still breathe in. I handed them to her.

"I hate to leave you," Angel said, grabbing my arm as I offered the box to her.

"I can't," I replied, thinking of the fax in my pocket. Would I have gone, without having read the message?

"Can I take you somewhere?"

I thought of Jess and Loren, wondering if they were still stuck at the hospital when we all knew they needed to be on the road out of town. Would they go to Loren's mom in Chicago? Or meet her somewhere? Angel didn't have time to run me around to try to find my friends, and what good would I be to anyone hanging out in the hospital, unable to call or be called? Did the hospital have emergency generators going for all they would need? Was power out there too? What about phones?

"I need to stay here."

"Alone?"

"I have Princess."

"You have weapons, I guess." She knew my parents. I thought of the recurve bow next to my bed, the rifle beneath it, machetes and axes and mattocks in the garage. Check.

I nodded vigorously.

"Can you board up the windows?"

I nodded again.

She was holding Jane, rocking her, like a younger child. "I don't feel good leaving you."

"You need to get Jane someplace safe. This flu. It's going to be bad. Make 1918 look mild."

Angel blanched. She pulled me in for a hug. Her large leather shoulder bag poked me. She readjusted and hugged me tight. Jane put her arm around me too.

"Your mom loves you," Angel whispered. "Don't ever doubt it. The way you love Levi, she loves both of you. That's the way it is with love. Some of us don't run out."

Finally, the tears came. Ones I had been holding in all morning. I cried for my family, for Angel and Jane—because I just didn't know—for Loren and her mom and Jess.

All the people who couldn't wait for the end to pop off, did they really have so little capacity to empathize with the potential quantity of loss we were facing? I cried because I didn't know what was going to happen, couldn't even pretend I saw a normal, boring future anymore. I suddenly felt tired, neither fight nor flight, but ready to sleep.

Finally we let each other go and said donadagohvi. I hoped I would see them again.

Angel had driven away before I remembered to ask her about the binder full of faxes that had been moved. The messages from Dad. At least, the last one I had in my pocket was from Dad. What about the others? I opened the shades in the office to see better. I wondered where Angel had set it. I started with the desk drawers, as that made the most sense. Nothing. I moved on to the closet. In the closet I found a large backpack and set it on the desk, but kept looking for the binder. I looked under the couch and even moved the fax machine. It was gone.

I sat down on the couch with the backpack to see what it held. Carabineered to the outside of the pack was a key chain to the hybrid truck in the garage. "That's not exactly useful," I said to Princess.

I began to unpack the bag.

The top held a space blanket. Beneath that was a plastic bag of laminated maps. I started pulling everything out and laying it on the couch. The gallon bag further in was full, heavy, and wedged in tight. I took it out and realized it was stuffed with cash. More than I had ever seen. Harriet Tubman's portrait on twenty-dollar bill after twenty-dollar bill. I set it to the side and kept emptying the bag, the remainder of which was packed full of typical camping gear. A solar charger, a world band radio that would pick up shortwave stations, a water filter, two cans of fuel gel, a multi-tool, a portable fishing kit, a first aid kit capable of treating gunshot wounds. But no binder.

I repacked everything but the radio and the solar charger. I pulled the fax from my pocket, looked at it one more time, then packed it too. I couldn't read it anymore. My guess was Adam and the *Ladder* would soon be gone. Was there more Angel wasn't telling me?

Were my parents headed back after they retrieved Levi? How was Levi going to get the lifesaving treatment he needed if the world fell apart? It was going to take a lot more than solar chargers and first aid kits to save him.

Levi was going to die. Why? If Adam could call my dad and tell him where they were, couldn't he explain why Levi couldn't stay in this timeline? And Mom? Between the two of them, couldn't they have convinced him? Could Adam show them the caverns?

The blood was pounding in my temples. A headache, pressure that seemed to start in my chest. I wanted to scream, but didn't want to frighten Princess. Instead I collapsed in Levi's bed and cried. I didn't have time to nap, to sleep, but I didn't care. I didn't want to think or dream. I just wanted everything to be different. I just wanted Levi to be saved. For that matter, I wished that for all of us. *There should be more time.*

When I woke up, it was full daylight. I sat up. Princess was curled up with me. She leaned over and licked the salt from my dried tears off my face. "Well, girl, those windows aren't going to cover themselves. Back on task."

First, though, I was going to set up the solar charger and hope that my phone would save me.

At
the
Party

There was a large work shed in the garage where plywood was stored. It was splintery and unwieldy. While my phone sat in the shade, but the solar charger sat in the sun, I worked as quietly as possible. Princess stood guard. The yard was damp, but no longer icy. The neighborhood was much quieter than I had ever heard it. It was so quiet, I heard the jingle of Princess's collar when she alerted to the sound of a car over a block away. It sounded like the distinctive putter of Loren's diesel engine—her mother's Volvo. I had listened for and heard it so many times before. My heart sang. I grabbed my phone and the charger, put a leash on Princess, and made it to the driveway before Loren pulled in. It was a good thing, too, because I had to help her get Jess into my house.

Jess was wearing brown Carhartt's. Rugged and new, with a white thermal under it.

I hugged them. "Have you really been in the hospital? You look amazing."

Jess looked over at Loren, pointing with their chin. "These are my break-out-of-the-hospital clothes Loren got me. But I need some sun."

They were both smiling. So big. So real. And for the first time in weeks, I couldn't stop smiling either. I hadn't seen

Jess and Loren together since Jess's parents banned Loren from the hospital. Now they were sitting on the couch together, clearly a couple. My third-wheel status was pretty solid right now. It was awesome.

"Um"—I gestured awkwardly—"what happened?"

Loren spoke, "Angel came by the hospital and told us we should get over here ASAP if we ever wanted to see you again."

I remembered the fax with the phone number I didn't recognize across the top of the page. "I need to make a phone call. Are your phones working?" Mine had charged enough to come on, but there were no bars or lines where there should have been lines and bars.

Loren just said, "Do you know what's happening out there?" She handed me her phone. There were no lines or bars on her phone either. "Domestic terrorists, attacks on cell towers and water treatment plants. We came to get you. We're going to meet my mom halfway between here and Chicago tomorrow."

"Do you need some maps?"

"You can bring them with you."

I shook my head.

"Why not?"

"Let's go inside."

Once we were sitting around the table, I caught them up on everything I hadn't had a chance to tell them. I skirted carefully around *Soulcraft*.

I wished I could show them the e-mail Adam had sent about the satellites. Showed them the dates and time stamps. All I had was the fax from my dad. Loren read it and then she handed it to Jess.

"What does it mean?" Jess asked.

"I don't really know," I said.

"So, now Levi isn't going into the future?" Loren asked. I thought she was going to cry.

"It looks like it."

We sat quietly for a long time.

"Loren told me what she could, but, still, wow," Jess whistled.

"The most unbelievable part is that you robbed a museum," Loren remarked.

"I want to see you in that blonde wig," they added.

I gestured my chin to where Jess and Loren were holding hands, their closeness that was closer than ever. "So, what's up with . . ."

Loren and Jess exchanged glances, talked without words, much like they often had. Finally, Jess said, "Well, you know my family was not very tolerant of . . . well . . . of much. So, since I almost died, I realized when I woke up I couldn't live without Loren. I prefer love to being alone and dead. Screw them."

They had never talked about their family like this before. Loren leaned over and kissed Jess on the forehead.

"If they hadn't made passes at me before and then pretended it never happened, I'd say it was just a head injury."

"But I did."

"She knows," said Loren.

Jess blushed. "Sometimes your friends know you better than you know yourself."

I stood up. "So, you think you can stay until tomorrow? You want some coffee or tea or water? We have a lot of bottled water."

When I returned from the kitchen, we talked a little more, made plans. Jess's head had begun to hurt so they went to lie down in my parents' room.

Loren pitched in with helping me finish boarding up the windows. We hinged a few of the boards in case I wanted to open them for light later. While we worked, we heard car and house alarms going off a few streets away. I could tell when each siren and alarm sounded it made Loren more anxious.

"So, you think Adam went home."

I shrugged. "That was the plan. If you knew what was coming and you could escape, what would bring you back? Dad said he would see me on the mountain."

Loren dropped what she was holding and hugged me. I couldn't cry anymore, but it was nice to be held. "You should go with me and Jess," she whispered.

"Dad said to wait. So, I'll wait."

She held off trying to talk me into it again until just before she joined Jess in my parents' room.

I got up early and made us breakfast: corn flour and chocolate chip pancakes with dried berries, coffee with powdered milk and sugar, and the last of the bananas Mom had bought, as green as possible, before she and Dad left. They needed eating or they'd be only good for banana bread or baby food. I set the table with nice plates instead of paper.

I put on a playlist of music that we all liked, something with only happy songs. We had always taken for granted that even if we couldn't hug each other, we could call, we could video chat, we could, at the worst, e-mail or even send a real piece of paper through the Postal Service. If we absolutely had to. Now even that was uncertain. How could we plan to see each other again if we had no idea where we were going? Is this the anxiety our ancestors felt when our people were rounded up and marched away—that fear that in separation there was an inevitability of loss? Did sadness weigh on my ancestors until perhaps the worst did or didn't happen?

If Adam was right about what was coming, I might never find them again. And God, I hoped he was wrong. Maybe that was why Dad told me to wait. Maybe something had changed—the timeline fluttered, shifted, a traveler saving us all, all the important art safe and in vaults. My family was coming back to me. This I wanted to believe. I wanted to hold my little brother's hand again and hug my mom and dad. I wanted Levi to grow up with me. Get treatment and be taken care of by his family.

Waiting is hard, doing nothing is harder, so I cooked. Loren and Jess came to the table. I'd let them sleep in. Once we were seated, I said a prayer.

"Wado, Unetlvnvhi, help us know your will and do your will." In Cherokee the word that gets used for "God" or "the creator" basically means "one who provides everything." So, it's not really God in the Western sense or

Greek or Norse, but a recognition that none of this is ours, we didn't create anything so much as riff on what we were given. And we really seemed to be bungling that one.

"And wado, Mom and Dad, for the food. For everything," I finished, my voice catching. That was all I could manage.

We were quiet for a few minutes. Then Loren spoke up.

"I want to tell you something." I felt Jess become as tense as I suddenly felt.

I waited.

"Jess already knows." They seemed to relax.

"Maybe I should have told your parents, I don't know. But when I told them I don't swim, they heard, 'I can't swim.' But . . . I can. I just choose not to. My mom made sure I could swim as soon as I was old enough to learn."

I began to laugh. Why hadn't I known this? I kept laughing. Jess and Loren were laughing too. I picked up my phone and put on "You Never Can Tell" by Chuck Berry. I stood up and gestured for Loren to get up and dance with me. Jess pointed at their concussed head and stayed seated. We all sang along. It seemed like the perfect song. "'C'est la vie,' say the old folks . . ."

Then we ate and we laughed and there were no more somber feelings. Finally, as we finished, Loren left the table and returned with a metal box. She handed it to me.

Inside was a small photo book. It had pictures of me, Jess, Loren, and our families. There were even two of Adam towards the end. The last one was of him and me standing under the *Ladder.* I didn't remember her taking it. I closed it, feeling all the things. Sad, grateful, in love, happy I had such wonderful people in my world, even if this was all.

Loren had never bothered with hard copies before; I realized this meant she no longer had faith in the system of cloud memory and off-site drives staying intact. That was what almost made me cry again.

The night before, we had talked about whether or not the best was behind us. "The best for who?" Loren had asked. It was a valid question. Hadn't I sent my own brother away in the belief he would be better off in a new society, a world where people were just human beings, where we recognized that race was a construction? That gender could be a spectrum? Native nations had known that. Christianity had tried to beat it out of us.

At six, Levi had already been called racist names by other kids, kids who learned it from their parents. It couldn't be undone and it was going to be worse before it got better, period. But maybe the world *would* truly get better, not just for my family—that kind of thinking is too small. Maybe it would get better for all people whose worth had been determined by how difficult or beneficial it was to exploit them and their land. Perhaps it would be better for other living things: the birds, the bugs, the dolphins, the whales. James Baldwin had said something like only a child believes they can become an adult painlessly. We were no longer children.

After Loren and Jess left, I cuddled on the couch with Princess. I looked through the photos Loren had given me. Then, I ran my finger over the route she had drawn for me on the map. She was going to meet her mother at family land in Kansas. I'd traced our route to Indian Territory on a map for her as well. I hoped we would all get where we were going before—before what? A big crash, a true World War, a plague, a failure of the system combined with environmental disasters? All of the above? The Biggest Blip.

I turned on the world band radio and listened to news from Africa and Europe. Even there, I could tell the off-world settlements were being advertised. It was the same commercial in a different language. I wondered if I should have given my friends the radio, despite wanting to believe the timeline I had written down from talks with Adam was accurate. It had been reliable so far, and Loren and Jess should be where they were going long before the big event. They had their car radio, which would run as long as the car battery lasted. Apparently, the no-electricity situation ended almost at the state's border with Oklahoma. Not because the storm hadn't hit there, but because the Choctaw and other tribes had buried the electrical lines that crossed the Reservation years ago.

I made a to-do list, based on the timeline. I had maybe a week more to wait around in relative safety. I started sorting through the things in my bedroom. There were boxes of notes between me and my friends, art projects, craft supplies, clothes that hadn't fit for years, free T-shirts with logos for everything from the at-large Cherokee community to a local turkey trot.

By the time I was done with my room, I had a trash bag full of stuffed animals and four separate cardboard boxes; a giveaway box, if there was anyone left to take it; trash; papers to burn; and a large box of photos and vinyl records still in their frames that would fit in the front seat of the truck. I gathered from the rest of the house until it was full. The truck's bed was packed tight, the hard plastic cover over it secure and locked. Ninety days of supplies for two careful people. Camping stuff, liquid and gas fuel, rain gear. Humans weren't made for constant wet, the chill damp that seeps into your shoes and toes, makes your fingers shrivel. Once the cold invades, it's hard to believe you'll ever be warm again.

I checked the backyard and took Princess out. I plugged in some old-fashioned headphones to the world band, as constantly charging my wireless headphones with the solar charger would be an annoyance. I checked the local fire and safety lines and local radio, which still seemed to be functioning normally despite the spreading outage. Now and then, a radio station would suddenly disappear and I would hover over other stations until I found one that was mostly business-as-usualing. Sometimes, when I heard a siren, I could tune to the emergency lines and identify the emergency, where it was coming from, the source of smoke and noise. Often, I couldn't. The incidents seemed to be increasing. Wrecks caused by downed traffic lights; lifesaving machines no longer up to the task of saving. At a certain point I shifted to far away stations broadcasting joyous music. My heart was no longer up for the blues.

I made sweet treats, feeding myself happiness, not caring about the eventual sugar crash. Vietnamese coffee with chicory and sweetened condensed milk. Moroccan mint tea with lots of sugar and mint from Grandmom's backyard gardens. Sweet crepes with balsamic strawberries. Music and food helped me forget the world was ending.

Texas
Sun

The next day the sun was back big-time from dawn to dusk, no evidence of any recent cold front left behind except in downed power lines and no electricity.

While I spent the day in the shade outside, the house stored up heat. The boarded-up windows were no help. I missed our old house, with its upstairs windows that could be opened to coax through an occasional breeze. I figured Loren and Jess were at Loren's family's land in Kansas by now. I hoped Loren's mom had made it there as well. It was an eight-hour drive to Kansas City, Kansas. They hadn't had to go quite that far. I hoped Angel had retrieved her mom.

I had a battery-powered fan and spent the evening napping in front of it, deleting trash and apps on my phone, reorganizing my photos, taking pictures and scans of objects I wasn't ready to let go of yet.

Unable to sleep, I stayed awake most of that night; Princess and I snuck outside where it was cooler. I let her run as long as she stayed quiet. I trusted her ears to cue into threats. I hoped the stray sounds we heard were raccoons and possums. I was pretty sure some were people taking the opportunity to go through the houses most of my neighbors had fled over the last week. I wondered where they had gone. To Oklahoma? Further northeast, to stay with friends and relatives, to live in hotels while they waited for the electrical grid to be repaired? What about the people with no place to go? When I felt brave enough, I ventured into the prairie with a taser and binoculars and saw the lines of car taillights and headlights on the highway. Tow trucks and emergency lights seemed to be constantly pulling and pushing vehicles off to the shoulder.

Reports on the radio talked about the abandoned vehicles and how many of them had windows smashed, anything of value taken. They warned drivers not to get on the road if they didn't have a full tank or charge. They reported that failed pumps and chargers had led to fights, even riots in places. Society will crumble with a bang, the whisper long having rang in our ears.

When Princess alerted me to a sound at the beginning of our street, I rushed her into the house. I picked up the battery-powered lantern and kept it next to me. My recurve bow was there, but I didn't load it.

We peeked outside. Someone was practically running in the dark with a baby stroller, the car seat kind. They had come down the hill fast. They stopped at the carport across the street. I knew the house was empty because it was Ida's and she had left with her son the first day of the power outage. They were headed back to the Choctaw Reservation. Lots of Choctaw people live and work in DFW, since it's the closest metroplex to the Choctaw Nation. Reservations weren't built with opportunities; tribes had to add those later. By the time they did, some of us had relocated to bigger cities. Mom had always wished we lived closer to Cherokee Nation.

I waited for the sound of breaking wood or windows, but there wasn't anything. I looked outside and saw the person disappear into the house. A few moments later she came back out for the stroller. Princess started to make a noise, but I petted her head.

"I think they have a key," I whispered. I wondered if it was Paka and her new baby.

With nothing else to see, we sat on the couch, waiting. At least until Princess begin to bark furiously.

Despite her vicious bark, there was a tentative knock on the door a few moments later. I snuck to the window and saw a woman holding a bundle on our porch.

"Hello!" she whispered, her soft voice barely audible. A baby's cry began and the woman shushed her. As I had suspected, it was Paka. The young mom who had grown up across the street with her grandmother.

She repeated, "Hello," her voice wavering with threatened tears.

I took a deep breath. I put Princess on her leash. Then I opened the door.

Paka had her two-month-old daughter with her and a black eye.

"I'm sorry to bother you." She had been crying. "Do you know where my grandma is?"

"Your uncle came and got her a few days ago."

Paka sounded as if she would choke. She was nearly shaking with either anger or fear.

"What happened?"

"I don't want to talk about it. I had to leave. I couldn't stay there anymore."

I knew Paka had been living a few blocks away with her husband, a man who had been her work manager before marrying her. I had only met him in the driveway of her grandmother's house once. I hazarded a guess.

"But won't he look for you there? I mean, if you had to—uh—escape."

At that, Paka began to really cry. The baby joined in.

No. No. No, I thought. We didn't need to be making this much noise. Not if Paka had just left an angry man.

I reached out and patted Paka's back, guided her into our house. I was awkward with her. With the lantern, I was able to guide her toward my little brother's room. She sat down in the rocking chair that had belonged to my mother since she was pregnant with me. Paka rocked Nihi gently, and the baby's eyes, at first, were anxious, looking around the dark room, the only light the battery-powered lantern I had. After a few minutes, the baby relaxed, closing her eyes to sleep.

"Let me bring you some tea," I said.

Paka nodded, but then shook her head, "No caffeine. I'm nursing."

"Want fenugreek?" I said, remembering my mother's regimen to encourage an unsteady milk flow brought on by stress.

Paka nodded. I hoped what we had was still good. Thinking of the herbal tea I had brought my mother years ago made Levi materialize in my brain, no longer an infant, but six years old. Suddenly I wanted to cry. Grief will sucker punch you every time. Kaboom. I missed my baby brother, the one I had held and rocked in this chair. I grieved him staying in this world to suffer.

I stopped myself. These rabbit holes were dangerous. They could break a mental ankle and leave you stranded in depression.

I returned to what the young woman in front of me needed. I thought of the shed in the yard. There were plastic boxes with toys and baby clothes. Mom had packed them away and forgotten them, meant to take them to the cousins back home, but they had been shuffled onto the wrong truck during the move and ended up in the backyard instead. I could go find things Nihi would need, Nihi could use. I'd go get the boxes and sort through them like mere objects in the gift shop. Wash what was useful and pitch the rest. I could do this now and make my potential grief productive. I could find toys and clothes for the baby, here, now. I took Paka her tea. Told her to rest; mommas have to sleep when babies sleep. That was all I knew right then. We would figure the rest out later.

Paka and I fell into a rhythm, cooking and talking, sleeping and reading. I was rereading a series by N. K. Jemison that began with *The City We Became*. We took turns listening to the radio, surveilling the abandoned block we had grown up on. Our dead end cul-de-sac reflected that phrase in a way it never had before. We seemed to be the only living people here.

Paka finally shared her story with me one night. Her husband had seemed like a good guy at first. After they married and she quit work he seemed to be purposely keeping her from spending time with her family, expected her to be home when he was home. Ida hadn't liked him. She missed Paka, I knew.

Then the electricity went out and there was no work to go to. Money was tight. The baby cried. Paka had enjoyed the quiet. Making dinner, playing in the yard with the baby. Then he'd lost his temper one day, yelling at her about the baby crying, getting pregnant in the first place. He shoved her into a door, her glasses catching and breaking, blacking her eye. He'd been sorry. Ever so sorry. But she was already gone. She just had to wait for him to fall asleep.

"I knew," she said, "I knew if I stayed, he'd talk me into forgiving him, because you would have to, wouldn't you, in order to stay? Then there would be another baby and in the background the sound of me being shoved into a window. You know, even if he never did it again, it would always be there. I would just be waiting for it." She paused. It was the most emotional she had gotten. "And what if he hurt Nihi? What if she grew up seeing him hurt me?" She shook her head. "No, I couldn't even consider staying."

I nodded. Sometimes you just have to shut up and let people tell their story.

"And, now, I just want to go home."

I understood. With my family and the people who loved me elsewhere, my house was no longer a home. Even the art that I had thought made the world a better place? It was more powerful in my memory, but still less important than Paka and Nihi. The baby made eye contact with me, smiled. My heart panged. Love is not something that lessens the more you love. Every hard thing I had gone through lately was for Levi. I knew Paka felt at least as much for her baby as I felt for my little brother. She would do anything to save her. I hoped I could help.

And so that was when I told her everything.

Nice Things

There were five houses in the cul-de-sac. Paka's grandma's was across from us. Paka had a key and went over a few times to gather some family photos, bring over some different canned food and dried beans and preserves. There was a lot of chicken noodle soup. We joked that if only cars ran on soup, we were set to travel the world.

There were three other houses in the circle between our houses. All seemed empty. At least the cars that normally sat in the driveway, or came and went, didn't. None of the houses had been boarded up and I never saw any candles or lights.

Paka and the baby slept in Levi's room. One night an explosion shattered the quiet. Paka came running out into the living room, the baby crying in her arms. We went to the backyard and saw flames shooting into the sky from the house two doors down. My heart was hopeful that when the emergency vehicles came, I could ask them for an update on the local situation. I didn't think the flu was spreading yet, but the information we were able to get on the radio wasn't much helpful anymore. In my own neighborhood I saw there were still power lines down, a dangerous situation if the power came back on. I wondered if that was what had happened to the burning house, though it hadn't popped on at my house.

I stood waiting outside the front door for emergency vehicles. I had a mask and gloves, to be on the safe side. Emergency personnel would be the first exposed to an unknown virus, wouldn't they? I promised to try to warn them when they came, even if I wasn't sure how, even if I knew they wouldn't believe me, might lock me away for my own safety.

The house burned. We checked the emergency radio and heard the fire spoken of, but no one was dispatched. Finally, we went back in, the smoke making its way into our sealed house anyway.

Paka sat back on the couch, playing with Nihi, kissing her toes, telling her what a good baby she was.

"Did you hear any sirens today either?" she finally asked as I turned off the radio.

"I didn't notice."

"I noticed it last night. I wondered if they were doing all their runs silently. No sirens during the night at all. The occasional gunfire, distant explosions like that house, but no rescue sounds."

I hadn't really thought about it, but yes, before that, they'd seemed to be nonstop.

"What do you think that means?" she pressed.

I thought of the stories about the future/past. "I think it means we have to save ourselves."

Paka nodded, leaned down, and kissed Nihi on her belly, before standing and picking her up. "So, what else is new?"

Stressed Out

Paka and I sat down and talked about our plans. She needed to go home, be with her family. The night before, with three days left, I drew a map on the dining room wall in pencil. Once Paka agreed it looked right, I filled it in with permanent marker. If my family couldn't make it to me before I headed out, I wanted them to understand the route I planned to take. I hoped Dad could forgive me. I assumed, from the existence of the fax, he had. Or at least he understood. Why else tell the girl who had tried to send his son two hundred years away to wait to be rescued? But I wanted to go to the Chickasaw Tribal headquarters first. Paka understood that the sacred item I still had in a cedar box in my closet needed to be delivered. Then I would take her to Choctaw Nation. From there I could go to Auntie's.

I didn't want my parents to panic if I wasn't at the house. I didn't want them wandering around, searching for me, tracking me, wasting Levi's valuable time. Since Levi hadn't gone to the future, he needed to be in a hospital, but that would be out of the question soon. What were we going to do? Under a ninety-day quarantine, Levi wouldn't get the care he needed. At first, Adam had told me, resources would be used on the futilely ill. Hospitals would be places of contagion. People with chronic illnesses would be most at risk. Health care had always been a struggle, even with insurance. Another pandemic we weren't prepared for wouldn't help.

The question kept sneaking up on me. Why had Adam called my dad? If he knew Dad wasn't going to believe him or Mom about time travel and the end of the world, why had he called? Suddenly, I thought I knew. Adam couldn't separate Levi and Dad like that, just as I couldn't send Levi alone with Adam until Mom called. It was one thing to believe you are willing to put a child through something because it's in their best interest. It is another thing to do it. Dad losing his son would break his heart. Better to bet on the world you know, than a fairy tale.

Studying maps and copying them onto note cards helped me stop thinking about things I didn't have answers for and couldn't fix.

I wanted to be able to guide us by memory, if needed. Was pretty sure GPS was not going to be an option. I thought of the Federal Road built over two centuries ago with an eye towards removing my people from our lands. Eventually, that road was paved, and could still be followed back to Cherokee land in the southeastern United States.

I worked into the evening while Paka slept. I wanted to be done when she got up. We were taking turns, watching the world outside, listening to broadcasts. We slept in shifts, had some meals together, now and then I cared for Nihi. There were fewer and fewer random cars on our street, but more people on foot. Gas and charges were in short supply. Stores weren't open. You couldn't run credit cards or surveil customers with no electricity. Why pay employees only to be robbed?

We couldn't wait much longer for rescue. Paka and I had decided to leave in two days, regardless.

I walked out to the garage, opening the back door to the yard to let in a little waning daylight. Princess ran out into the backyard for a minute, then came back in. As soon as I opened the front door for the truck, she leaped in, always ready to go. I started rearranging things. I'd need to remember to grab the rifle and ammo when it was time to go. It was going to be tight. There was really no room anymore for my box of framed photos and my favorite vinyl.

As soon as I sat in the driver's seat, I forgot about that. I held the wheel and mimicked the motions of starting the truck. It began to feel like my chest had been cut open and was filling with cold air. My heart hammered and I couldn't hear anything outside my own body. Tears brimmed in my eyes and began to flow down my cheeks. I wrapped my arms around my body and began to rock back and forth. I couldn't do this. Even if I doubled up on my meds. They already made me sleepy; I couldn't drive drowsy. That would just make things worse. I felt cold, clammy all over. I got out of the truck and went into the house, exhausted. I prayed my family would make it home first.

Take Care of Me

Paka startled me awake.

"He's at Grandma's."

"What?"

"Frank. He's trying to break into Grandma's house."

I got up, my pajama top and shorts sticky with sweat. I looked out the window.

"Are you sure it's him?"

"Yeah, he was yelling when he first banged on the door." On cue, he shouted Paka's name again, yelling at her to open the door. Princess growled. I didn't want her to bark, so I commanded her to be quiet. She let out a nervous whimper and then stood in front of the door, her teeth showing as she growled softly.

"What should we do?" Paka asked. Frank hadn't come empty-handed. He had a crowbar that he was using on the side door under the carport.

"Let's go," I said. "When he goes in the house, we open the garage door and get out of here."

Paka nodded and grabbed Nihi's things. I was glad the baby stroller and seat were in the garage. I grabbed the rifle from my room and ran out to the truck.

The passenger seat still held the box of photos and records. I pulled them out and set them on the floor, trading them for the car seat. Paka was right behind me with Nihi. She buckled her in calmly but quickly.

"You can drive, yeah?"

"I've been driving since I was twelve," Paka said.

"Good." I handed her the keys. "Hop in."

I watched out the garage door window for Frank to disappear into Paka's grandma's house. Once he was well inside, I pulled the garage door open as fast as I could. I slid into the passenger seat and got my seat belt on. Princess hopped into the space beneath the dash. We were crowded, but we were all in.

In the moonlight we could see the street well enough, so Paka didn't turn on the headlights yet. I prayed we wouldn't hit anything. She gunned the truck and it fishtailed out of the driveway. She kept her eyes on the road, but I looked in the mirror and saw her husband run out of the house, a futile attempt to chase us down the road. Paka flipped on the headlights at the end of the street. She never looked back.

Heathens

Choctaw Nation was closer than the Chickasaw Cultural Center, but I couldn't afford to backtrack after I returned Paka to her family. So we headed to the Chickasaw Reservation first. The drive was normally less than two hours from our house. But once we got off the neighborhood streets, there was nothing but stop-and-go traffic ahead. People on the side of the road would wave and sometimes run out ahead. Paka swerved expertly around them. I was so grateful she was driving. Grateful for the hybrid truck, recharging itself while we drove on the diesel in the two large tanks.

While we drove we talked and then listened to music. I wanted to put on an audiobook, but finding one we both wanted to listen to had proved a challenge previously. Music was easier to agree on, once we found a genre we both liked. Nothing sad. Unremitting dancing and optimism was what the end of the world called for.

It was dawn when we got there. Much too early for employees like my curator friend, Kabi', to be at work. If they were even still working. The Cultural Center had a campus that included a pre-contact village. The sun was rising over the pointed log fence just as we pulled into the parking lot. Nihi was asleep, so Paka opted to stay in the truck with her and Princess.

"I don't know if anyone is here . . ." I said. We had passed some cars in the employee parking lot, so I was more hopeful than I sounded. Princess whined and I put her on a leash and let her do her morning business.

"That dog has the right idea. If you don't hurry back, I'm gonna step into those bushes over there."

I pointed to the cameras at the top of the fence. "Just watch where they're looking," I said.

"World ends and I still have to sneak around to pee," Paka muttered.

We had caught one of Brandon's broadcasts during the night drive, having trouble finding the frequency as we drove. But he had said more roads would be closing later that day. We had been lucky to get out before the one between Texas and Oklahoma shut. I wondered if the flu was already here, carried by wild birds and ducks to small chicken flocks and zoos. How many times had I seen wild birds trapped in buildings? The leap would be in sneezes of animals handled, contaminants on fingers, doorknobs that were touched before noses and eyes. It would be sudden and airborne and passed by vaccinated children, and devastating to unvaccinated people and those a few years past their latest booster.

I stopped thinking about that. I needed to get this "Found in collection" object to Kabi' and get us back on the road. Paka to her family, me to mine. Kabi' was a musician and an artist who hunted ducks and carved beautiful decoys out of wood. I shuddered. Ducks for sure would carry it, their mucous membranes a bird flu factory.

My friend was devoted, first to his family, second to the Cultural Center and language preservation. I reached the museum's front door and found a printed sign that read "Closed." I walked around to a side door for the Center, a long walk around the traditional village, which was padlocked.

I noticed another camera with a blinking light following me. I waved and hollered. I jumped up and down.

"Chinchokma?" I yelled. The world was quiet enough that I heard the click of a door.

"Stevie?"

From back where I had come, I heard the voice of my friend. I gently touched the bag that hung at my side, holding the cedar box, the extra object I had swiped from the museum when I helped take the headdress. The piece, "Found in collection," that had been stolen from a dying Chickasaw—that should have been buried with him, not left on a shelf in a museum miles and miles from his home.

I'd decided to tell Kabi' everything. I hoped the object would help him believe me. At the very least he could get it where it belonged, treat it as it needed to be treated.

Kabi' opened the locked gates of the village. "What the heck are you doing on the road, Stevie? You should be home. Or somewhere? The reports out of your state are kind of scary."

"It's going to get worse. But I have to tell you a real quick story."

I did. And after, I handed him the bag and the papers I had photographed in the museum.

His eyes skimmed the paper.

"This is what's in here?"

I nodded.

Kabi' set it in the middle of a table. We were both quiet for a few minutes.

"Sacred, huh?" I asked.

He nodded, looking over the paperwork again.

"There's more."

"You liberated more things?" His eyes were wide and he stepped back. I had a feeling he would smudge the room as soon as I left.

"No, there are more things I need to tell you." Then I told him what I had been told about the future; the next ninety days. I told him about my friend, Adam, the art thief and time traveler.

He took this oddly in stride too. "So, what's next for you?"

"Taking my friend to her people in the Choctaw Nation. Then going to mine in Cherokee Nation."

"Reservations are going to close." He didn't say it like a question. It suddenly occurred to me that I hadn't seen any of the Chickasaw Lighthorse posted around the museum. Kabi' was the only person holding down the center, while we had passed several officers monitoring the roads into and out of the Rez.

"Soon, yeah?" Again, it wasn't really a question.

I told him about Brandon's broadcast, the call numbers. He wrote them down. I wondered if he always won at cards.

"You better get on the road," he said. "Long day ahead of you."

I stood up. Kabi' picked up a radio. "Come in Lighthorse Chick 214274. Over."

"This is Lighthorse Chick 214274."

"There's a green diesel truck headed your way. Two women, a baby, a dog. Definitely not art thieves." He kind of laughed when he said it. "Let them pass. They're headed to Choctaw. Over."

"Ten-four," the woman said.

"You should get yourself through Tulsa as quick as possible," he said. "The Indian Nations are coordinating with the feds. Ain't that a hoot? But cities and states will start making up their own rules before long." I had the feeling Kabi' knew a lot more than he was letting on.

Adam had told me the Indian Nations and reservations would become unlikely allies—though historically equal entities—cooperating when the cyberattacks took down systems of banking, energy, and hospitals. Basically, infrastructure not being able to communicate would create a heck of a mess. This continent was going to break up into a quilt of countries that would replace state governments. It would be more like Europe in that way than ever before, but divided in a variety of ways, not necessarily by ethnic groups or religion; though some would self-segregate, perpetuate the divided world they were comfortable with, while others would choose to live in places they loved, with people they loved, and welcome the interruption of the hustle where money was the true God. Native nations would assert their reservation boundaries and laws, expelling citizens and non-citizens who chose not to respect their nationhood status and belief that the land was for everyone, and no one could take more than they needed. Many people would leave, sell out, go buy more elsewhere, while more would join the exodus of planet colonization than ever before. More people than ever before would create communities, some in former summer camps, some in abandoned apartment buildings. It would be a lot of fooling around and finding out for years.

Meanwhile, the uber-wealthy would flee to their own cruise ships in space, as if a world without earth, water, and trees was better when it was all-inclusive. As if the vacation could last forever.

I wondered if they would have a Coney I-Lander, but I doubted it. There are some things you can only get in Tulsa.

"My friend needs to come in and use the facilities."

"Send her in," Kabi' said. "I'm gonna draw you up a map. I'll send it out with her. There are no deputies available, but follow the roads I note for you. It's gonna slow you down, but it's safe. Since you have a Choctaw citizen with you, maybe they won't give you any trouble. If they do, tell them to call the Choctaw Assistant Chief's office."

I nodded.

"You know, some of our spiritual leaders saw this coming over a hundred years ago."

I nodded. That's what my mom told me she'd heard in stories from elders as a kid. How had I forgotten? These things were written of in wampum belts older than my nation.

"We were a little worried it was going to get us Ghost Dance levels of attention. But I don't think it's a surprise at the national and international security levels. They seem ready to keep order."

"Maybe too ready?"

"Well, maybe to maintain the status quo. Not for everything to change."

We were both quiet.

"So, would you say it's like the dominoes aren't so much falling in some places, as being pushed?"

"Yeah, with the plan to put everything back like it was. But . . . there's not going to be a return to normal."

"What is normal?"

"Normal wasn't so great for so many."

I nodded.

School massacres were normal.

Genocide was normal.

Corporations replacing families was normal.

Drugging kids to make them obedient was normal.

Dying because health care was unaffordable and too complicated and drugs that cost $13 sold for $1300 was normal.

Not being able to take off work when someone you loved was dying was normal.

Normal will kill you. I realized I was tired of normal.

Kabi' asked if I wanted to pray and smudge before I got on the road. I did.

Kabi' walked me back to the door. He checked his watch, "I'll feel better when my family gets here. I could really use a nap."

I didn't know when I would feel better. But I didn't put that on my friend. I found Paka doing the potty dance while holding Nihi. Nihi seemed to love it.

I took the baby and she ran to the entrance of the building.

She walked back slow and chill a few minutes later.

"Cultural Center is nice. Too bad the restaurant is closed."

"Wanting some grape dumplings or corn soup?"

"Yeah, I wanted to compare it to our restaurant. Pretty sure Choctaw's better."

I laughed. I wasn't going to take a side on that. If I did, I'd have to defend the honor of the Cherokee fusion food that was served in our nation's restaurant. I didn't think it was really a competition. But, hey, I am Cherokee.

Garden
Dove

The trip from Chickasaw took about two hours. Only forty minutes longer than it normally would have since we were cutting through small Oklahoma towns.

When we got there, we found that the Choctaw Nation had closed the hotels and the casino. Armed Oklahoma National Guard were turning non-Native residents of Texas back. It was a tense situation that didn't promise good things to come.

A state of emergency had been declared by Texas and all the bordering states, including Oklahoma. Choctaw Nation was being forced to deal with the refugees first. There were few cars driving the other direction. Cell phone service was still out.

Paka waited in a line to check in. The Lighthorse were guarding roads into the Reservation. Only residents were being allowed in for the foreseeable future. I was glad we had left when we did.

We were waved in to talk to an Assistant Chief in the Lighthorse offices. Paka had asked me to speak with someone about what I knew. But I was terrified to tell anyone in a position of authority anything. What if I was wrong? And how could I even believe that, with the confirmation I'd had over the last month? Still, I was afraid. It was one thing to live believing I had to be ready for the end of what was deemed civilization. It was quite another to tell people who had power over a sovereign nation, or who might recommend I be locked away.

We sat down in the chairs in front of a large wooden desk, waiting for the Assistant Chief. Instead, Brandon walked in.

"Siyo, Stevie."

"Oh, wow." I was stunned. "Osiyo, ginalii."

Paka looked back and forth between us.

"Oh, Paka, this is my friend, Brandon."

"From the radio?"

"From the future . . ." I replied quietly.

We sat in silence.

Eventually, I spoke. "So, who are you staying for?"

Brandon smiled. "You remember Octavia at the museum in Philadelphia?

I nodded. Remembering she had told me to tell Brandon "Halito."

"She's Choctaw. She came home a few days ago." He smiled. And sort of blushed. "We're staying in a honeymoon suite. In the Paris part of the casino."

I took this in. Brandon had chosen to stay. Adam had gone on.

I breathed deep and stood up.

"Well, Paka, I think my work here is done."

"Yeah, I have things covered here," Brandon replied. "Y'all need to get on the road, Stevie."

Paka stood up and leaned forward and shook Brandon's hand. "Nice to meet you. Yakoke."

Brandon nodded. "We radioed the Lighthorse to let you through to your grandparents' place. They let them know you're coming. If you have your Choctaw ID, things will go faster."

"I do."

"When this is over, bring Nihi in for her ID."

Paka laughed and turned to walk out.

"Stevie, hang on a sec."

I remained where I was and Brandon came around from behind the desk. He sat down in the leather chair, gestured for me to sit down as well, so I did.

"I'm sorry. I'm sorry so much was asked of you. I'm sorry you had to do a lot of hard stuff on your own. Alone."

I could only nod.

"All I can promise is there will be enough good people left to change things, to make the world a better place, to choose actions that will make things better . . . not seven generations from now, but soon."

Tears began to spill down my cheeks.

"You won't be alone. I promise."

We both stood up and he hugged me. I wiped my face.

"Wado," he said. "Donadagohvi."

"Howa, donadagohvi," I answered, turning to leave. Yes, let's see each other again. It was a prayer. A plea to Unetlanvhi, the one who provides everything. And a hope.

Older

It was noon before we made it to Paka's family's land. A large gate and horse fence surrounded the place, which was one of the ranches that provided bison meat sold by the Choctaw Tribe. We passed a small part of the herd as we drove up the long road to the gate, where one of her uncles met us.

Paka stopped the truck and hopped out. Her uncle came to the truck and hugged her. I had met him at Paka's grandma's on more than one occasion.

"Halito, Moshi," Paka said to her uncle.

"Lord, girl, you look just like my sister when she had you," he said. His voice was both happy and sad. "Let me see that baby."

Paka reached in and took Nihi out and handed him to her uncle. I got out and Princess hopped out with me. I went over to the driver's side of the truck. Her uncle leaned down and breathed deep, smelling the warm scent of Nihi's fluffy hair. His sparse whiskers must have tickled because Nihi laughed.

Paka and I looked at each other and Paka burst into tears.

Her uncle looked perplexed.

"It's the first time Nihi has laughed," I explained.

"Oh, that's a good thing, yeah?" He cuddled Nihi and bounced her gently.

I unhooked the car seat from the truck's front seat and handed it to Paka.

"Well," I said after a moment. "I better hit the road."

Paka's uncle looked up. "Nothing doing. Ida wants to see you. If I don't bring you back there, I can't come home."

I looked at Paka, tallying up the hours I had in front of me, before total lockdown kicked in.

"Just for an hour or so," Paka said.

"Come up to the house and eat, at least," added her uncle. "We're breaking out the green onions."

I laughed. "Wow, bringing out the big guns. I can't say no to that." Wild onion dinners were normally a spring thing. I wondered what spring would be like for us next year. Would we be able to be in community by then? How much community would be left? Where would I be? Would Levi be alive? I stopped. I came back to where I was. I couldn't worry about things that hadn't happened yet. May never happen. I needed to enjoy the wild onions while I could.

Paka reached out and hugged me again. Tight.

She said a lot with that hug.

An
Echo

Paka's family had enough warning to throw together a party for her and the baby and me. Outside, her uncles were cooking bison ribs and steaks on a charcoal grill, while inside her aunties were frosting a pink strawberry cake.

Poor Paka burst into tears again when her grandma got out of her recliner and came to hug her. They whispered to each other for several minutes while I was introduced to various family members. The scent of cooking beans and green onions and eggs vied for my heart. Tanchi labona, what the Choctaw called their version of corn soup, boiled on the stove too. Paka's grandma took the baby from her and sat back down in what I could tell was HER recliner and gestured to me to come over. I leaned down and hugged her.

"Yakoke, Stevie, for bringing Paka home. We went by her house when we left, but no one answered the door." Ida paused, made a face as if she tasted something bad. "That man."

"Hawa, elisi," I said. I had called her grandma when I was little, when I thought all mothers of mothers were called elisi, not just Cherokee grandmothers.

"I'm glad you're here." She paused. "Did you drive?"

"No, Paka did."

She nodded, "You can stay here. You're welcome. Big storm coming. Who knows what else? Prepare for the worst, hope for the best, yeah?"

I nodded. It was tempting. The house and the people, it was like being with my aunties; the smells were the same and the décor was similar. Aunts were busy, uncles were standing outside talking, keeping eyes on the kids who were running around. When I heard them speaking Choctaw, it was like hearing but not understanding my own language. Which I needed to learn. I shook my head.

"My family is expecting me. I have to get on the road."

"After we eat."

"Hawa, elisi."

Cousin after cousin, neighbor after neighbor had shown up for Paka and her baby's homecoming. But the event seemed to serve more than one purpose. People came in and saw Paka's grandma, then hugged Paka, sometimes bearing a gift for the baby. Most of the children never even entered the house, immediately swept into the games happening outside. But the parents had a worried look. They whispered in low voices. Preserves were traded. Meat was taken outside to be stored in the freezer that was attached to the solar power array over the barn. Ammunition exchanged hands, along with batteries.

I overheard the words *masks, walkie-talkies,* and *Lighthorse* a lot.

Someone told a story they had heard that morning. A truck driver with a tanker truck of insecticide had been killed while stopped at a Texas rest stop the night before. His truck was missing.

"What would someone do with a tanker full of bug spray," someone muttered. I thought of the stories Adam told me. Some people think when the system goes down, they'll get to be in charge. And some people think other people aren't people—just obstacles in the way of their chance to be a millionaire, a king. I shuddered. I went back to hold Nihi so Ida and Paka could eat. So I could feel love.

After a round of eating, Ida called me over. "Maybe you should go out and practice driving, then? Before you go?"

I laughed. She was right. Always preparing for the worst, hoping for the best.

As We
Drive By

I went out to the truck. Princess was hanging out with the windows down, waiting for me. She was thrilled to see me. Dogs were like that: like they never expected you to return and were so happy you decided to come back to them. I took her leash and led her to the pen. She cried for a moment and then lay down, curled up in a corner, nested in the hay.

The keys were still in the truck. I took a deep breath and got in the driver's seat.

I turned it on and was annoyed that there was no rumble of an engine. "Just like the video games," I told myself. "It's on," I continued. "Now checking the dashboard."

I was grateful for the backing camera. I didn't know how people managed without one in a world with toddlers and small animals. I turned the wheel slowly and swung into the road, driving a section that seemed to lead back to the portion of the ranch where we had spotted the bison herd in the distance. I wanted to see them up close one more time. I had asked if it would be okay, and an uncle suggested I leave Princess and not get out of the truck.

I drove slowly, more slowly than I would be able to drive on the highway if traffic was proceeding at normal speeds.

When I got close to the bison herd, I slowed down. They were large creatures, slow moving when unconcerned. I stopped the truck and watched a momma and her baby. There were at least three babies in this herd. From a distance a male watched me. He was eating bluestem grass, thoughtful. I put my windows down. The breeze wafted over them. Overhead, clouds were building up. But all summer they had done that, only teasing us with the promise of rain. I could smell the grass and the bison. It was a comfort.

The male wandered down into the road, watching me, not letting me drive any further. A few others followed him. I got the message.

"I'm not a threat to your family," I said.

He looked unconvinced. Then I let myself think about why I hadn't driven for two years and I began to cry.

The real reason I stopped driving was because I killed someone. Not in the actual wreck, but in the aftermath. I sideswiped an older woman when I turned out onto the highway on my way to shop at some thrift stores for books and clothes. A jaunt. A totally unnecessary trip. I hit the gas instead of the brake, driving hard into and down the side of her car. Then I pulled over to the side of the road, too afraid to get out or move. Because of the way I hit her car, neither of us could open our driver's side doors.

The other driver was Nedra Nicks, mother to a daughter she had survived, and mother and grandmother to Eleanor Nicks. I was sixteen and probably should have gotten a ticket. I sat in the car and cried until the ambulance got there. Well, I was still crying when the ambulance got there, just no longer in the car. The air bags had gone off and the smell of sulfur was in the air. Instead of yelling at me, Nedra hugged me, said it was okay, said insurance would fix her car.

Then Nedra went home and had a heart attack alone. Her granddaughter, Eleanor, in Tulsa couldn't reach her on the phone that night. The next day, she called a neighbor to check on her.

I knew Eleanor hated me.

My family and friends had comforted me, assured me that it was an accident and bad luck. They'd never even thought of holding it against me. But every morning after, I woke up sick and ashamed. I wished there had been some way to keep Nedra from dying; to keep Eleanor from losing the woman who had raised her. A stranger to me, who was trying to get home while I was just out buying things I didn't really need.

I had never told her granddaughter I was sorry.

I was about to run out of chances.

I drove more quickly back to Paka's family. There was an unplanned trip to Tulsa to be made, if it was the last thing I ever did.

I went back to the house and ate well. After, Paka came out to the pen with me to get Princess and I told her what I was going to do. That way at least someone would know.

She frowned. "You don't have to do that. It was an accident. Only you blame you."

"I never even tried to tell her I was sorry. And I think she probably blames me. Wouldn't you, if . . . ?" I didn't need to finish.

Paka nodded. She reached into the leather satchel she had hanging at her side. I was surprised to see a pistol. Paka had been armed for self-defense the entire time.

"Take this. You look cool with that recurve bow and rifle and all, but this is more sensible for the front seat of the truck."

We were standing at the truck. I reached into the back seat and grabbed two boxes of masks. One for adults and one for children. "Y'all use these if anyone shows up. Put new folks in quarantine, somewhere comfortable, but don't risk getting sick. It's going to be bad. The younger children will have some immunity, just because they were immunized recently. Something in those vaccines. But not kids with asthma, and not most of the adults who care for them."

Paka nodded. Once more, we hugged.

We both heard the rattling of the old pickup truck before we saw it. He parked nearby.

"Can't believe that didn't shake every bolt off that old thing."

"He was driving fast, yeah?"

An old, white-haired man stepped out of the truck and placed his straw cowboy hat on his head. His face was red.

"Who's that?"

"That's Danney."

"Is he Choctaw?"

"Naw, his kids are. His wife was the daughter of Mr. Sunday."

I nodded, as if I had a clue what Paka was talking about.

Paka saw me. Laughed. "Choctaw preacher. Spiritual leader."

"He's a good man. Rancher in the area. He's part of the community."

"What's going on, you think?"

Paka shrugged. "I'll go see. Don't dine and dash. Take Princess for a walk before you go, but stay close. You're not the only nervous Native around."

Princess and I walked along the gravel road. When we heard several more trucks roar to life, I turned to see what was going on.

Paka waved us back to the house. We jogged back. "It's getting real out there. A group of local non-Choctaw ranchers are trying to rustle some of the bison herd."

"Oh, wow."

"'Oh, wow' is right. That's a lot of jerky. You better get on the road. Grandma had the aunties pack you up some food. You better grab it and go. Get in there and say your halitos and such."

"My donadagohvis," I murmured.

"We will. You're my baby's auntie now. You better bet we'll see you again. Birthdays, holidays," she teased.

I suddenly couldn't speak. A week ago I wouldn't have thought I was auntie-ready. But now . . .

My voice kind of caught, though I was trying hard to keep it light. "You have enough masks for the babies."

Paka patted her chest. "And lots of sustenance."

I laughed. Then I reached out and grabbed Paka and pulled her to me.

"Love you, sis," Paka said.

I nodded. I was already tired of saying goodbye. I knew there would be more. And I knew I wouldn't see all of them again. There just weren't that many happy endings in the many alternative timelines. This was life, wasn't it? Not a horror story, but not a fantasy either.

"Donadagohvi," I whispered.

"Chi pisa la chike," she whispered back.

I packed the food Paka's aunties had set aside for me into an ice chest. When I got into the truck, I held my breath. It had been two years since I had driven, other than up and down the mountain. That's why Dad had told me to wait at the house, wasn't it? Even with everything there to help me get out of town, he was going to have to be the one to save me, because I couldn't be trusted to save myself? Mom had been right. Someday I would be on my own. I would have to be my own hero. This truck wasn't going to drive itself.

I turned the key. It should have roared like a thing with teeth. But it was quiet.

"Too quiet," I muttered.

I checked my mirrors. I held my breath.

Then I drove.

Very slowly.

Teeth
Agape

I forgot how sleepy I sometimes got when I was driving. I turned off Mona Awad's book *Bunny* and put on an album by Medicine Horse. "Now, if I fall asleep to Cherokee heavy metal," I said, looking over at Princess.

Princess responded with a yawn.

"Girl, you cut that out."

Princess looked ashamed. Then looked out the window.

I kept talking to her. "There's a reservoir up here. Maybe we can find a place to park and take a catnap."

Princess frowned with her black brows.

"Don't look at me. I didn't invent the phrase. Not even my language," I muttered as I pulled over to the side of the road. I had taken one less-traveled, but felt super exposed. I thought of all the stuff in the back of the truck I was planning to deliver. I considered skipping Nedra's granddaughter, but only long enough to feel guilty.

"Well, heck," I said. "Let's make for the trees. Maybe you can get a swim in. Can you swim, girl? Can all dogs swim? Do y'all sometimes have to take lessons?"

Okay, now I was definitely getting goofy. I pulled in between some old-growth cedars. One had fallen backwards, its roots pointing accusingly at the reservoir, the sky, a gnarled hundred-year-old claw. Its fallen top gave us cover from the road. I pulled in and put the windows down. I set my alarm. "No more than forty-five minutes." Time was not slowing down. I fell asleep quickly, my hand on Princess's head in my lap. When I began to dream about motorboats, I startled awake. Princess was growling lowly, shoving her nose out the gap in the windows.

"Hush, girl," I said. I grabbed the backpack and pulled out the binoculars. On the road, a tanker truck was backing towards the gates that protected the gangplank on top of the reservoir. Signs around the reservoir indicated this was the plant that treated the water for the farmlands and homes of the Muscogee Reservation.

They didn't belong. The symbols on the tank were familiar: pesticide, hazardous. One man carried a rifle, the other bolt cutters. I swallowed. This was the truck I'd heard about at Ida's. The driver killed, and the semi stolen.

They were in camo clothing. Survivalist types who were anxious to kick off the anarchy they felt they were prepared for. The kind of men who had cellars full of food and exercise equipment they didn't use.

But who needs to run when you have a gun? I thought. Then I remembered my own rifle in the truck. The sirens connected to the spinning lights on the top of the water treatment plant began to howl. Had someone seen them? What evil idiot poisons drinking water? Did they not understand that water can't be isolated? Did they not understand that water becomes rain and returns to the planet, and that the food you eat lives on that poisoned water?

Or dies?

"The rain falls on the just and the unjust, both." I went to the back of the truck. Would they be able to get it into the water if they couldn't back their truck in? They had killed a man. They meant to kill a lot more. I got into the cab and loaded the rifle. I could hit a deer in the heart if I had to. A slow-moving man would be easier, camouflaged or not. I took a deep breath.

I backed out of the cedars as gently as possible. I stopped before leaving our hiding space. I commanded Princess to get on the floor. I wedged the rifle where it wouldn't slide around while I drove, made sure the safety was on. Once I reached the edge of the cedars, I stopped. The .30-06 had eight shells. It was a bolt action rifle. Could the truck back towards the water with all the tires on one side flat? And if the one with the rifle turned his sight on me?

I stopped thinking. I used the truck's mirror to keep the heavy rifle steady. I thought through the order of shots. Back tire, front tires, middles. If that guy pointed his rifle at me, he would be bumped into the list. I repeated the order to myself as I chambered the first round. *Don't come for me,* I prayed.

He didn't. When the first tire exploded, he dropped to the ground like I'd hit him. His partner shifted the truck out of reverse and tried to drive away. I aimed and hit another tire. Rubber exploded and the truck tilted hazardously towards the ditch. The man on the ground stood up and grabbed his knee. He went down again. He began to use his rifle as a crutch, but as he stood he pulled the trigger, shooting into the ground, enough of a backfire and fright that he fell back over. I returned my attention to the tires in the middle. The driver stopped and struggled to get out of the cab, then the whole thing fell over on its side. His friend was up again, hollering for help. Limping worse than before.

"That ACL might need some surgery. Good luck with that during a pandemic," I muttered. The driver ran down the road, leaving his partner behind. I breathed with relief. The tank of hazardous chemicals was resting safely on its side in the grass.

Tulsa

We made our getaway quickly. Who knew how many more of those murderers were out there? What if they had back-up down the road? I drove faster than I had ever driven. I rolled the windows down and Princess stuck her head out the window.

"Take me back to Tulsa," I sang. The truck tried.

I needed to get further down the road. I couldn't get caught up in this mess. I hoped the alarms I'd heard at the reservoir would be followed up quickly by the Lighthorse. By the time I got to the highway, I saw a Lighthorse vehicle headed the direction I came.

I stopped once at a rest area and asked a Lighthorse-woman, who was actually on a horse, about entering Tulsa. She marked my map for me, writing the road numbers to the side so I would be less likely to miss them. I had to stop at the Muscogee Nation checkpoints, too, but Choctaw Nation had radioed ahead for me and once I showed my Cherokee ID card, they let me through.

The closer I got to Tulsa, the more the sky looked pregnant with rain. Looking back towards the west, the sky burned red, a smoky sky, beautiful, an ombre of oranges and reds and yellows with violet edges that touched what seemed like rain-heavy clouds. When the world burns, the sunsets will be amazing.

Unbidden, I thought of the last rainstorm I'd stood in. A first kiss.

Nedra Nicks had grown up across the street from the Tulsa Fairgrounds. At the entrance to the building honoring past oil expos stood a seventy-five-foot-tall gold-painted plaster-and-concrete statue of an oil worker. It was in the list of tallest ten statues in the United States. Its long shadow kept her house cool in the summer, even while the industry it honored helped heat up the world.

My mom had grown up in Tulsa, too, at the same time Nedra's daughter had lived in that house, a house they would pass on to Eleanor Nicks. Their paths hadn't crossed. We knew a bit about the family from the obituary and social media posts.

I exited the highway and drove past the Coney I-Landers, Swan Lake, the upscale shopping center, and the sprawling university campus, until finally, I, too, was in the shadow of the golden oilman who watched over the sometimes–fried food festival, sometimes–amusement park of my mother's youth. I drove past the house, swung around the block driving slowly. Finally, on the third pass, I pulled into the driveway.

But then I couldn't move.

Probably the last thing she wanted to see was me behind the wheel of another car.

I took a deep breath and rolled the windows down, then saw Eleanor step out onto the front porch.

"Can I help you?" she asked as I finally stepped out of the car.

"I'm sorry." I was going to make excuses about why I hadn't gotten in touch earlier, but I couldn't speak.

"What?"

"I'm sorry," I repeated.

"What for?"

"The world is ending," I stammered.

"Well, no kidding. But why are you at my house?"

"I was the other driver." I had stepped a little closer.

We were both silent.

"Ah. I know who you are."

I didn't know how to respond.

"I came to help you?" This was not going well. Suddenly everything I could think to say was wrong—too many long stories, things which were maybe just a coincidence, nothing that would make sense to anyone but me.

"I'm sorry," I tried again.

"I can't say I didn't blame you," Eleanor said at last. "First, my mom died too early, then my grandmother. I went from being a spoiled granddaughter to being an orphan my senior year in college." Her voice shook.

I looked away from her towards the street. How strange that the anarchy that had overtaken my neighborhood was mere insulated quiet in this city. The street wasn't deserted, nor yet the chaos it would become, nor the martial law that would follow soon enough. I felt dizzy, unable to tell Eleanor anything.

But then I tried.

"This city is in better shape than the one I was in," I started.

She shrugged. "I've already lost everything in my freezer. The power stays on for businesses and stoplights. No point in refilling it yet."

"No point for a while," I went on.

"Yeah?"

"Everything is going to fall apart. Drones, cyberattacks, state militias. A perfect storm of climate and people. A hurricane of sorts, without water, though eventually there will be some of that too."

"Rain? We haven't had but one good rain this year."

I thought of that storm and Adam's perfect kiss. Perfect, because there would be no way for him to disappoint me two hundred years away. A kiss between friends that would never lead to more, except in my imagination. I willed myself not to think of him—not to blush.

I looked up at the sky and checked the old wind-up watch Adam had given me.

"Sunset, tonight," I said.

She looked at me for a moment. "Okay, Nostradamus."

"Then tomorrow, martial law, because of the new flu."

"Maybe Cassandra is more like it. Tell me about this new flu."

"Fabricated chicken factory-related. It will be common knowledge tomorrow."

"Okay, I think you should go. First you kill the woman who raised me, now you're scaring me to death. You ruined my life, but I kept telling myself it was an accident, you were a stupid kid, kids do stupid, thoughtless things. I did stupid, thoughtless things. But this is next level. What is wrong with you?"

From the truck, Princess barked.

"I want to show you something." I got my keys to unlock the plastic cover over the truck's bed.

Eleanor hesitated, but then walked around me to the truck. I opened the cover.

She surveyed the contents. I stood out of the way while she touched the various boxes and bags and containers in the truck's bed.

"You actually believe this, don't you? That's why your truck is packed with food and water, and Sterno, and gasoline? What is this?"

"Ninety days of supplies," I said.

"What makes you think this is going to happen?"

I thought hard. I knew there would be rain around sunset, but I had to be home by then. I went to the car and pulled out the world band radio. I didn't know if she would believe Brandon or not. Might she believe I was a believer in conspiracies, easily led? Was I?

"In ten minutes or so this broadcast will come on. This guy, Brandon, will say everything I just said." I handed her the radio.

She turned it on. Static hummed. "But that just tells me why you believe it. Doesn't make it true."

I didn't know what else to say. Tulsa seemed so normal compared to what I had left behind in Texas. The wails of emergency sirens still pierced the air, the sounds of a city ticking along, no smoke from abandoned, burning houses. Standing there, I, too, could believe the world wasn't set to catch fire and flood. It was surreal. Is this what it was like to flee a war-ravaged country? To lose everything, and then cross a border and stand amidst a population that took the next glass of clean water for granted? For years the images of countries devastated by drought and civil war had hung in museums, served as trauma porn on screens, lessons, distractions from the privileged life I had lived. It had been unthinkable that it could happen here. But it had, before. The land had been invaded and taken from people who had called it home for thousands of years. It could happen again, on a much smaller time frame.

"Apocalypse" is such a strange word. My mother always said that Indigenous people and people with roots in Africa were post-apocalyptic populations. As were people in Vietnam, India . . . anywhere Indigenous people had been murdered for resources, extracted and exploited. But the Greek bits of the word mean "to uncover" and "to reveal," as in "a revelation." What was this decimation of the human population going to reveal?

Eleanor turned the knob on the radio. I resisted the urge to ask her to wait, to not lose the signal, but let her rotate through the various stations of the world. She stopped on a station where the announcer was speaking quickly in Spanish. I didn't understand much. I recognized the sounds of formal Spanish spoken in Spain. I watched Eleanor's face.

"Do you speak?" she asked quietly.

"Not really."

She frowned. The voice on the radio was fast and breathy. I caught the words "gripe aviar Americano."

"What is he saying?"

She put her finger in front of her lips. She looked like a librarian. Her face was pale as a second voice joined the broadcast.

I checked my watch. It was almost time for Brandon's broadcast.

"You're wrong," Eleanor spoke up, still listening attentively. "It's already started."

"What?"

"In Spain, they just announced it. They're already calling it the 'American Bird Flu.'"

She handed the radio to me. I tried finding Brandon's station. Still only static. He wasn't there.

"I don't need to hear that."

I turned the radio off.

"You know the 1918 flu was called the Spanish Flu for a long time. It caused people from Spain problems for a while, even though it may probably started on U.S. soil— Kansas, even. But because the recordkeeping in Spain was good, that was where it was first well-documented and reported. So, Spain was blamed. And anyone who spoke Spanish, really." She paused. "Guess they're making sure they don't get blamed this time."

My head swam. It was too early. Yes, Topsy, Oklahoma, was only two hours away, but if this was broadcasting from Spain, there were dominoes already down.

"You really think this is the end of the world?"

I nodded. "For ninety days."

"And what do you think coming here, mere hours before all this breaks, has accomplished? Do you think this makes up for killing my grandma, when there's nothing I can do?"

What had I thought this would accomplish? Last night, sitting in the truck in the dark, driving for the first time—then crying—it had seemed like a good idea.

She was raising her voice now. "Everything in my fridge is ruined. I have maybe two weeks' worth of canned food, and some stuff to make sourdough bread, and you're telling me I have to lay low for ninety days? It's a little late for a grocery run!" She was starting to cry. "What am I supposed to do?"

That was a good question. What was anyone supposed to do? I couldn't ask her to drive me to Topsy and then try to make it home. If the flu was already being mentioned on international news, things were out of whack. The timeline had tightened in unforeseen ways, a skipping minute-hand was leading to a skipping hour-hand, and we had lost at least a day. Somewhere, maybe, a breaking of the rules had rewritten the future. I wondered if somehow it was my fault. I took a deep breath.

"Keep my truck."

"What?"

"There's more than enough for ninety days. Should be enough for two, you know. In case."

I saw Eleanor considering this. Saw how the addition of one more person gave her pause. Who would she save? Who did she love?

"What about you?"

I shrugged. "You got a bicycle?"

Eleanor gave me a look. Then she walked over to her garage. She leaned down and pulled the garage door up. Lord, did she have a bike she was going to give me? I hoped she had a helmet too. The door slowly revealed a small bus, wrapped with the logo of the local library, books and animals with glasses reading them. "Reading Rabbits and Book Bunnies would like a word or three!" the décor suggested.

I stared. Princess barked again.

"We can trade," Eleanor said. "But if you're wrong? It's stolen, as far as I'm concerned."

She walked into the garage and returned with the keys.

I took mine from my pocket and we exchanged sets. "Good trade," I said. I handed the radio back to her, then returned to the truck to get Princess and my backpack. I remembered the cash in my bag and pulled it out, handing it to her too.

Her mouth dropped open.

Then she slowly reached out and took it. "I was going to argue with you," she said. "Then I remembered you killed my grandma."

I winced. "Ouch."

Eleanor took a deep breath. "Bus is electric. It's still charged. But no detours. Maybe two hours' worth of juice."

She pushed open the door. Princess jumped up onto the old-fashioned bench seat, tried to get comfortable, then hopped down and curled up on the floor.

"Credit cards will be bricks for a while. All the banks are going offline soon."

"Take care of the Book Bunny," she replied. Then she went and backed the truck out so I could back out the bookmobile. I took a deep breath before climbing in, didn't want her to see how nervous I was. I was grateful for the backing camera on the bus, but went ever slow. It was tight. I held my breath like that would make us smaller and inched out. I had never driven anything so big. Once out of the garage, I reached out and popped the large mirror back out as far as it would go. Sweat was exiting all the places it exits when you're terrified.

I looked down at Princess. "When you think you can't do something, pretend you are someone who does that thing all the time," I muttered, paraphrasing one of my favorite authors. Princess raised a black eyebrow. Then I repeated it to myself over and over and I backed into the ever busying street. Eleanor and I exchanged glances.

"Donadagohvi," I hollered. She just nodded back, before driving away in the truck. I wondered who she would save.

I drove less than a block before turning across the street into the parking lot underneath the gold roughneck. I wondered if another statue would take its place, one who hadn't seen over microplastics, warm polar bears, and poison red algae in lakes like the oil idol. Would it be a variation on the art in the future, a reminder of what short-term, money-centered thinking would do?

I thought of the Statue of Liberty in *Planet of the Apes*, buried, sticking up out of the ground, a symbol of a lost world. I thought of Adam and the ladder he'd rescued, removed to a future where it wouldn't be worshiped or prayed to, but would might be a reminder that for too long, a human being's potential was determined by the color of their skin.

When you really love someone, you want them to be happy and cared for; you don't want them to suffer; you don't want them to be teased or bullied or killed for their skin color, religion, who they love or who they are. I missed him now, and mourned that my brother was on this planet, guaranteed suffering that none of us could relieve. I wanted him to be safe and happy. I didn't want to worry that he would die too early or be murdered on his way home.

Remembering my family was on their way to me, I put the bus back into drive. It was big. Too big for me. But it was full of books. Statistics suggested at least ten percent of them were great. You could do worse than head into an apocalypse with a bus full of books. I hoped there were a few Levi might like.

Coming Home

I drove the book truck around the parking lot a little, briefly getting to know it, practicing turns and stops. I focused on driving, trying not to think about time or the future or where my family was now. Looking for me in Texas? It was hard. As much as I had promised myself that I would be present when I got behind the wheel, it was hard. Thoughts intruded. Feelings insisted they be felt. I was grateful for my medication more than ever.

Then I laughed out loud. Princess gave me a worried look. I knew what story my mom would tell as soon as she saw me driving a book truck.

"When I was in community college, I had a teacher named Dr. Blubaugh who drove trucks as a side hustle. He had a friend who drove a Hot Chip truck. He said whenever they met for lunch, he never locked the book truck, but someone always tried to break into the Hot Chip truck in spite of all the locks. He'd say, 'Kids will steal chips, but books were safe.'"

Well, if Professor Blubaugh could see me now.

That laughing brought tears to my eyes. I took a deep breath.

"You ready, girl?" I asked Princess.

In reply Princess settled in for a nap.

I figured I was a little safer seated up high, able to see further and above the other cars. I had a back end full of books keeping me insulated from the cars behind me. I tried not to think too hard, worry about the other drivers. In the time I spent in the parking lot, I'd noticed an uptick in traffic around me. Some people were masked up, some in bandannas, filling up extra gas containers at the gas stations I could see from the highway, filling the parking lots of grocery stores and home improvement stores. This was what my town had looked like weeks ago. It had been strange to enter a semi-normal city, but that was changing. A few years ago, during the preamble to a lockdown and pandemic, Mom, Levi, and I had seen a fight over the last jug of water during our grocery run. After that, she'd made me stay home with baby Levi.

I was glad Eleanor didn't have to worry about going out into that.

I got in the far-right lane and drove the speed limit while cars raced past. When I reached the city's edge, there was less traffic. Still, I wanted to get off the highway. One wreck and we could all be trapped on that road for hours. I pulled to the side and checked my map. I turned the radio on, now just a listing of one disaster after another. I tried not to think about the people. The closing of state borders was spreading from the southwest to the east and north. The nighttime curfew I had expected was coming a day early. Things were happening faster than they should. I thought about the time travelers Brandon and Adam had told me about, the ones who couldn't wait for things to kick off too, and wondered if they were already two hundred years away or if they'd stuck around to see the show. I wondered if they walked through a couple of chicken factories collecting diseased birds themselves.

Princess was panting. I was afraid to stop or get out, so I gave her some water in a travel mug. I turned the bus away from the highway and took a side road that would cut through dying towns and farms. I watched for the county road I needed that would eventually take me to Topsy. I was nervous, second-guessing myself that maybe I was messing up.

When I turned onto a road that was more dirt than gravel, I stopped. About the distance of a city block away was a red jeep, the hood up, steam rolling off it.

"Well, that blows," I told Princess.

I pulled out the binoculars and saw a motorcycle was parked next to the jeep. A helmeted man sat astride it, his hands in the air, with a man on foot pointing a gun at him. I saw the motorcycle guy move his hands ever so slowly, reaching up to remove his helmet, revealing black hair in one long braid.

A chill started at my ears and sliced my body crosswise.

I slowly drove up.

Cloudbusting

"It can't be," I muttered to Princess. Or maybe to myself. Talking to my dog made me feel less alone.

Parking, I placed my hand on the doorknob. I thought of the gun Paka had given me. It was tucked into the glove compartment. I reached over and discreetly pulled it out. The man with the gun, seeing me, had put the motorcyclist between us, watching both the bus and the motorcycle rider.

I breathed slowly, terrified to hold the weapon while shaking. It was loaded. It was deadly. I didn't want to use it. But if you are going to touch a gun, you must assume it will do what it was made to do. And this was not a rifle or recurve bow situation.

Was it him? Would I step out of the safety of the bus for a stranger? Would a second weapon make an already dangerous situation explode? I made sure the safety was on, then slipped it into the pocket of my hoodie. It was an awkward, obvious weight. I pulled at the door handle. I didn't consider Princess.

She leaped across me, her back legs trampolining off my thighs, knocking the door open with a metal clang.

"Princess, no!" I screamed.

Adam turned my way. It was him. It was always him.

The man pivoted his weapon to my dog, his face contorting from threatening to terrified as she launched. The gun didn't go off. Down he went.

I hurried over to where Princess stood growling now, reaching for her leash while Adam picked the gun off the ground. He put it in one of his saddlebags. The man tried to keep both his hands and throat protected from Princess's bared teeth as she kept growling into his face.

I was pulling hard on her leash and trying to talk to her calmly when, from behind us, a child screamed, "Daddy!"

"I'm sorry. I just need to get home," the man blubbered from the ground, unable to keep from crying. "I just want to get my daughter home."

I turned and looked towards the jeep and saw a small girl crying too, unable to decide whether to stay in the car or run to her father. Adam leaned down and helped the man to his feet, at which point Princess then ran in between them, her whole body leaning into Adam, waiting for him to return the attention. The man backed away. The little girl ran to the man, wrapping her arms around his legs, pressing her crying face into her father's body.

"So, you and your kid are more important than anyone else?"

The man looked away. "I've got a jeep full of baby formula and food for my brother's family too."

"That wasn't going to fit on his bike." I was angry. I was glad I hadn't pulled out the pistol; I was shaking so hard it might have gone off.

Adam was stooped down, talking to Princess, who just kept licking his face and hands and wagging her docked tail. "Guess you should have bought some coolant on your supply run, too, if you were only going to look out for yourself."

Adam looked tired. Even tired, he was more beautiful than I remembered. And he was standing in front of me, not two hundred years in the future.

"Get back in your jeep, dude."

"Can I have my gun?"

Adam and I both looked at each other, then at the stranger.

"Just get back in your car, mister."

The man sighed. He was no longer crying. He leaned down and picked up his still-crying daughter, his embrace giving her permission to escalate the volume of her sobs, though her tear-stained face stayed buried in his shoulder now. They got back in the car.

Adam pulled back the gun's slide to see if anything was chambered. Then he popped the clip out of the .45.

"Is it?"

"Not loaded."

I leaned down and hugged Princess. She was happy. But she was pretty much always happy. Yet her body now practically hummed with joy.

"Where is Levi?"

Adam took a deep breath. Checked his watch. Then he went to his saddlebags. He pulled out his phone.

"Proof of life," he said. My mom, dad, and Levi stood in front of a mountain. I couldn't recognize where. I felt like I had been kicked in the chest. I felt Adam grab my arm, not letting me collapse on the ground too hard. I couldn't believe I had planned to send him away without letting my parents say goodbye.

I stared at the family photo, the picture I wasn't in. They were all smiling, happy, Levi laughing in the arms of his father.

"They're good. They're safe. Angel brought the faxes to your dad. Whatever was in them made him a believer."

"Who went with Levi?"

"I don't know. It should have been Walt, but maybe, since your mom is there, her? We won't know until one of them shows up back here. Free will and all. But one of them will come back, Stevie. They promised."

I tried not to think about Dad saying they would see me on our mountain in Cherokee Nation. Surely he had known that wasn't true. All the earlier faxes being from Dad made sense, if he went. All along, future-Dad had been guiding my mother, and making present-Dad crazy. But, even now, could that change? How would Mom change the future, the world, going forward with the information she had? Would she be the one sending the faxes in another timeline? And would one of them really come back to live with me?

"And you're here?" I said it like a question, like I didn't believe it. "How did you find me?"

"Your mother drew me a map to get me to Topsy, Oklahoma. And, well, swipe left. I made a pit stop."

I did. There was a picture of the route that I'd thought I was going to use, drawn on the wall for my family. I swiped left again and saw scans of the family pictures I had left behind in the box in the garage. There were copies of all of them. Then I saw some of the self-portraits I had left in my room. Adam reached for the phone. He was blushing. "I thought you might like those . . ." I felt my own cheeks warm up.

I took a breath, not wanting him to hear what I was feeling in my voice. But voices will betray you every time.

"And, your vinyl records . . . they're in the saddlebags. Had to toss my food and blanket."

"Well, I guess I came along at the right time."

Adam shrugged. "I would have found you anyway. Even if I had to walk."

I was gonna need a minute. I handed him back the phone. Suddenly I felt the weight of my gun in my pocket. "Can you take this? Mine is definitely loaded."

Princess barked. We looked over and saw the guy was exiting his vehicle.

"What are we going to do about him?"

"I think I can get that jeep going. Good thing it's older."

I believed him. Adam was good with his hands.

"Wonderful, because I'm pretty attached to my bookmobile?"

Adam laughed. "You would bring a bookmobile to an apocalypse. What else you have in there?"

"I have no idea."

"Let's hope there's book tape or coolant."

"Might be a Chilton's auto repair book on jeeps?"

"Fingers crossed," Adam said, before disappearing into the mobile library.

Adam found some book tape and repaired the jeep's split hose. He added water to what was left of the coolant in the radiator's reserve tank. Then we watched the guy drive away.

Once he was gone, we loaded the motorcycle into the back of the book truck.

"You're driving now?"

"I am."

He looked at me. He had known. He had known all along why I was sad, scared, and afraid. He had known that every time I left the house, I wondered if living life was as important as not dying. He knew that I took everything seriously, that I worried all the time, that I would have wrapped the people I loved in bubble wrap and not let them go anywhere if that was the only way to keep them safe. He had known that I felt like a murderer who got away with it, but never felt free or unafraid. And still, he had come back to be with me.

"Good deal," he finally replied, smiling. He opened the door to let Princess in the cab. "Because I could use a nap."

"Well, the book bus awaits."

Once we were buckled in, Princess squeezed up onto the bench seat between us. Adam stretched his legs out and leaned back against Princess, close to me, but not quite touching. Close enough to feel the warmth of his shoulder. We were both too tired to talk. I hoped there would be time. I drove faster than I had on the highway until we turned off the blacktop road onto gravel. Soon, we were driving through thick woods.

Now and then I reached down to pat Princess, who was gently snoring, her head on Adam's thigh. As my hand drifted from the top of her head down her neck, I felt

Adam's hand bump into mine. I held my breath, trying to keep my eyes on the road, afraid to look over. Then he put his hand over mine, his fingers twining between my fingers, resting, waves of electrical tension racing up my arm and into the rest of my body. I wondered if the nearly invisible hair on my arms was standing up. I was hot and cold at the same time. I was a cliché in a rom-com. If that rom-com was set at the end of the world.

The bus suddenly came to a halt.

The sudden end of forward motion awoke Princess and startled Adam. He leaned over and looked at the flickering lights on the dashboard.

"Downside of an electric vehicle."

"Needs charge?"

"Yup." He opened the door and got out. The sound of thunder rolled through the woods and shook the trees in the surrounding woods.

"How much further to your aunties'?" He looked up at the sky.

I looked up the road. "It goes around the mountain aways. Probably a twenty-minute drive. Maybe an hour hike."

"In the rain."

"Maybe we take your bike. Try and race it."

"You said your dad vetoed you riding on the back of a bike?"

"Ideally, I should have my own."

"Noted."

We opened the back of the truck and unloaded the motorcycle. Adam handed me the helmet. I put the backpack Mom had left me on my back, locking everything else up. We took off Princess's leash so she could run behind us. Then I climbed on, my arms wrapped tightly around Adam's waist.

I began to cry, thinking about how my life had changed. I was grateful for the helmet to hide my tears, but still worried Adam could feel the shaking in my body. Six months ago, I had thought my mother was being overprotective, when I just wanted to go to college away from her and the habits of my life, the responsibilities of helping raise my little brother when she and Dad were busy with work. I had thought building a new life would fill the void—my fear of driving, of living, of losing. I was suddenly grateful that my parents were there to choose for Levi, to hold him one last time; that I hadn't denied them that painful goodbye. I knew they would have chosen this pain a million times. To know that Levi would live a longer, healthier life; once they had the knowledge I had, they would have chosen the same way I did, always. We all loved him more than we loved ourselves.

We were almost at the top of the mountain when the tears on the inside were matched by the rain striking the outside. Adam pulled the bike off the road under the pines that were tall and close together. A Christmas tree farm that someone forgot to harvest.

I took the helmet off and set it on the back of the bike. Miles away, lightning struck the ground. We both watched, waiting for the lightning's heartbeat.

"It's all happening, just like you said. Why did you come back?"

"For you." Adam leaned down and pulled me to him, his face leaning close to mine. "What do they say in *Paradise Lost*, without you even heaven would be hell?"

"Are you only kissing me because it's tradition?" I whispered.

"I'm kissing you because I want you to be my person. My best friend. I've wanted you to be my person since we met. Every time I had something I wanted to say, I wanted to say it to you first."

He kissed me.

"How could I have gone into a future without this?" His lips pressed into mine, warmer and more tender than I could have imagined. I never wanted him to stop. I reached up and drifted my hands over his hair, down to the back of his neck, following his braid down to shoulders. I pulled myself against his chest. Finally, I had to take a breath. I turned my head and breathed in the scent and warmth of his body.

"Are you sure it's not because you've tasted Pepsi?"

Adam laughed. "Well, that too."

Lightning struck the ground again, closer this time. Close enough to be concerned.

"Can you promise me something?"

Adam looked at me, waiting.

"Promise to kiss me like that when it's not raining? There are droughts, and then there are *droughts*."

Adam laughed. He reached down and took my hands in his before bringing them to his lips.

"I promise."

"Me too," I replied. I pulled him to me and kissed him again.

The rain was coming down even harder, but if the world hadn't been ending, I think we'd still be standing there kissing in the thunder and lightning.

We had to take the road carefully. When I was a kid and it was dark outside, the stars were brighter than almost anywhere I had ever been. Still, the road going up always seemed to take forever. I remembered being impatient for the car trip to end. To be running around the house with my cousins, eating the food my grandmother and Aunt Geneva had made. Now, holding on to Adam, I didn't mind the journey. I didn't even think I was hungry for the beans and cornbread I knew would be waiting.

Suddenly, I remembered this would be the first time Adam would meet my aunts and uncles and my cousins. He would sit at the table and become part of my life. His whole life, he had been trained to do one thing, to save a few of the artifacts of the world that were worth saving; to preserve works that transcended words. Now, too, his life had completely shifted. He had been raised to complete a mission he was given. He would have to figure out what he wanted to do, who he was going to become.

"We're going to build a better world, aren't we?" I asked.

I felt him nod. I stepped back and looked into his eyes.

He leaned in and kissed the top of my head. "We already are."

Donadagohvi.

Remember Me

Letter 1

Dear Levi,

How do I speak to you in the future? How old will you be when you read this letter? What is your dog's name? I can hazard a guess.

How strange to feel like both your sister and your ancestor. Of course, I was there for your raising. I always felt like you were a little bit my child, more than my brother. I would have died for you. I would have done anything to not see you suffer or be hurt or die early.

I guess I did.

Your mother did, too. She has written her own letters. We speak of you often.

Your father sacrificed, too. I am glad you are together. Dad is always the most kind and loving guide.

I see Loren and Jess regularly. Of course, you remember them, especially Loren. I can't tell her story, but I know she has written you as well.

I want you to do a few things for me. Go to the creek on the land near our old home. Do you remember when we walked there when you were little? Do you remember the garbage and the foam from the fertilizer that built up, spun in the stream when there was water in it? Do you remember how Mom said there was a brief period when it was full of minnows, frogs, the trees alive with chirping? But whenever we were there, the only seemingly living things were water and leeches? Can you step into that creek now? Can you swim in the crisp, clear water? Do the frogs and fish flee from you?

I'm being rhetorical.

I can see it, as it is for you, because Adam has shown me in words and art. He has sculpted the creatures and the flora for me in cedar.

Collect the water from that creek and take it to the Chapel of The Ladder. Leave it there for me. Or pour it into the water feature.

Know that we are with you, and you are always in my heart.

Love,
Stevie

The End (sort of)

Side A:
Who Do You Love?
By The Jesus and Mary Chain

Turning Tide	by Medicine Horse
A City of Fire	by Louis W. Ballard
Stay in My Corner	by The Arcs
Come and Get Your Love	by Redbone
Space Age Love Song	by A Flock of Seagulls
24 Frames	by Jason Isbell
Motorbike	by Leon Bridges
Garageland	by The Clash
Heaven Sent	by Parker Millsap
Ancestor Song	by Robbie Robertson
Dearly Departed	by Shakey Graves
What's Going On	by Marvin Gaye
Elephants	by Austin Basham
The Day Texas Sank to the Bottom of the Sea	by Micah P. Hinson
A Lie Nation	by The Halluci Nation, John Trudell, Lido Pimienta, Tanya Tagaq, Northern Voice
Landslide	by The Chicks or Stevie Nicks
Creep	by Radiohead
Heartaches and Pain by Charles Bradley Judadatla Tsisqwa (Spotted Bird)	by Kalyn Fay
Can't Take It	by Pretendians Band
Red Dirt Boogie, Brother	by Jesse Ed Davis
Satellite	by Guster

Oh, Spaceman	by Micah P. Hinson
Retribution	by Tanya Tagaq
One Piece at a Time	by Johnny Cash
Black Is the Color of My True Love's Hair	by Nina Simone
You Always Hurt the One You Love	by The Mills Brothers
Waltz Across Texas	by Brave Combo
I'm Sorry	by Brenda Lee

Side B:
Summer's End By John Prine

Anyone Who Knows What Love Is (Will Understand)	by Irma Thomas
Solo	by Gathering of Nations Pow Wow, featuring Fawn Wood
World Burns	by Lokel
At the Party	by Black Belt Eagle Scout
Texas Sun	by Leon Bridges
Nice Things	Hayes Carll
Stressed Out	by Twenty One Pilots
Take Care of Me	by Ailani
Heathens	by Twenty One Pilots
Garden Dove	by Samantha Crain
Older	by Mato Wayuhi
An Echo	by Samantha Crain
As We Drive By	by Whiskey Folk Ramblers
Teeth Agape	by Tanya Tagaq
Tulsa	by Kalyn Fay
Coming Home	by Leon Bridges
Cloudbusting	by Kate Bush
Remember Me	by Fawn Wood

Acknowledgments

In 2008, I went to see Martin Puryear's *Ladder for Booker T. Washington* not realizing it was on loan to the National Gallery. Walking into the room where it always hung and seeing it no longer there was one of the seeds of this story. My unconditional love for my siblings and my children is another. Since that day, I wrote a lot, but I read more.

More than any other literary movement, Afrofuturism impacted the crafting of this story. Big debt there. Without Octavia Butler's groundwork, I never even know how to try. To that end, the expertise of Dr. Constance Bailey and her Afrofuturism course was the most important class I ever sat in. There was even a special appearance by Victor LaValle! And, wado, Dr. Sean Dempsey, for a whole semester on the history of the crafting of souls and letting me talk about Shelley's *Modern Prometheus*. Wado, Nicole Rikard for always being only a text away. Dr. Krishen Samuel, thanks for all the musicals.

When I first imagined this story, I thought it was about the importance of art and how it can be medicine for the world. I believe that. But medicine isn't worth much without people and love. A good, supportive community is so important. If you haven't found yours, I hope you do.

Being an older sister is as integral to this story as being a parent, so, wado, Mom and Dad, for giving me Jess and Angel to care for and love unconditionally. If I could time travel, I'd be sitting in a room listening to records with my dad. I miss you every day, Baba.

This Cherokee Futurism doesn't exist without Cherokee Nation or without Levine Querido. Editor Nick Thomas has been such a gift. Wado, also, to Arthur Levine, Antonio Gonzalez Cerna, Irene Vázquez, Arely Guzmán, Danielle Maldonado, Kerry Taylor. Thanks to Cherokee artist and illustrator Rebecca Lee Kunz for saying "Osiyo" at Cherokee Holiday. Thank you, also, to Meghan and Anne.

Thank you to my agent, Emily Sylvan Kim, and Ellen Brescia of Prospect Agency.

Thank you to Martin Puryear for your work. I sat in front of your *Ladder* so many times. Wado, Marla and Lydia (jigesa) for the museum gig in Tulsa. Thanks, Laura Pegram and Carolyn Steinhoff Smith, for helping me get to New York.

Any errors or mistakes are my own. Thank you to Carole Lindstrom and Ryan Chamberlain. Starting writing days debriefing with you got the manuscript finished, as did the cool reusable journal from Elena Henry, talks with Ana Henry (an early reader) and conversations with Heath and AJ Henry.

I will be forever grateful to readers who put eyes on this early on. Wado, Lokosh (Joshua D. Hinson, Chickasaw), Ari Tison (Bribri), Stacy Wells (Choctaw), and Leslie Stall Widener (Choctaw).

Wado to Native Writers and their work. I read futurisms and speculative fictions and genius stuff. Angeline Boulley's *Warrior Girl Unearthed* is a must read. Rematriate the bones and art. Our ancestors don't belong in storage. Works by Louise Erdrich, Kelli Jo Ford, Lee Francis IV, Stephen Graham

Jones, Daniel Heath Justice, Terese Mailhot, Tommy Orange, Mona Susan Power, Waub Rice, Cynthia Leitich Smith, Drew Hayden Taylor, Gerald Vizenor, Chelsea Vowel, Joshua Whitehead, and Dan Wilson are some of the best things out there.

I am so grateful to be part of a growing Native writing community. Please support these gifted writers and their work. Wado, Kaua Māhoe Adams, Haleigh Baker, Marcella Bell, Patricia Buckley, Michelle Cronin, Annette Saunooke Clapsaddle, Stacie Shannon Denetsosie, Christine Derr, A.J. Eversole, Tehya Foussat, Laurel Goodluck, Kate Hart, Emmy Her Many Horses, Shane Hawk, Millie Kingbird, Dr. Denise Lajimodiere, Vanessa Lillie, Dr. Darcie Little Badger, Jillian Metchooyeah, Dr. Devon Mihesuah, Trisha Moquino, Ruby Hansen Murray, Danica Nava, Andrea Page, Gretchen Potter, Dawn Quigley, Marcie Rendon, Kim Rogers, Monique Gray Smith, Traci Sorell, Dr. Blue Tarpalachee, and Stephanie Zackery for writing.

If you liked, shared, checked out, hand sold, reviewed, or read *Man Made Monsters*, wado. I hope you know how grateful I am that you let us into your world or spent time in ours! Artist Jeff Edwards made me and the book better. Thanks to WNDB for honoring *MMM*. Thanks to Vampires Library, Kayleigh Creates, and Kimberly Basso Davis. Never underestimate how much your long distance kindness and support means to me.

Finally, thanks to my student Maddie who told me, "You put the fun in funerals."

Some Notes on this Book's Production

Art for the jacket, case, and interiors was drawn by Rebecca Lee Kunz, who used layered painting and collage techniques to create the illustrations while including archetypal symbolism and historical Cherokee icons to represent aspects of the story. The text was set by Westchester Publishing Services, in Danbury, CT, in Freight. Designed by Joshua Darden, the family is inspired by the warmth and pragmatism found in 18th-century Dutch typefaces. The displays were set in Freight and PP Editorial, the latter a narrow serif designed by Mathieu Desjardins and Francesca Bolognini for Pangram Pangram. The book was printed on FSC™-certified 98gsm Yunshidai Ivory paper and bound in China.

Production supervised by Freesia Blizard
Assistant Managing Editor: Danielle Maldonado
Book designed by Jonathan Yamakami
Editor: Nick Thomas

LQ

LEVINE QUERIDO